This book is to be returned on or before the last date stamped below.

-7 JAN AN

17 MAR AN

14 APR AN

15 MAY AN

16 JUN AN

-6 AUG AN

26 AUG AN

11 JAN AN

12 FEB AN

15 APR A

-6 JUN AN

-2 JUL AN

17 SEP AN

2

D0536647

20 JUL AN

15 NOV 90

MAR

16. JUL

DUMFRIES AND GALLOWAY LIBRARIES

WITHDRAWN

DOYLE, ARTHUR CONAN
THE FINAL ADVENTURES OF SHERLOCK HOLMES. ANNAN

F

LARGE PRINT

DUMFRIES AND GALLOWAY REGIONAL LIBRARY SERVICE

Catherine Street, Dumfries. Tel. Dfs 53820

CO 192934

THE FINAL
ADVENTURES OF
SHERLOCK HOLMES

Also available in Crescent

Dear Stranger
The Hour Before
   Midnight
It's Been a Lot of Fun
The Still Storm
The Falklands Whale
Deathwatch
Shattered
The Wrong Face
Love Child
The Gironde Incident
The House on Prague
   Street
The Stratford Story
A Presence in an Empty
   Room
I Sent a Letter to My
   Love
Outrage
Phoenix Rising
Delilah's Fortune

None Shall Spurn
Mysterious Railway
   Stories
Death Mail
Season of Change
The Cold Room
The Whitehall Sanction
Minnie Ashe at War
The Breadwinner
Incidental Music
The Domino Vendetta
Never Forgive, Never
   Forget
King's Wench
It's a Funny Game
Uninvited: The Visitation
It's Cold Next Door
The Confession
Katharine Hepburn
Golgotha
Spring at Brookfield

THE FINAL ADVENTURES OF SHERLOCK HOLMES

Completing the Canon

by Sir Arthur Conan Doyle

Collected and introduced by
Peter Haining

A CRESCENT BOOK

This selection and introduction copyright ©
Peter Haining, 1981
First published in Great Britain by
W. H. Allen & Co. Plc, 1981

This Crescent edition published 1986

Phototypeset by Galleon Photosetting
Printed and bound in Great Britain by
The Garden City Press Ltd, Letchworth, Herts.
for the publishers, W. H. Allen & Co. Plc,
44 Hill Street, London W1X 8LB

This book is sold subject to the condition that it shall not, by
way of trade or otherwise, be lent, re-sold, hired out or
otherwise circulated without the publisher's prior consent in any
form of binding or cover other than that in which it is published
and without a similar condition, including this condition, being
imposed upon the subsequent purchaser.

British Library Cataloguing in Publication Data
————————————

ANNAN

Doyle, *Sir* Arthur Conan
  [Short stories. *Selections*] The final
  adventures of Sherlock Holmes: completing
  the Canon.
  I. Title   II. Haining, Peter
  823'.912[F]   PR4621

ISBN 1-85188-026-7

Contents

'There has been some debate as to whether the Adventures of Holmes, or the narrative powers of Watson, declined with the passage of the years. When the same string is still harped upon, however cunningly one may vary the melody, there is still the danger of monotony. The mind of the reader is less fresh and responsive, which may unjustly prejudice him against the writer. To compare great things to small, Scott in his autobiographical notes has remarked that each of Voltaire's later pamphlets was declared to be a declension from the last one, and yet when the collected works were assembled they were found to be among the most brilliant. Scott was also depreciated by critics for some of his most solid work. Therefore, with such illustrious examples before one, let me preserve the hope that he who in days to come may read my series backwards will not find that his impressions are very different from those of his neighbour who reads them forwards.'

From 'Mr Sherlock Holmes to his Readers', STRAND magazine, March 1927, and deleted by Sir Arthur Conan Doyle when he used the essay as the Preface to THE CASEBOOK OF SHERLOCK HOLMES.

For
John Bennett Shaw
'Keeper of the Records'
&
W. O. G. Lofts
'Master of Researchers'

Introduction

'Somewhere in the vaults of the bank of Cox & Company, at Charing Cross, there is a travel-worn and battered tin dispatch box with my name upon the lid. It is crammed with papers, nearly all of which are records of cases to illustrate the curious problems which Mr Sherlock Holmes had at various times to examine.'

So wrote Dr Watson in 'The Problem of Thor Bridge', and one of the most deeply-felt wishes of Sherlockians everywhere has long been that these illusive documents might come to light and at last be published. Of course, many another writer apart from the revered Sir Arthur Conan Doyle has attempted to create new Adventures for the Master of Detectives and his faithful chronicler – not a few of these tales based on hints and clues contained in the existing stories – but as in the case of all great originals (which Holmes undeniably is) no substitute can ever surplant the model. For would anyone deny that in under a century Sherlock Holmes has become one of the three most famous characters in literature, the other two being Hamlet and Robinson Crusoe?

According to the generally accepted viewpoint

7

the Complete Adventures of Sherlock Holmes consist of sixty cases – fifty-six short stores and four novel-length tales. But, as this book will show and as more than one Sherlockian expert has already proclaimed,[1] there are in fact *twelve* more Sherlock Holmes items which should rightly be included in the canon. What, in fact, Sir Arthur Conan Doyle left us of his immortal sleuth was seventy-two items which are all essential to a full understanding of the genius of Holmes. The reasons for these twelve items being omitted will be discussed here in detail, item by item. They are all being collected together in one volume for the very first time, and as such form an essential addition to the existing definitive two-volume edition of the stories. The assembling of these rare and difficult-to-obtain items has naturally called for considerable detective work of its own – such has been their obscurity – and fellow-Sherlockians in both Britain and America have assisted me so that we can at last make easily available the complete canon of Sherlock Holmes

[1] An important study of these remaining items is the two-part essay, 'Completing the Canon', by Peter Richard, which appeared in *The Sherlock Holmes Journal*, Winter 1962 and Winter 1963 issues. There was also a 'Postscript' in the Spring 1964 issue. In these articles Mr Richard skilfully argues the claims for each additional story, and I am happy to acknowledge my debt to his work in conducting my own research and reaching my own conclusions for this collection.

Adventures. It is also satisfying to be publishing these illusive items on the fiftieth anniversary of the death of Conan Doyle (he was born in May 1859 and died in July 1930), and it is the passing of his work into the Public Domain which has assisted in their publication.

If, first, we examine these remaining items, they may be categorized as follows:

a. Two commentaries by Conan Doyle on his famous detective: 'The Truth About Sherlock Holmes' and 'Some Personalia About Sherlock Holmes'.

b. Two Conan Doyle parodies featuring Holmes: 'The Field Bazaar' and 'How Watson Learned The Trick'.

c. Two Sherlockian cases: 'The Adventure of the Tall Man' (completed by another writer) and 'The Case of the Man Who Was Wanted' (which is the subject of some controversy as to its authorship).

d. Two short stories by Conan Doyle, in which Holmes emerges as the writer of important letters to the Press and which help solve baffling mysteries.

e. Two plays, a one-act drama – 'The Crown Diamond' – and a comedy sketch – 'The Painful Predicament of Sherlock Holmes' – in which the actor William Gillette may have had a hand.

f. An early Conan Doyle story, 'The Mystery of Uncle Jeremy's Household', in which the prototypes of Holmes and Watson make their bow; and a poem, 'The Case of the Inferior Sleuth', in which Conan Doyle disassociates himself from Holmes's view of other literary detectives.

Should any fervent Sherlockian immediately dispute the inclusion of two of the items listed, namely 'The Case of the Man Who Was Wanted' and 'The Painful Predicament of Sherlock Holmes', the total of twelve extra items still holds good, for there are also in existence two other full-length plays by Conan Doyle – 'Sherlock Holmes' and 'The Speckled Band'. 'Sherlock Holmes' was certainly written by Conan Doyle though William Gillette who made it famous may well have amended parts of it, while 'The Speckled Band' was all his own work, a three-act drama based on the short story of the same title. These are not included in this collection, although they are undeniably part of the Sherlockian canon, for the simple reasons that they would have made this volume prohibitively long and, more importantly, both are readily available in editions published by Samuel French Ltd. So instead I have, as you will find, included in the book by way of an Appendix three other items of Sherlockiana, all by Conan Doyle. They each have a special relevance to completing our picture of the Great Detective.

For the sake of this completeness, I believe I should also mention one or two other items found among Conan Doyle's papers by his biographer, John Dickson Carr, while he was researching his *Life of Sir Arthur Conan Doyle* (1949), though neither could in my opinion be justifiably given a place in this book. In a packet marked 'Envelope XXIX', Carr tells us, he found a 'Map of Holmes's and Watson's Clash with the Enemy' – but before anyone can get excited at such a potentially important discovery he adds, 'This is a joke, not of Holmesian relevance.' More interesting, however, were three exercise books bound in thick cardboard which he came across among a collection of more than fifty of Doyle's notebooks and commonplace books. They contained a three-act play entitled 'Angels of Darkness', written in the author's neat and distinctive hand. Of this, Dickson Carr says:

'He had written the first two acts at Southsea in 1889, the third in 1890, when Sherlock Holmes seemed to have no possible future. "Angels of Darkness" is chiefly a reconstruction of the Utah scenes in "A Study in Scarlet"; the whole action takes place in the United States. Holmes does not appear in it. But Dr John H. Watson does very much appear.

'"Angels of Darkness" presents a problem to any biographer. The biographer, in theory at least, must be an unrelenting Gradgrind; he should not indulge in those glorious Holmes-Watson speculations which have caused controversy on both sides of the Atlantic. But the devil of temptation prods horribly. Anyone who turns over the pages of "Angels in Darkness", then, will be electrified to find that Watson

11

has been concealing from us many important episodes in his life.

'Watson, in fact, once practised medicine in San Francisco. And his reticence can be understood; he acted discreditably. Those who have suspected Watson of black perfidy in his relations with women will find their worst suspicions justified. Either he had a wife before he married Mary Morstan, or else he heartlessly jilted the poor girl whom he holds in his arms as the curtain falls on "Angels in Darkness".

'The name of the girl? There lies our difficulty. To give her name, a well-known one, would be to betray the author as well as the character. At best it would impeach Watson in matters other than matrimonial; at worst it would upset the whole saga, and pose a problem which the keenest deductive wits of the Baker Street Irregulars could not unravel.

'Conan Doyle . . . knew he must put aside that play forever. There were good things in it, notably the comic scenes not present in "A Study in Scarlet"; but a play about Watson without Sherlock Holmes would leave the public aghast; and it has not been published even yet.'

Dickson Carr's verdict is certainly one that all Sherlockians will, I am sure, share!

But I have dwelt long enough on items which have no place here; let me now sketch in the background to the twelve items which do complete the canon. I have arranged them in chronological order of publication, from 'The Mystery of Uncle Jeremy's Household' in 1887

12

to 'How Watson Learned The Trick' written in 1924 (excluding, of course, 'The Truth About Sherlock Holmes' which Conan Doyle wrote in 1923, but which reads more conveniently at the beginning of the collection) and this more than spans the whole period of the saga from when it was begun in 1887 with 'A Study in Scarlet' to 'His Last Bow' which appeared in 1917. If these contributions are added to the sixty Adventures we already have, they at long last bring to a triumphant finale the authentic life and cases of the 'Master of Detectives'.

THE TRUTH ABOUT SHERLOCK HOLMES (1923)

I think it would be difficult to find anything more suitable than this essay by Conan Doyle to open a collection of his last writings about Sherlock Holmes – save, of course, arranging for him to compose a completely new Introduction from beyond the grave. He actually wrote it back in 1923 for Collier's, the American magazine firm who published many of the Holmes stories, and it appeared in their journal, *The National Weekly* in the pre-Christmas issue of 29 December 1923. In the piece he describes how he created Holmes, the initial difficulties he had in finding a publisher, and then his genuine amazement at how the public took to his detective. This popularity in turn created its own problems as far as his literary career was concerned, and he deals with this quandary in a frank and engaging way. Sir Arthur later utilized the facts in this essay in his long out-of-print autobiography, *Memories and Adventures* (1924), but this marks its first republication in its original form.

THE MYSTERY OF UNCLE JEREMY'S HOUSEHOLD (1887)

As Conan Doyle has admitted, Holmes and Watson did not spring fully finished into his mind, but rather developed from his musing on his old university Professor, Dr Joseph Bell, and the detective story genre as a whole. Their first appearance in the form we now know and value was, of course, in the novel, *A Study in Scarlet*, published in *Beeton's Christmas Annual* of 1887. But they were actually taking shape before this and made their first bow in prototype in a tale Conan Doyle called 'The Mystery of Uncle Jeremy's Household' published in *Boy's Own Paper* almost twelve months prior to *Beeton*. It is significant to note that in his essay, 'The Truth About Sherlock Holmes', Conan Doyle makes reference to the fact that he wrote some of his earliest stories for several journals, including *Boy's Own Paper*, but dismisses all these efforts and trusts they will remain 'forever in oblivion'. On examination of 'The Mystery of Uncle Jeremy's Household', published in seven episodes during January and February, 1887, a reason for this attitude immediately becomes apparent: the tale is actually an early working of the idea of an intelligent and resourceful detective, complete with partner, solving a baffling mystery – the self-same format which was to make the Holmes and Watson stories so successful. Examination of Conan Doyle's work shows that he, in fact, recycled several of his early themes in later works: 'The Mystery of Sasassa Valley', for instance, which is reprinted later in this book, has at its heart a 'frightful fiend with glowing eyes', which turns out to be a rather more commonplace object. The parallel with the story of 'The Hound of the Baskervilles' will be obvious to the reader. My opinion concerning 'The Mystery of Uncle Jeremy's Household' is also shared by a distinguished Sherlockian, James Edward Holroyd, who has also had a chance to read the now extremely rare and coveted issues of the *BOP* in which the Conan Doyle detective story appeared. In the *Sherlock Holmes Journal* of spring 1967 he says the story is 'remarkable as containing various echoes of Holmes and Watson before the first Baker Street adventure appeared in print.' He goes on:

'In the story, Hugh Lawrence, the narrator, had lodgings in Baker Street. His friend was John H. Thurston. Sherlockians will scarcely need to be reminded that Watson's front names were John H. and that Thurston was the name of the man with whom he played billiards at the club. Lawrence, like Watson, studied medicine, while Thurston, like Holmes, was devoted to chemistry, spent his time "happily among his test-tubes and solutions" and even had "an acid-stained finger" . . . If Uncle Jeremy's

Household was indeed written, or conceived before *A Study in Scarlet*, all the parallels I have quoted would become precursors of the Saga and would answer the question, "Did Sherlock Holmes originate in BOP?" '

In reading this fascinating story, brought back into print for the first time in almost a hundred years, the reader will also find some other Sherlockian parallels not quoted by Holroyd. Hugh Lawrence, like Holmes, makes a practice of studying people to discern their characters, is good as cross-examination, and is quite indifferent to the charms of women. He is also strong, brave and resourceful and prefers to solve the mysterious goings-on in the household himself rather than call in the police. The reader will, I believe, find many other features in 'The Mystery of Uncle Jeremy's Household' that were repeated in *A Study in Scarlet* and later Holmes's adventures, thereby making it a legitimate precursor to the saga and qualifying it for a place in the canon.

THE MEMOIRS OF SHERLOCK HOLMES:
'The Field Bazaar' (1896)
'The Field Bazaar', which Conan Doyle wrote in 1896, is not only a genuine early Sherlockian adventure, but also one of the first parodies of Holmes and Watson – the type of story which subsequently became very popular with other writers, and has exercised pens as diverse as those of J. M. Barrie, Bret Harte, O. Henry, Stephen Leacock, R. C. Lehmann, A. A. Milne

and Mark Twain to mention just a few. The parody is one of only two that Doyle himself wrote, the other being 'How Watson Learned The Trick' which is also republished in this collection. 'The Field Bazaar' is an amusing piece about a conversation between Holmes and Watson over their breakfast table and was written by Conan Doyle to help raise funds at Edinburgh University where from 1876 to 1881 he had studied to become a doctor. (The money was to help enlarge the University cricket ground and Conan Doyle was, as we know, a great cricket enthusiast.) It appeared in the university magazine, *The Student* on 20 November 1896, and has subsequently been referred to, because of its elusiveness, as a 'lost adventure'.

THE STORY OF THE MAN WITH
THE WATCHES (1898)
THE STORY OF THE LOST SPECIAL (1898)
These two detective stories by Conan Doyle which appeared in the *Strand* within a month of each other (July and August, 1898) have been exercising the minds of Sherlockians for almost fifty years. As far back as 1936 they were being described as 'Two suppressed Holmes episodes' by the noted authority Christopher Morley, and ever since argument has waged back and forward about their place in the canon. I myself have never been in any doubt, and this view-point is emphatically supported by perhaps the greatest expert on the saga, the American Edgar

17

W. Smith, editor of *The Baker Street Journal*, who in 1956 wrote: ' "The Lost Special" and "The Man with the Watches" are certainly, in my opinion, Canon-fodder. I am convinced that these accounts were written by Holmes, as were "The Adventures of the Lion's Mane" and "The Adventure of the Blanched Soldier". The style is certainly not Watson's; but it reminds me very much of "His Last Bow" which many, including myself, now believe to have been written by Holmes.'

Knowing the delight of Sherlockians in discussing any contentious points concerning 'The Master', it is no surprise to find that there have been quite a number of articles published over the years on this issue, but almost to a man the writers support the view that both stories *are* part of the canon. That eminent English Sherlockian, Lord Donegall, is a strong advocate and has cited two particular quotations in the stories which he believes settle the matter beyond dispute. Writing in the *Sherlock Holmes Journal*, Winter 1969, he deals first with the case of 'The Lost Special' and says, 'But there can be no doubt, even in the face of Watson's silence, that the "amateur reasoner of some celebrity" [referred to in the story] who volunteered a solution of the case in a letter printed in the London *Times* on 3 July 1890, was indeed the sage of Baker Street. On this point, the evidence of the opening sentence of the letter as it has come down to us is final and conclusive.' Lord Donegall then turns to the other story:

'Nor can there be any doubt that the "well-known criminal investigator" [mentioned in the tale] who similarly volunteered a solution of the baffling mystery of "The Man with the Watches", two years later, was also Sherlock Holmes. Here again the explanation offered – in a letter to the *Daily Gazette*, written probably late in March or early in April 1892 – did not jibe exactly with the facts as ultimately revealed; and here again the Watsonian reticence may be condoned both on this ground and on the ground of Holmes's preoccupation with other more pregnant things. But the letter itself rings true – the cold, systematic logic of the synthetic reasoning employed, and the condescending didacticism which marks the style and method of expression throughout, attest unerringly to the Master's hand.' In the light of such convincing argument, I find it impossible to deny that these two stories are not both deserved and important parts of the complete Sherlockian canon. (As a matter of record, both stories have for many years been included in all French editions of the Complete Adventures.)

THE ADVENTURES OF THE TALL MAN (*c.* 1900)
This is a particularly unusual and interesting item of Sherlockiana for it is the plot outline for a Holmes Adventure which Conan Doyle never wrote in full. It was discovered by another of Conan Doyle's biographers, Hesketh Pearson, while he was burrowing among the author's voluminous papers in the early 1940s. Most

appropriately, he chose the pages of the *Strand* magazine to announce his discovery, revealing in the issue of August 1943: 'Among Doyle's papers I discovered the scenario for an unwritten Sherlock Holmes story, in which the detective, baffled by the criminal's cunning, is reduced to the strategem of frightening the villain into a confession of guilt. This is done with the help of an actor, who makes himself up to resemble the murdered man, pokes his ghost-like head into the bedroom window of the murderer and cries out his name in "a ghastly sepulchral voice". The criminal gibbers with fright and gives the game away.' When this announcement was made by Pearson there were some who immediately expressed doubts about the authenticity of the outline – yet these were soon swept aside by Edgar W. Smith, who retorted in *The Baker Street Journal*, 'I think the plot is authentic. Yes, this doubtless came from the deed-box at Cox and Co!' The item is reprinted here just as Conan Doyle left it, and apart from its intrinsic value in providing us with details of yet another case of deduction by the Master, it also gives us a fascinating insight into the way the author wrote his stories, first mapping out his characters, plot and denouement before writing the actual tale. In 1947, another well-known American Sherlockian, Robert A. Cutter, took on the difficult task of clothing this literary skeleton with flesh: it is included here and is, I think, a work of which Conan Doyle would have approved.

The Painful Predicament of Sherlock Holmes (1905)

This is another illusive and puzzling piece of Sherlockiana – a one-act play in which Holmes solves a mystery without speaking a word! It is illusive because copies have been of the utmost rarity for over half a century, and puzzling because we cannot be sure whether the author was Conan Doyle or William Gillette, the American actor who first brought Holmes to the stage in New York in 1899. Of this original four-act drama, to which I referred earlier, Peter Richard tells us: 'In 1897 Doyle wrote his Sherlock Holmes play. Both Henry Irving and Beerbohm Tree considered producing it – but eventually the play was put aside until Charles Frohman procured the rights for the American actor, William Gillette . . . It had a long and successful history, Gillette playing the part in many revivals for some thirty-five years, including a London run at the Lyceum Theatre in 1901.'

It was in 1905, when the play, 'Sherlock Holmes', was already an established favourite with audiences, that 'The Painful Predicament of Sherlock Holmes' was first performed in London, with Gillette in the title rôle. At the time the American actor was appearing in a new comedy entitled 'Clarice', but wanted a short curtain-raiser to amuse his audience. According to a contemporary report he had planned to use a humorous sketch entitled 'The Silent System' but this apparently became unavailable and a

21

substitute had to be found. Gillette decided to look no further than the character with whom he was already becoming identified and who had aided his career immeasurably – Sherlock Holmes. And at this point the speculation begins. Some Sherlockians are of the opinion that Gillette himself dashed off the 'Painful Predicament' although there is no manuscript in existence in his hand to substantiate this, while others, notably Edgar W. Smith, feel the actor may well have called on Conan Doyle – with whom he was already friendly – to whip up something quickly for him. We do know for certain that Doyle wrote several plays and pastiches at this time (for example the already mentioned 'Sherlock Holmes' and 'The Field Bazaar') and it seems not unreasonable to speculate he could easily have produced this light-hearted sketch in a matter of days, if not hours. It is also a fact that Holmes was protected by copyright in England and Conan Doyle would have had to have been consulted. In any event, the play was staged on 23 March 1905, with Gillette and a Miss Barrymore as Holmes's talkative client. Just how hastily the production had been put on was revealed in a review in the *New York Times* the following day: 'Miss Barrymore played her part after only twenty minutes' study, a remarkable feat of memory, and only once did she slip up on her lines. During the whole course of the playlet, Mr Gillette did not speak once, but he has certain business of writing on slips of paper and handing them to

Miss Barrymore. By this means he was enabled to write the cues out for her!' As an interesting footnote to this long-forgotten play, the actor who played the only other important character in the sketch, a page boy named Billy, was destined to enjoy a form of immortality more than equalling that of Sherlock Holmes. His name was Master Charles Chaplin.

THE CASE OF THE MAN WHO WAS WANTED
(*c*. 1914)

This is without doubt the most controversial of all the Holmes items associated with the canon. It was discovered among Conan Doyle's papers by Hesketh Pearson, and later published in America with the recorded permission of the Executors of the Conan Doyle Estate – and yet it is claimed that the story was actually the work of a retired English architect, Arthur Whitaker, who sold it for its plot to Conan Doyle for the ridiculous sum of £10! Let us, though, examine the facts. Pearson revealed his discovery in the same issue of the *Strand* (August 1943) in which he had reported finding the outline for 'The Adventure of the Tall Man'. He wrote, 'Another discovery of mine was more interesting: a complete adventure of the great detective called "The Man Who Was Wanted". It is not up to par, and Doyle showed wisdom in leaving it unpublished; though when news of my discovery reached America the threat of its suppression almost created an international incident, one Holmes fan going so far as to suggest that the future relationship between the two countries might be imperilled if this addition to the Sherlock saga was not given to the world.' Despite his lack of enthusiasm for the quality of the story, Pearson did add significantly, 'The opening scene between Holmes and Watson betrays the hand of the Master . . . By the time he wrote that story, Doyle was thoroughly sick of Sherlock Holmes.' John Dickson Carr also refers to the story in his *Life of Conan Doyle* (1949): 'He never tried to force a story. One Holmes story, "The Man Who Was Wanted" he rejected and put away. Since it has not been published, those of us who have read it can say that the central plot-idea – how a man may disappear from ship-board, under the eyes of witnesses – is worthy of that unwritten tale of Mr James Phillimore . . . But it is written casually, almost impatiently, with its author's mind and heart turned towards other matters.' Carr was not quite correct in one of his assertions, however, because 'The Man Who Was Wanted' *had* been published, albeit only in America. Ever since the news of Pearson's find had become common knowledge, American magazine publishers had relentlessly pursued Denis Conan Doyle, the Literary Executor of his father's Estate, for permission to reprint this 'lost adventure'. Finally, Denis succumbed to the advances of the giant Hearst Group in New York and granted permission for them to run it in their enormously popular magazine, *The Cosmopolitan*, in August 1948. Naturally enough, the story was heralded by a striking announcement: 'The most famous detective of all time solves his last case! A recently discovered and heretofore unpublished novelette starring the immortal Sherlock Holmes.' From that day to this the argument about the authorship has continued, although the disbelievers of its authenticity would appear to be in the stronger position as a result of the Executors actually making a payment of royalties to Mr Arthur Whitaker. Despite all that has been said and written about 'The Man Who Was Wanted', I still cannot help wondering whether Conan Doyle did not figure in its creation somehow. Sadly, neither Arthur Whitaker nor Denis Conan Doyle are still alive so that we might go over the matter anew. Perhaps, though, Sir Arthur might have had something to do with the concept or even written part of it (*vide* Hesketh Pearson's comment), and I find myself unable to dismiss the story as spurious as many Sherlockians have done. There is no denying the mystery surrounding 'The Man Who Was Wanted', but all the same I feel it deserves a place here. I trust you will agree.

SOME PERSONALIA ABOUT MR SHERLOCK HOLMES (1917)

Sherlock Holmes was a world-wide favourite when the Editor of the *Strand*, Greenhough Smith, anxious to keep the detective's name featuring in the magazine, persuaded Conan Doyle to write this article about the legend he had created. The essay makes a particular point of the belief that had grown up regarding Holmes being a real person, and cites a number of instances of people writing to the sleuth of Baker Street imploring him to help them solve real-life crimes of one sort or another. Understandably, Conan Doyle also mentions the occasions when he found himself being asked to play Sherlock Holmes, with results quite as spectacular as those enjoyed by the Great Detective! 'Some Personalia About Mr Sherlock Holmes' was first published in the December 1917 issue of the *Strand* and has remained difficult to find ever since.

THE CASE OF THE INFERIOR SLEUTH (*c.* 1919)

In Holmes's first book, *A Study in Scarlet*, he addresses some rather unflattering remarks about two of his predecessors in detective fiction: C. Auguste Dupin, created in 1841 by Edgar Allan Poe, and Monsieur Lecoq, devised by the French writer, Emile Gaboriau, in 1866. Conan Doyle, of course, admitted that he drew considerable inspiration from the works of Poe and Gaboriau in creating Holmes, so it should be born carefully in mind that it is Sherlock who speaks these lines in that first story:

Sherlock Holmes rose and lit his pipe. 'No doubt you think that you are complimenting me in comparing me to Dupin,' he observed. 'Now, in my opinion, Dupin was a very inferior fellow. That trick of his of breaking

26

in on his friends' thoughts with an apropos remark after a quarter of an hour's silence is really very showy and superficial. He had some analytical genius, no doubt; but he was by no means such a phenomenon as Poe appeared to imagine.'

'Have you read Gaboriau's works?' I asked. 'Does Lecoq come up to your idea of a detective?'

Sherlock Holmes sniffed sardonically. 'Lecoq was a miserable bungler,' he said in an angry voice; 'he had only one thing to recommend him, and that was his energy. That book made me positively ill. The question was how to identify an unknown prisoner. I could have done it in twenty-four hours. Lecoq took six months or more. It might be made a text-book for detectives to teach them what to avoid.'

Watson, apparently, was not the only one to be perturbed by such ungenerous remarks about two literary characters he admired. In 1915 the American critic and poet, Arthur Guiterman, addressed some strong lines of complaint to Conan Doyle. Poor Sir Arthur saw at once that the words he had put into the mouth of his character had been attributed equally to himself. He took up his pen to defend himself in a like manner. These two poems now form a unique and important addition to the canon – Conan Doyle's lines comprising the only Sherlockian verse he ever wrote – and in them the author sets the record straight once and for all on his opinion of Holmes's literary predecessors. The Guiterman poem first appeared in a collection of light verse called *The Laughing Muse*, and Doyle's riposte was published some years later in Lincoln Springfield's reminiscences, *Some Piquant People* (1924). This is the first time they have appeared together in a collection.

THE CROWN DIAMOND: AN EVENING WITH SHERLOCK HOLMES (1921)

'The Crown Diamond' is the second of Conan Doyle's short plays featuring Sherlock Holmes and is unique among his work in that it was later turned *into* one of the Holmes cases, 'The Adventure of the Mazarin Stone', rather than having been adapted *from* existing material. Records indicate that this 'Evening with Sherlock Holmes' was given its first trial performance at the Bristol Hippodrome on 2 May 1921, and then transferred to London, opening there at the Coliseum on 16 May. Although the run continued, with one break, until the end of August, there is no indication that it has ever been performed again in England, and it has certainly never been staged in America. All the evidence points to the fact that Doyle astutely adapted the play into a short story for the *Strand* while it was still running at the Coliseum: in any event it appeared in the magazine in the October 1921 issue. Doyle also made certain changes to the story in the transition from stage to printed page, the most important one being that the villain of the play, the notorious Colonel Sebastian Moran, became Count Negretto Sylvius in the story. Though no one would claim that Conan Doyle was an outstanding playwright, his Holmes and Watson plays do have a sense of theatre about them which must have made their performances well worth attending, and it would indeed be nice to see them revived today. It is a particular pleasure to be rescuing 'The Crown Diamond' from obscurity and placing it in the Sherlockian canon as it has only once ever been printed – and that was in a private edition of just fifty-nine copies.

HOW WATSON LEARNED THE TRICK (1924)

The writing of this Holmes and Watson parody, which Conan Doyle undertook towards the very end of his life, may well be the most curious story in the saga. In 1924 a remarkable doll's house belonging to the then Queen of England, was being put on exhibition in London. The beautifully made toy, with its exquisite miniature furniture and fittings, possessed a small library with rows of tiny books. At the time none of these books contained any text, and the idea was mooted to invite the leading literary figures of the day to write short stories which could then be painstakingly reprinted in the little volumes. Not surprisingly Sir Arthur was one of the authors who was approached and – staunch patriot that was – agreed soon thereafter producing a story he knew would be acceptable: a brief Sherlock Holmes episode called 'How Watson Learned The Trick'. On its receipt, says a contemporary report, it was 'printed and bound in one of the miniature volumes comprising the library of this elaborate Lilliputan structure.' Although the story naturally generated a considerable amount of interest while the exhibition was on, once the doors of the doll's house had been closed to the public it was soon forgotten and the text has since become excessively rare. It was briefly rescued from this obscurity in April 1951 when it appeared in a typewritten copy in *The Baker Street Journal* – from which it has been taken for this book. Aside from its rarity, 'How Watson Learned The Trick' is interesting because it seems to confirm the belief that Sherlock Holmes was born in Surrey. During the course of the episode, which takes place while the two friends are at breakfast, Holmes exclaims at the success of Surrey in a game of cricket. Commenting on this in his essay, 'Completing the Canon', Peter Richard says, 'Although a man may have only "small experience of cricket clubs" (as Holmes admits in "The Field Bazaar"), it is not unusual for him to follow his home County side with interest, even enthusiasm. It therefore seems probable that Holmes's birthplace was in Surrey – possible, in fact, that his ancestors, being country squires and Reigate being in Surrey, that they were indeed the original Reigate Squires!' In hindsight, it seems most fitting that in the last uncollected adventure which Conan Doyle left us he should have presented a clue to the very birthplace of his by then immortal sleuth.

The Appendix to this volume brings together three rare and fascinating pieces of Holmesian material that, like the first twelve items, are all by Conan Doyle and similarly help broaden our knowledge of the Great Detective as well as his creator.

A GAUDY DEATH: CONAN DOYLE TELLS THE TRUE STORY OF SHERLOCK HOLMES'S END (1900)
This section of the book begins with a particularly rare item which has escaped the attention of many Sherlockians. It appeared in the year 1900 in the British weekly magazine *Tit-Bits*, which, as it name suggests, was a pot-pourri of stories, articles, essays, interviews, puzzles and snippets of news and information all presented in a lively style to appeal to a mass readership. The publishers were George Newnes Ltd, who also owned the *Strand* magazine, and when *Tit-Bits* reached its thousandth Issue and decided to celebrate the fact, they utilized this association to obtain a scoop for which any other journal would have paid a fortune – an interview with the notoriously publicity shy, Dr Conan Doyle.

Conan Doyle had, of course, already dispatched Holmes over the Reichenbach Falls and was apparently anxious that he should remain there despite the continuing pressure from his readers. Hence the interview, which is given in Conan Doyle's own words and was almost certainly vetted by him before publication, is all the more interesting because of the light it throws on how he planned the 'killing' of Holmes, and because a crack is alredy beginning to show in his resolve to leave his detective in his watery grave in Switzerland. This item has not been reprinted since its original appearance in that special issue of *Tit-Bits* dated 15 December 1900.

THE MYSTERY OF SASASSA VALLEY (1879)

I have already briefly mentioned this story, which was the first Conan Doyle succeeded in getting published and which earned him the princely sum of three guineas. It is, however, more important than it at first seems because it uses for the first time an idea that later became central to the most famous of all the Sherlock Holmes Adventures, 'The Hound of the Baskervilles'. In the light of this fact it's perhaps not surprising that Conan Doyle makes no specific mention of the tale of his autobiography, *Memories and Adventures*, written in 1924, merely informing us: 'During the years before my marriage I had from time to time written short stories which were good enough to be marketable at very small prices – £4 on average – but not good enough to reproduce. They are scattered about the pages of *London Society*, *All The Year Round*, *Temple Bar*, *The Boy's Own*

Paper and other journals. There let them lie.' In fact, 'The Mystery of Sasassa Valley' was submitted to the popular magazine *Chambers's Journal* in the spring of 1879 and after the usual interminable delay was accepted for publiction. The struggling young doctor was delighted to accept and the story duly appeared, anonymously, in the October issue. (It was *Chamber's* policy to credit only their most famous contributors). At the time, we learn, Conan Doyle expressed only one regret about the publication – that the Editor had cut out his use of the word 'damn' in several conversations! With the passing of the years, however, he was no doubt glad the story was not easily attributable to him for, as you will read, it is based on a superstition about a demon-like creature with glowing eyes which eventually turns out to be . . . but I will not spoil your interest by revealing the ending. Nonetheless, the similarity with the idea of the 'demon hound' of Dartmoor will be evident to anyone who has read the Holmes story. This publication marks the mystery's first return to print in almost a hundred years.

MY FAVOURITE SHERLOCK HOLMES ADVENTURE (1927)

In March 1927, some months prior to the publication of the fifth and final volume of the short Holmes Adventures, *The Casebook of Sherlock Holmes*, Sir Arthur Conan Doyle took up his pen for the last time to write about his famous sleuth. Appropriately it was for the self-same magazine in which the Great Detective had been 'born', the *Strand*. The occasion was the announcement of a competition in which readers were invited to pick their favourite Holmes Adventure, and Sir Arthur had agreed to provide the definitive list. Seemingly he could not resist the opportunity for a last parting shot at the character who had made him famous and wealthy, but had also overshadowed every other achievement of his lifetime. 'I fear,' he wrote in the article, which was entitled 'Mr Sherlock Holmes to His Readers', 'that Mr Sherlock Holmes may become like one of those popular tenors who, having outlived their time, are still tempted to make repeated farewell bows to their indulgent audiences. This must cease and he must go the way of all flesh, material or imaginary. One likes to think that there is some fantastic limbo for the children of imagination, some strange, impossible place where the beaux of Fielding may still make love to the belles of Richardson, where Scott's heroes still may strut, Dickens's delightful Cockneys still raise a laugh, and Thackeray's worldlings continue to carry on their reprehensible careers. Perhaps in some humble corner of such a Valhalla, Sherlock and his Watson may for a time find a place, while some more astute sleuth with some even less astute comrade may fill the stage which they have vacated.'

Although by this time Holmes had literally dozens of rivals clamouring after his position of pre-eminence in the detective field, the passing years were certainly not going to oblige his creator: the two men from Baker Street were already numbered among the immortals of literature and there they were destined to remain. In the rest of his article Conan Doyle again went over the facts of Holmes's career and commented on the views which were reaching him that some readers felt the standard of the Adventures had declined in the later years. He concluded, 'It is as a little test of the opinion of the public that I inaugurate the small competition announced here. I have drawn up a list of the twelve short stories contained in the four published volumes[1] which I consider to be the best, and I should like to know to what extent my choice agrees with that of *Strand* readers. I have left my list in a sealed envelope with the Editor of the *Strand*.' Three months after the appearance of this article, in the June issue, Conan Doyle ended the speculation by publishing his list – or perhaps it would be more accurate to say that he really began the arguments that have continued unabated to this day about the respective merits of the stories.

Later that year Sir Arthur used his essay 'Mr Sherlock Holmes to His Readers' as the Preface

[1] The four volumes of stories referred to by Conan Doyle are *The Adventures of Sherlock Holmes*, *The Memoirs of Sherlock Holmes*, *The Return of Sherlock Holmes* and *His Last Bow*. The remaining twelve stories were still to appear as *The Casebook of Sherlock Holmes*.

to *The Casebook of Sherlock Holmes*, just deleting the reference to the competition and, for some strange reason best known to himself, the very relevant comment about the quality of the stories I have reprinted at the front of this book. With this list of his twelve favourite stories, Conan Doyle had finally done with Sherlock Holmes: he was never to write another word about him in the three short years of life which remained to him. Perhaps, though, there was no need to say any more, for his last paragraph in the address to readers was as good a finale as any author might hope to write about a character he had created and his particular ambitions for that character. So in bringing together this final collection of Sherlock Holmes material by Sir Arthur Conan Doyle, I can think of no better way of concluding my own remarks than by quoting his words one last time.

'And so, reader, farewell to Sherlock Holmes! I thank you for your constancy, and can but hope that some return has been made in the shape of that distraction from the worries of life and stimulating change of thought which can only be found in the fairy kingdom of romance.'

PETER HAINING

The Truth About Sherlock Holmes

When Sir Arthur Conan Doyle deliberately killed Sherlock Holmes the vehement protests which came from all quarters made him realize, to his amazement, how completely the great detective had captured the world's imagination. In this essay Sir Arthur answers all our questions about Holmes – how he was born and developed and why it became necessary to kill him. It is amusing to read here that Dr Bell, Holmes's prototype, was never able to help Doyle in contriving the stories. And he tells the story of that disastrous flyer in comic opera with Sir James Barrie, out of which came one good thing – Barrie's delightful parody on Sherlock Holmes which he wrote to console Doyle and which is also included here.

COLLIER'S *The National Weekly*
29 DECEMBER 1923

It was in October, 1876 that I began my medical course at the University of Edinburgh. The most notable of the characters whom I met was one Joseph Bell, surgeon at the Edinburgh Infirmary. Bell was a very remarkable man in body and mind. He was thin, wiry, dark with a

37

high-nosed, acute face, penetrating grey eyes, angular shoulders, and a jerky way of walking. His voice was high and discordant. He was a very skilful surgeon, but his strong point was diagnosis, not only of disease, but of occupation and character. For some reason which I have never understood he singled me out from the drove of students who frequented his wards and made me his out-patient clerk, which meant that I had to array his out-patients, make simple notes of their cases, and then show them in, one by one, to the large room in which Bell sat in state surrounded by his dressers and students. Then I had ample chance of studying his methods and in noticing that he often learned more of the patient by a few quick glances than I had done by my questions. Occasionally the results were very dramatic, though there were times when he blundered. In one of the best cases he said to a civilian patient:

'Well, my man, you've served in the army?'

'Aye, sir.'

'Not long discharged?'

'No sir.'

'A Highland regiment?'

'Aye, sir.'

'A noncom officer?'

'Aye, sir.'

'Stationed at Barbados?'

'Aye, sir.'

'You see, gentlemen,' he would explain, 'the man was a respectful man, but did not remove his hat. They do not in the army, but he would have learned civilian ways had be been long discharged. He has an air of authority and he is obviously Scottish. As to Barbados, his complaint is elephantiasis, which is West Indian and not British.' To his audience of Watsons it all seemed most miraculous until it was explained, and then it became simple enough. It is no wonder that after the study of such a character I used and amplified his methods when in later life I tried to build up a scientific detective who solved cases on his own merits and not through the folly of the criminal. Bell took a keen interest in these detective tales and made suggestions, which were not, I am bound to say, very practical.

The Twopenny Box

I endeavoured almost from the first to compress the classes for a year into half a year, so as to have some months in which to earn a little money. It was at this time that I first learned that shillings might be earned in other ways than by filling phials. Some friend remarked to me that my letters were very vivid, and surely I could write some things to sell. I may say that the general aspiration toward literature was tremendously strong upon me, and that my mind was reaching out in what seemed an aimless way in all sorts of directions. I used to be allowed twopence for my lunch, that being the price of a mutton pie, but near the pie shop was a second-hand bookshop with a barrel full of old books and the legend, 'Your choice for 2d', stuck above it. Often the price of my luncheon used to be spent on some sample out of this barrel, and I have within reach of my arm, as I write these lines, copies of Gordon's *Tacitus*, Temple's works, Pope's *Homer*, Addison's *Spectator* and Swift's works, which all came out of the twopenny box.

Anyone observing my actions and tastes would have said that so strong a spring would certainly overflow, but for my own part I never dreamed I could myself produce decent prose, and the remark of my friend, who was by no means given to flattery, took me greatly by surprise. I sat down, however, and I wrote a little adventure story which I called 'The Mystery of the Sasassa Valley'. To my great joy and surprise, it was accepted by *Chambers's Journal*, and I received three guineas. It mattered not that other attempts failed. I had done it once and I cheered myself by the thought that I could do it again.

Upon emerging from Edinburgh as a bachelor of medicine in 1881, my plans were all exceedingly fluid and I was ready to join army, navy, Indian service, or anything which offered an opening. But after taking a trip in a cargo vessel along the west coast of Africa, I finally settled down to practice in Plymouth.

I had at this time contributed several stories to *London Society*, a magazine now defunct, but then flourishing under the editorship of a Mr Hogg. It had never entered my head yet that literature might give me a career, or anything beyond a little casual pocket money, but already it was a deciding factor in my life, for I could not have held on, and must have either starved or given in but for the few pounds which Mr Hogg sent me.

During the years before my marriage I had from time to time written short stories which were good enough to be marketable at very small prices – five pounds on average – but not good enough to reproduce. They are scattered about amid the pages of *London Society*, of *All the Year Round*, of *Temple Bar*, the *Boys' Own Paper* and other journals. There let them lie. They served their purpose in relieving me of a little of that financial burden which always pressed upon me. I can hardly have earned more than ten or fifteen pounds a year from this source, so that the idea of making a living by it never occurred to me. But though I was not putting out, I was taking in. I still have notebooks full of all sorts of knowledge which I acquired during that time. It is a great mistake to start putting out cargo when you have hardly stowed any on board.

Enter Holmes and Watson

I had for some time from 1884 onward been engaged upon a sensational book of adventure which I had called *The Firm of Girdlestone*, which represented my first attempt at a connected narrative. Save for occasional patches, it is a worthless book. I felt now that I was capable of something cleaner and crisper and more workmanlike. Gaboriau had rather attracted me by the neat dovetailing of his plots, and Poe's masterful detective, Mr. Dupin, had from my boyhood been one of my heroes. But could I bring an addition of my own? I thought of my old teacher Joe Bell, of his eagle face, of his curious ways, of his eerie trick of spotting details. If he were a detective he would surely reduce this fascinating but unorganized business to something nearer to an exact science. I would try if I could get this effect. It was surely possible in real life, so why should I not make it plausible in fiction? It is all very well to say that a man is clever, but the reader wants to see examples of it – such examples as Bell gave us every day in the wards.

The idea amused me. What should I call the fellow? I still possess the leaf of a notebook with various alternative names. One rebelled against the elementary art which gives some inkling of character in the name, and creates Mr Sharps or Mr Ferrets. First it was Sherringford Holmes; then it was Sherlock Holmes. He could not tell his own exploits, so he must have a commonplace comrade as a foil – an educated man of action who could both join in the exploits and narrate them. A drab, quiet name for this unostentatious man. Watson would do. And so I had my purpose and wrote my *Study in Scarlet*.

I knew that the book was as good as I could make it and I had high hopes. When *Girdlestone* used to come circling back with the precision of a homing pigeon I was grieved but not surprised, for I acquiesced in the decision. But when my little Holmes book began also to do the circular tour I was hurt, for I knew that it deserved a better fate. James Payn applauded, but found it both too short and too long, which was true enough. Arrowsmith received it in May 1886, and returned it unread in July. Two or three others sniffed and turned away. Finally, as Ward, Lock & Co. made a specialty of cheap and often sensational literature, I sent it to them. They said:

DEAR SIR – *We have read your story and are pleased with it. We could not publish it this year, as the market is flooded at present with cheap fiction, but if you do not object to its being held over till next year, we will give you twenty-five pounds for the copyright.*

Yours faithfully,

WARD, LOCK & CO.

Oct. 30, 1886.

It was not a very tempting offer, and even I, poor as I was, hesitated to accept it. It was not merely the small sum offered, but it was the long delay, for this book might open a road for me. I was heartsick, however, at repeated disappointments, and I felt that perhaps it was true wisdom to make sure of publicity, however late. Therefore I accepted, and the book became Beeton's Christmas Annual of 1887.

It was in consequence of a publishers' dinner, at which I was a guest, that I wrote *The Sign of the Four*, in which Holmes made his second appearance. But thereafter for a time he was laid on the shelf, for, encouraged by the kind reception which 'Micah Clarke' had received from the critics, I now determined upon an even bolder and more ambitious flight.

Hence came my two books. *The White Company*, written in 1889, and *Sir Nigel*, written fourteen years later. Of the two I consider the latter the better book, but I have no hesitation in saying that the two of them taken together did thoroughly achieve my purpose, that they made an accurate picture of that great age, and that, as a single piece of work, they form the most complete, satisfying, and ambitious thing that I have ever done. All things find their level, but I believe that if I had never touched Holmes, who has tended to obscure my higher work, my position in literature would at the present moment be a more commanding one. The work needed much research and I have still got my notebooks full of all sorts of lore. I cultivate a simple style and avoid long words so far as possible, and it may be that this surface of ease has sometimes caused the reader to under-rate the amount of real research which lies in my historical novels. It is not a matter which troubles me, however, for I have always felt that justice is done in the end, and that the real merit of any work is never permanently lost.

I remember that as I wrote the last words of *The White Company* I felt a wave of exultation and, with a cry of 'That's done it!' I hurled my inky pen across the room, where it left a black smudge upon the duck's-egg wall paper. I knew in my heart that the book would live and that it would illuminate our national traditions. Now that it has passed through fifty editions I suppose I may say with all modesty that my forecast has proved to be correct. This was the last book which I wrote in my days of doctoring at Southsea, and marks an epoch in my life, so I can now hark back to some other phases of my last years at Bush Villa before I broke away into a new existence.

A number of monthly magazines were coming out at that time, notable among which was the *Strand* then, as now, under the very able editorship of Greenhough Smith. Considering these various journals with their disconnected stories, it had struck me that a single character running through a series, if only it engaged the attention of the reader, would bind that reader to that particular magazine.

Looking round for my central character, I felt that Sherlock Holmes, whom I had already handled in two little books, would easily lend himself to a succession of short stories. These I began in the long hours of waiting in my consulting room. Smith liked them from the first, and encouraged me to go ahead with them.

It was at this time that I definitely saw how foolish I was to waste my literary earnings in keeping up an oculist's room in Wimpole Street, and I determined with a wild rush of joy to cut the painter and to trust forever to my power of writing. So I settled down with a stout heart to do some literary work worthy of the name. The difficulty of the Holmes work was that every story really needed as clear-cut and original a plot as a longish book would do. One cannot without effort spin plots at such a rate. They are apt to become thin or to break. I was determined, now that I had no longer the excuse of absolute pecuniary pressure, never again to write anything which was not as good as I could possibly make it, and therefore I would not write a Holmes story without a worthy plot and without a problem which interested my own mind, for that is the first requisite before you can interest anyone else. If I have been able to sustain this character for a long time, and if the public find, as they will find, that the last story is as good as the first, it is entirely due to the fact that I never, or hardly ever, forced a story. Some have thought there was a falling off in the stories, and the criticism was neatly expressed by a Cornish boatman who said to me, 'I think, sir, when Holmes fell over that cliff, he may not have killed himself, but all the same he was never quite the same man afterwards.'

I was weary, however, of inventing plots and I set myself now to do some work which would certainly be less remunerative but would be more ambitious from a literary point of view. I had long been attracted by the epoch of Louis XIV and by those Huguenots who were the French equivalents of our Puritans. I had a good knowledge of the memoirs of that date, and many notes already prepared, so that it did not take me long to write *The Refugees*.

Yet it was still the Sherlock Holmes stories for which the public clamoured, and these from time to time I endeavoured to supply. At last, after I had done two series of them, I saw that I was in danger of having my hand forced, and of being entirely identified with what I regarded as a lower stratum of literary achievement. Therefore, as a sign of my resolution, I determined to end the life of my hero. The idea was in my mind when I went with my wife for a short holiday in Switzerland, in the course of which we walked down the Lauterbrunnen Valley. I saw there the wonderful falls of Reichenbach, a terrible place, and that, I thought, would make a worthy tomb for poor Sherlock, even if I buried my banking account along with him. So there I laid him, fully determined that he should stay there – as indeed for some twenty years he did.

I was amazed at the concern expressed by the public. They say that a man is never properly appreciated until he is dead, and the general protest against my summary execution of Holmes taught me how many and how numerous were his friends. 'You brute' was the beginning of the letter of remonstrance which one lady sent me, and I expect she spoke for others beside herself. I heard of many who wept. I fear I was utterly callous myself.

★

James Barrie is one of my oldest literary friends, and I knew him within a year or two of the time when we both came to London. He and I had one most unfortunate venture together. The facts were that he had promised Mr D'Oyly Carte that he would provide the libretto of a light opera for the Savoy. I was brought into the matter because Barrie's health failed on account of some family bereavement. I had an urgent telegram from him. I found him worried because he had bound himself by contract, and he felt in his present state unable to go forward with it. There were to be two acts, and he had written the first one, and had the rough scenario of the second. Would I come in with him and help him to complete it as part author? I did my best and wrote the lyrics for the second act, and much of the dialogue, but it had to take the predestined shape. The result was not good, and on the first night I felt inclined, like Charles Lamb, to hiss it from my box. The opera, *Jane Annie*, was one of the few failures in Barrie's brilliant career. We were well abused by the critics, but Barrie took all of it in the bravest spirit, and I still retain the comic verses of consolation which I received from him next morning.

There followed a parody on Holmes, written on the flyleaves of one of his books. It ran thus:

The adventure of the two collaborators
In bringing to a close the adventures of my friend Sherlock Holmes I am perforce reminded

that he never, save on the occasion which, as you will now hear, brought his singular career to an end, consented to act in any mystery which was concerned with persons who made a livelihood by their pen. 'I am not particular about the people I mix among for business purposes,' he would say, 'but at literary characters I draw the line.'

We were in our rooms in Baker Street one evening. I was (I remember) by the centre table writing out 'The Adventure of the Man Without a Cork Leg' (which had so puzzled the Royal Society and all the other scientific bodies of Europe), and Holmes was amusing himself with a little revolver practice.

It was his custom of a summer evening to fire round my head, just shaving my face, until he had made a photograph of me on the opposite wall, and it is a slight proof of his skill that many of these portraits in pistol shots are considered admirable likenesses.

I happened to look out of the window, and, perceiving two gentlemen advancing rapidly along Baker Street, asked him who they were. He immediately lit his pipe, and, twisting himself on a chair into a figure 8, replied:

'They are two collaborators in comic opera, and their play has not been a triumph.'

I sprang from my chair to the ceiling in amazement, and he then explained:

'My dear Watson, they are obviously men who follow some low calling. That much even you should be able to read in their faces. Those little pieces of blue paper which they fling angrily from them are Durrant's Press Notices. Of these they have obviously hundreds about their person (see how their pockets bulge). They would not dance on them if they were pleasant reading.'

I again sprang to the ceiling (which is much dented) and shouted: 'Amazing! But they may be mere authors.'

'No,' said Holmes, 'for mere authors only get one press notice a week. Only criminals, dramatists, and actors get them by the hundred.'

'Then they may be actors.'

'No, actors would come in a carriage.'

'Can you tell me anything else about them?'

'A great deal. From the mud on the boots of the tall one I perceive that he comes from South Norwood. The other is obviously a Scotch author.'

'How can you tell that?'

'He is carrying in his pocket a book called (I clearly see) "Auld Licht Something". Would anyone but the author be likely to carry about a book with such a title?'

I had to confess that this was improbable.

It was now evident that the two men (if such they can be called) were seeking our lodgings. I have said (often) that Holmes seldom gave way to emotion of any kind, but he now turned livid with passion. Presently this gave place to a strange look of triumph.

'Watson,' he said, 'that big fellow has for

years taken the credit for my most remarkable doings, but at last I have him – at last!'

Up I went to the ceiling, and when I returned the strangers were in the room.

'I perceive, gentlemen,' said Mr Sherlock Holmes, 'that you are at present afflicted by an extraordinary novelty.'

The handsomer of our visitors asked in amazement how he knew this, but the big one only scowled.

'You forget that you wear a ring on your fourth finger,' replied Mr Holmes calmly.

I was about to jump to the ceiling when the big brute interposed.

'That tommyrot is all very well for the public, Holmes,' said he, 'but you can drop it before me. And, Watson, if you go up to the ceiling again I shall make you stay there.'

Here I observed a curious phenomenon. My friend Sherlock Holmes *shrank*. He became small before my eyes. I looked longingly at the ceiling, but dared not.

'Let us cut out the first four pages,' said the big man, 'and proceed to business. I want to know why—'

'Allow me,' said Mr Holmes, with some of his old courage. 'You want to know why the public does not go to your opera.'

'Exactly,' said the other ironically, 'as you perceive by my shirt stud.' He added more gravely: 'And as you can only find out in one way I must insist on your witnessing an entire performance of the piece.'

It was an anxious moment for me. I shuddered, for I knew that if Holmes went I should have to go with him. But my friend had a heart of gold. 'Never!' he cried fiercely. 'I will do anything for you save that.'

'Your continued existence depends on it,' said the big man menacingly.

'I would rather melt into air,' replied Holmes proudly, taking another chair. 'But I can tell you why the public don't go to your piece without sitting the thing out myself.'

'Why?'

'Because,' replied Holmes calmly, 'they prefer to stay away.'

A dead silence followed that extraordinary remark. For a moment the two intruders gazed with awe upon the man who had unravelled their mystery so wonderfully. Then, drawing their knives –

Holmes grew less and less, until nothing was left save a ring of smoke which slowly circled to the ceiling.

The last words of great men are often noteworthy. These were the last words of Sherlock Holmes: 'Fool, fool! I have kept you in luxury for years. By my help you have ridden extensively in cabs where no author was ever seen before. *Henceforth you will ride in buses!*'

The brute sank into a chair aghast. The other author did not turn a hair.

To A. Conan Doyle
From his friend, J. M. BARRIE

Dangerous Ground

This parody, the best of all the numerous parodies, may be taken as an example, not only of the author's wit, but of his debonair courage, for it was written immediately after our joint failure, which at the moment was a bitter thought for both of us. There is, indeed, nothing more miserable than a theatrical failure, for you feel how many others who have backed you have been affected. It was, I am glad to say, my only experience of it, and I have no doubt that Barrie could say the same.

Before I leave the subject of the many impersonations of Holmes, I may say that all of them, and all the drawings, are very unlike my own original idea of the man. I saw him as very tall – 'over six feet, but so excessively lean that he seemed considerably taller,' said *A Study in Scarlet*. He had, as I imagined him, a thin razorlike face, with a great hawk's-bill of a nose, and two small eyes, set close together on either side of it. Such was my conception. It chanced, however, that poor Arthur Paget, who, before his premature death, drew all the original pictures, had a younger brother whose name, I think, was Harold, who served him as a model. The handsome Harold took the place of the more powerful but uglier Sherlock, and, perhaps from the point of view of my lady readers, it was as well. The stage has followed the type set up by the pictures.

People have often asked me whether I knew the end of a Holmes story before I started it. Of course I did. One could not possibly steer a course if one did not know one's destination. The first thing is to get your idea. We will suppose that this idea is that a woman, as in the last story, is suspected of biting a wound in her child, when she was really sucking that wound for fear of poison injected by some one else. Having got the key idea, one's next task is to conceal it and lay emphasis upon everything which can make for a different explanation. Holmes, however, can see all the fallacies of the alternatives, and arrives more or less dramatically at the true solution by steps which he can describe and justify.

He shows his powers by what the South Americans now call 'Sherlocholmitos', which means clever little deductions, which often have nothing to do with the matter in hand, but impress the reader with a general sense of power. The same effect is gained by his off-hand allusion to other cases. Heaven knows how many titles I have thrown about in a casual way, and how many readers have begged me to satisfy their curiosity as to 'Rigoletto and His Abominable Wife', 'The Adventure of the Tired Captain', or 'The Curious Experience of the Patterson Family in the Island of Uffa'. Once or twice, as in 'The Adventure of the Second Stain', which in my judgment is one of the neatest of the stories, I did actually use the title years before I wrote a story to correspond.

There are some questions concerned with particular stories which turn up periodically from every quarter of the globe. In 'The Adventure of the Priory School', Holmes remarks in his offhand way that by looking at a bicycle track on a damp moor one can say which way it is heading. I had so many remonstrances upon this point varying from pity to anger, that I took out my bicycle and tried. I had imagined that the observations of the way in which the track of the hind wheel overlaid the track of the front one when the machine was not running dead straight would show the direction. I found that my correspondents were right and I was wrong, for this would be the same whichever way the cycle was moving. On the other hand, the real solution was much simpler, for on an undulating moor the wheels make a deeper impression uphill and a more shallow one downhill, so Holmes was justified of his wisdom after all.

Sometimes I have got upon dangerous ground, where I have taken risks through my own want of knowledge of the correct atmosphere. I have, for example, never been a racing man, and yet I ventured to write 'Silver Blaze', where the mystery depends upon the laws of training and racing. The story is all right, and Holmes may have been at the top of his form, but my ignorance cries aloud to Heaven. I read an excellent and very damaging criticism of the story in some sporting paper, written clearly by a man who *did* know, in which he explained the exact penalties which would have come upon all concerned if they had acted as I described.

Half would have been in jail and the other half warned off the turf forever. However, I have never been nervous about details, and one must be masterful sometimes. When an alarmed editor wrote to me once: 'There is no second line of rails at this point,' I answered: 'I make one.' On the other hand, there are cases where accuracy is essential.

I do not wish to be ungrateful to Holmes, who has been a good friend to me in many ways. If I have sometimes been inclined to weary of him, it is because his character admits of no light or shade. He is a calculating machine, and anything you add to that simply weakens the effect. Thus the variety of the stories must depend upon the romance and compact handling of the plots. I would say a word for Watson also, who in the course of seven volumes never knows one gleam of humour or makes a single joke. To make a real character one must sacrifice everything to consistency and remember Goldsmith's criticism of Johnson that 'he would make the little fishes talk like whales.'

The Critic and the Snake

The impression that Holmes was a real person of flesh and blood may have been intensified by his frequent appearance upon the stage. After the withdrawal of my dramatization of 'Rodney Stone' from a theatre upon which I held a six months' lease I determined to play a bold and energetic game and certainly I never played a bolder. When I saw the course that things were taking I shut myself up and devoted my whole mind to making a sensational Sherlock Holmes drama. I wrote it in a week and called it 'The Speckled Band', after the short story of that name. I do not think that I exaggerate if I say that within a fortnight of the one play shutting down I had a company working upon the rehearsals of the other. It was a considerable success.

We had a fine boa to play the title rôle, a snake which was the pride of my heart, so one can imagine my disgust when I saw that the critic of the *Daily Telegraph* ended his disparaging review by the words: 'The crisis of the play was produced by the appearance of a palpably artificial serpent.' I was inclined to offer him a goodly sum if he would undertake to go to bed with it. We had several snakes at different times, but they were all inclined either to hang down from the hole in the wall like inanimate bell pulls, or else to turn back through the hole and get even with the stage carpenter, who pinched their tails in order to make them more lively. Finally we used artificial snakes, and everyone, including the stage carpenter, agreed that it was more satisfactory.

I have had many letters addressed to Holmes with requests that I forward them. Watson has also had a number of letters in which he has been asked for the address or for the autograph of his more brilliant confrère. A press-cutting

57

agency wrote to Watson asking whether Holmes would not wish to subscribe. When Holmes retired, several elderly ladies were ready to keep house for him, and one sought to ingratiate herself by assuring me that she knew all about bee-keeping and could 'segregate the queen'. I had considerable offers also for Holmes if he would examine and solve various family mysteries.

I have often been asked whether I had myself the qualities which I depicted, or whether I was merely the Watson that I look. Of course I am well aware that it is one thing to grapple with a practical problem and quite another thing when you are allowed to solve it under your own conditions. At the same time a man cannot spin a character out of his own inner consciousness and make it really life-like unless he has some possibilities of that character within him – which is a dangerous admission for one who has drawn so many villains as I.

I do not think that I ever realized what a living actual personality Holmes had become to the more guileless readers until I heard of the very pleasing story of the char-à-bancs of French schoolboys who, when asked what they wanted to see first in London, replied unanimously that they wanted to see Mr Holmes's lodgings in Baker Street. Many have asked me which house it is, but that is a point which, for excellent reasons, I will not decide.

The Mystery of Uncle Jeremy's Household

My life has been a somewhat chequered one, and it has fallen to my lot during the course of it to have had several unusual experiences. There is one episode, however, which is so surpassingly strange that whenever I look back to it it reduces the others to insignificance. It looms up out of the mists of the past, gloomy and fantastic, overshadowing the eventless years which preceded and which followed it.

It is not a story which I have often told. A few, but only a few, who know me well have heard the facts from my lips. I have been asked from time to time by these to narrate them to some assemblage of friends, but I have invariably refused, for I have no desire to gain a reputation as an amateur Munchausen. I have yielded to their wishes, however, so far as to draw up this written statement of the facts in connection with my visit to Dunkelthwaite.

Here is John Thurston's first letter to me. It is dated April, 1862. I take it from my desk and copy it as it stands:

My dear Lawrence, – If you knew my utter loneliness and complete *ennui* I am sure you would have pity upon me and come up to share my solitude. You have often made vague promises of visiting Dunkelthwaite and having a look at the Yorkshire Fells. What time could suit you better than the present? Of course I understand that you are hard at work, but as you are not actually taking out classes you can read just as well here as in Baker Street. Pack up your books, like a good fellow, and come along! We have a snug little room, with writing-desk and armchair, which will just do for your study. Let me know when we may expect you.

When I say that I am lonely I do not mean that there is any lack of people in the house. On the contrary, we form rather a large household. First and foremost, of course, comes my poor Uncle Jeremy, garrulous and imbecile, shuffling about in his list slippers, and composing, as is his wont, innumerable bad verses. I think I told you when last we met of that trait in his character. It has attained such a pitch that he has an amanuensis, whose sole duty it is to copy down and preserve these effusions. This fellow, whose name is Copperthorne, has become as necessary to the old man as his foolscap or as the 'Universal Rhyming Dictionary'. I can't say I care for him myself, but then I have always shared Caesar's prejudice against lean men – though, by the way, little Julius was rather inclined that way himself if we may believe the medals. Then we have the two children of my Uncle Samuel, who were adopted by Jeremy – there were three of them, but one has gone the way of all flesh – and their governess, a stylish-looking brunette with Indian blood in her veins. Besides all these, there are three maidservants and the old groom, so you see we have quite a little world of our own in this out-of-the way corner. For all that, my dear Hugh, I long for a familiar face and for a congenial companion. I am deep in chemistry myself, so I won't interrupt your studies. Write by return to your isolated friend,

JOHN H. THURSTON.

At the time that I received this letter I was in London, and was working hard for the final examination which should make me a qualified medical man. Thurston and I had been close friends at Cambridge before I took to the study of medicine, and I had a great desire to see him again. On the other hand, I was rather afraid that, in spite of his assurances, my studies might suffer by the change. I pictured to myself the childish old man, the lean secretary, the stylish governess, the two children, probably spoiled and noisy, and I came to the conclusion that when we were all cooped together in one country house there would be very little room for quiet reading. At the end of two days' cogitation I had almost made up my mind to refuse the invitation, when I received another letter from Yorkshire even more pressing than the first.

'We expect to hear from you by every post,' my friend said, 'and there is never a knock that I do not think it is a telegram announcing your train. Your room is all ready, and I think you will find it comfortable. Uncle Jeremy bids me say how very happy he will be to see you. He would have written, but he is absorbed in a great epic poem of five thousand lines or so, and he spends his day trotting about the rooms, while Copperthorne stalks behind him like the monster in Frankenstein, with note-book and pencil, jotting down the words of wisdom as they drop from his lips. By the way, I think I mentioned the brunettish governess to you. I might throw her out as a bait to you if you retain your taste for ethnological studies. She is the child of an Indian chieftain, whose wife was an Englishwoman. He was killed in the mutiny, fighting against us, and, his estates being seized by Government, his daughter, then fifteen, was left almost destitute. Some charitable German merchant in Calcutta adopted her, it seems, and brought her over to Europe with him together with his own daughter. The latter died, and then Miss Warrender – as we call her, after her mother – answered uncle's advertisement; and here she is. Now, my dear boy, stand not upon the order of your coming, but come at once.'

There were other things in this second letter which prevent me from quoting it in full.

There was no resisting the importunity of my old friend, so, with many inward grumbles,

62

I hastily packed up my books, and, having telegraphed overnight, started for Yorkshire the first thing in the morning. I well remember that it was a miserable day, and that the journey seemed to be an interminable one as I sat huddled up in a corner of the draughty carriage, revolving in my mind many problems of surgery and of medicine. I had been warned that the little wayside station of Ingleton, some fifteen miles from Carnforth, was the nearest to my destination, and there I alighted just as John Thurston came dashing down the country road in a high dog-cart. He waved his whip enthusiastically at the sight of me, and pulling up his horse with a jerk, sprang out and on to the platform.

'My dear Hugh,' he cried, 'I'm so delighted to see you! It's so kind of you to come!' He wrung my hand until my arm ached.

'I'm afraid you'll find me very bad company now that I am here,' I answered; 'I am up to my eyes in work.'

'Of course, of course,' he said, in his good-humoured way. 'I reckoned on this. We'll have time for a crack at the rabbits for all that. It's a longish drive, and you must be bitterly cold, so let's start for home at once.'

We rattled off along the dusty road.

'I think you'll like your room,' my friend remarked. 'You'll soon find yourself at home. You know it is not often that I visit Dunkel-thwaite myself, and I am only just beginning to settle down and get my laboratory into working order. I have been here a fortnight. It's an open secret that I occupy a prominent position in old Uncle Jeremy's will, so my father thought it only right that I should come up and be polite. Under the circumstances I can hardly do less than put myself out a little now and again.'

'Certainly not,' I said.

'And besides, he's a very good old fellow. You'll be amused at our ménage. A princess for governess – it sounds well, doesn't it? I think our imperturbable secretary is somewhat gone in that direction. Turn up your coat-collar, for the wind is very sharp.

The road ran over a succession of low bleak hills, which were devoid of all vegetation save a few scattered gorse-bushes and thin covering of stiff wiry grass, which gave nourishment to a scattered flock of lean, hungry-looking sheep. Alternatively we dipped down into a hollow or rose to the summit of an eminence from which we could see the road winding as a thin white track over successive hills beyond. Every here and there the monotony of the landscape was broken by jagged scarps, where the grey granite peeped grimly out, as though nature had been sorely wounded until her gaunt bones protruded through their covering. In the distance lay a range of mountains, with one great peak shooting up from amongst them coquettishly draped in a wreath of clouds which reflected the ruddy light of the setting sun.

'That's Ingleborough,' my companion said,

indicating the mountain with his whip, 'and these are the Yorkshire Fells. You won't find a wilder, bleaker place in all England. They breed a good race of men. The raw militia who beat the Scotch chivalry at the Battle of the Standard came from this part of the country. Just jump down, old fellow and open the gate.'

We had pulled up at a place where a long moss-grown wall ran parallel to the road. It was broken by a dilapidated iron gate, flanked by two pillars, on the summit of which were stone devices which appeared to represent some heraldic animal, though wind and rain had reduced them to shapeless blocks. A ruined cottage, which may have served at some time as a lodge, stood on one side. I pushed the gate open and we drove up a long, winding avenue, grass-grown and uneven, but lined by magnificent oaks, which shot their branches so thickly over us that the evening twilight deepened suddenly into darkness.

'I'm afraid our avenue won't impress you much,' Thurston said, with a laugh. 'It's one of the old man's whims to let nature have her way in everything. Here we are at last at Dunkelthwaite.'

As he spoke we swung round a curve in the avenue marked by a patriarchal oak which towered high above the others, and came upon a great square whitewashed house with a lawn in front of it. The lower part of the building was all in shadow, but up at the top a row of bloodshot windows glimmered out at the setting sun. At the sound of the wheels an old man in livery ran out and seized the horse's head when we pulled up.

'You can put her up, Elijah,' my friend said, as we jumped down. 'Hugh, let me introduce you to my Uncle Jeremy.'

'How d'ye do? How d'ye do?' cried a wheezy cracked voice, and looking up I saw a little red-faced man who was standing waiting for us in the porch. He wore a cotton cloth tied round his head after the fashion of Pope and other eighteenth-century celebrities, and was further distinguished by a pair of enormous slippers. These contrasted so strangely with his thin spindle shanks that he appeared to be wearing snowshoes, a resemblance which was heightened by the fact that when he walked he was compelled to slide his feet along the ground in order to retain his grip of these unwieldy appendages.

'You must be tired, sir. Yes, and cold, sir,' he said, in a strange jerky way, as he shook me by the hand. 'We must be hospitable to you, we must indeed. Hospitality is one of the old-world virtues which we still retain. Let me see, what are those lines? "Ready and strong the Yorkshire arm, but oh, the York-shire heart is warm." Neat and terse, sir. That comes from one of my poems. What poem is it, Copperthorne?'

'The Harrying of Borrodaile,' said a voice behind him, and a tall, long-visaged man stepped forward into the circle of light which

66

was thrown by the lamp above the porch. John introduced us, and I remember that his hand as I shook it was cold and unpleasantly clammy.

This ceremony over, my friend led the way to my room, passing through many passages and corridors connected by old-fashioned and irregular staircases. I noticed as I passed the thickness of the walls and the strange slants and angles of the ceilings, suggestive of mysterious spaces above. The chamber set apart for me proved, as John had said, to be a cheery little sanctum with a crackling fire and a well-stocked bookcase. I began to think as I pulled on my slippers that I might have done worse after all than accept this Yorkshire invitation.

II

When we descended to the dining-room the rest of the household had already assembled for dinner. Old Jeremy, still wearing his quaint headgear, sat at the head of the table. Next to him, on his right, sat a very dark young lady with black hair and eyes, who was introduced to me as Miss Warrender. Beside her were two pretty children, a boy and a girl, who were evidently her charges. I sat opposite her, with Copperthorne on my left, while John faced his uncle. I can almost fancy now that I can see the yellow glare of the great oil lamp throwing Rembrandt-like lights and shades upon the ring of faces, some of which were soon to have so strange an interest for me.

It was a pleasant meal, apart from the excellence of the viands and the fact that the long journey had sharpened my appetite. Uncle Jeremy overflowed with anecdote and quotation, delighted to have found a new listener. Neither Miss Warrender nor Copperthorne spoke much, but all that the latter said bespoke the thoughtful and educated man. As to John, he had so much to say of college reminiscences and subsequent events that I fear his dinner was a scanty one.

When the dessert was put on the table Miss Warrender took the children away, and Uncle Jeremy withdrew into the library, where we could hear the dull murmur of his voice as he dictated to his amanuensis. My old friend and I sat for some time before the fire discussing the many things which had happened to both of us since our last meeting.

'And what do you think of our household?' he asked at last, with a smile.

I answered that I was very much interested with what I had seen of it. 'Your uncle,' I said, 'is quite a character. I like him very much.'

'Yes; he has a warm heart behind all his peculiarities. Your coming seems to have cheered him up, for he's never been quite himself since little Ethel's death. She was the youngest of Uncle Sam's children, and came here with the others, but she had a fit or something in the shrubbery a couple of months ago. They found her lying dead there in the evening. It was a great blow to the old man.'

'It must have been to Miss Warrender too?' I remarked.

'Yes; she was very much cut up. She had only been here a week or two at the time. She had driven over to Kirkby Lonsdale that day to buy something.'

'I was very much interested,' I said, 'in all that you told me about her. You were not chaffing, I suppose?'

'No, no; it's all true as gospel. Her father was Achmet Genghis Khan, a semi-independent chieftain somewhere in the Central Provinces. He was a bit of a heathen fanatic in spite of his Christian wife, and he became chummy with the Nana, and mixed himself up in the Cawnpore business, so Government came down heavily on him.'

'She must have been quite a woman before she left her tribe,' I said. 'What view of religion does she take? Does she side with her father or mother?'

'We never press that question,' my friend answered. 'Between ourselves don't think she's very orthodox. Her mother must have been a good woman, and besides teaching her English, she is a good French scholar, and plays remarkably well. Why, there she goes!'

As he spoke the sound of a piano was heard from the next room, and we both paused to listen. At first the player struck a few isolated notes, as though uncertain how to proceed. Then came a series of clanging chords and jarring discords, until out of the chaos there suddenly swelled a strange barbaric march, with blare of trumpet and crash of cymbal. Louder and louder it pealed forth in a gust of wild melody, and then died away once more into the jerky chords which had preceded it. Then we heard the sound of the shutting of the piano, and the music was at an end.

'She does that every night,' my friend remarked; 'I suppose it is some Indian reminiscence. Picturesque, don't you think so? Now don't stay here longer than you wish. Your room is ready whenever you would like to study.'

I took my companion at his word and left him with his uncle and Copperthorne, who had returned into the room, while I went upstairs and read Medical Jurisprudence for a couple of hours. I imagined that I should see no more of the inhabitants of Dunkelthwaite that night, but I was mistaken, for about ten o'clock Uncle Jeremy thrust his little red face into the room.

'All comfortable?' he asked.

'Excellent, thanks,' I answered.

'That's right. Keep at it. Sure to succeed,' he said, in his spasmodic way. 'Good night!'

'Good night!' I answered.

'Good night!' said another voice from the passage; and looking out I saw the tall figure of the secretary gliding along at the old man's heels like a long dark shadow.

I went back to my desk and worked for another hour, after which I retired to bed, where I pondered for some time before I dropped to sleep over the curious household of which I had become a member.

III

I was up betimes in the morning and out on the lawn, where I found Miss Warrender, who was picking primroses and making them into a little bunch for the breakfast-table. I approached her before she saw me, and I could not help admiring the beautiful litheness of her figure as she stooped over the flowers. There was a feline grace about her every movement such as I never remember to have seen in any woman. I recalled Thurston's words as to the impression which she had made upon the secretary, and ceased to wonder at it. As she heard my step she stood up and turned her dark handsome face towards me.

'Good morning, Miss Warrender,' I said. 'You are an early riser, like myself.'

'Yes,' she answered. 'I have been accustomed to rise at daybreak.'

'What a strange, wild view!' I remarked, looking out over the wide stretch of fells. 'I am a stranger to this part of the country, like yourself. How do you like it?'

'I don't like it,' she said, frankly. 'I detest it. It is cold and bleak and wretched. Look at these' – holding up her bunch of primroses – 'they call these things flowers. They have not even a smell.'

'You have been used to a more genial climate and a tropical vegetation?'

'Oh, then, Mr Thurston has been telling you about me,' she said, with a smile. 'Yes, I have been used to something better than this.'

We were standing together when a shadow fell between us, and looking round I found that Copperthorne was standing close behind us. He held out his thin white hand to me with a constrained smile.

'You seem to be able to find your way about already,' he remarked, glancing backwards and forwards from my face to that of Miss Warrender. 'Let me hold your flowers for you, miss.'

'No, thank you,' the other said, coldly. 'I have picked enough and I am going inside.'

She swept past him and across the lawn to the house. Copperthorne looked after her with a frowning brow.

'You are a student of medicine, Mr Lawrence?' he said, turning towards me and stamping one of his feet up and down in a jerky, nervous fashion, as he spoke.

'Yes, I am.'

'Oh, we have heard of you students of medicine,' he cried in a raised voice, with a little crackling laugh. 'You are dreadful fellows, are you not? We have heard of you. There is no standing against you.'

'A medical student, sir,' I answered, 'is usually a gentleman.

'Quite so,' he said, in a changed voice. 'Of

course I was only joking.' Nevertheless I could not help noticing that at breakfast he kept his eyes persistently fixed upon me while Miss Warrender was speaking, and if I chanced to make a remark he would flash a glance round at her as though to read in our faces what our thoughts were of each other. It was clear that he took a more than common interest in the beautiful governess, and it seemed to me to be equally evident that his feelings were by no means reciprocated.

We had an illustration that morning of the simple nature of these primitive Yorkshire folk. It appears that the housemaid and the cook, who slept together, were alarmed during the night by something which their superstitious minds contorted into an apparition. I was sitting after breakfast with Uncle Jeremy, who, with the help of continual promptings from his secretary, was reciting some Border poetry, when there was a tap at the door and the housemaid appeared. Close at her heels came the cook, buxom but timorous, the two mutually encouraging and abetting each other. They told their story in a strophe and antistrophe, like a Greek chorus, Jane talking until her breath failed, when the narrative was taken up by the cook, who, in turn, was supplanted by the other. Much of what they said was almost unintelligible to me owing to their extraordinary dialect, but I could make out the main thread of their story. It appears that in the early morning the cook had been awakened by something touching her face, and starting up had seen a shadowy figure standing by her bed, which figure had at once glided noiselessly from the room. The housemaid was awakened by the cook's cry, and averred stoutly that she had seen the apparition. No amount of cross-examination or reasoning could shake them, and they wound up by both giving notice, which was a practical way of showing that they were honestly scared. They seemed considerably indignant at our want of belief, and ended by bouncing out of the room, leaving Uncle Jeremy angry, Copperthorne contemptuous, and myself very much amused.

I spent nearly the whole of the second day of my visit in my room, and got over a considerable amount of work. In the evening John and I went down to the rabbit-warren with our guns. I told John as we came back of the absurd scene with the servants in the morning, but it did not seem to strike him in the same ridiculous light that it had me.

'The fact is,' he said, 'in very old houses like ours, where you have the timber rotten and warped, you get curious effects sometimes which predispose the mind to superstition. I have heard one or two things at night during this visit which might have frightened a nervous man, and still more an uneducated servant. Of course all this about apparitions is mere nonsense, but when once the imagination is excited there's no checking it.'

'What have you heard, then?' I asked with interest.

'Oh, nothing of any importance,' he answered. 'Here are the youngsters and Miss Warrender. We mustn't talk about these things before her, or else we shall have her giving warning too, and that would be a loss to the establishment.'

She was sitting on a little stile which stood on the outskirts of the wood which surrounds Dunkelthwaite, and the two children were leaning up against her, one on either side, with their hands clasped round her arms, and their chubby faces turned up to hers. It was a pretty picture and we paused to look at it. She had heard our approach, however, and springing lightly down she came towards us, with the two little ones toddling behind her.

'You must aid me with the weight of your authority,' she said to John. 'These little rebels are fond of the night air and won't be persuaded to come indoors.'

'Don't want to come,' said the boy, with decision. 'Want to hear the rest of the story.'

'Yes – the 'tory,' lisped the younger one.

'You shall hear the rest of the story tomorrow if you are good. Here is Mr Lawrence, who is a doctor – he will tell you how bad it is for little boys and girls to be out when the dew falls.'

'So you have been hearing a story?' John said as we moved on together.

'Yes – such a good story!' the little chap said with enthusiasm. 'Uncle Jeremy tells us stories, but they are in po'try and they are not nearly so nice as Miss Warrender's stories.

This one was about elephants—'

'And tigers – and gold—' said the other.

'Yes, and wars and fighting, and the king of the Cheroots—'

'Rajpoots, my dear,' said the governess.

'And the scattered tribes that know each other by signs, and the man that was killed in the wood. She knows splendid stories. Why don't you make her tell you some, Cousin John?'

'Really, Miss Warrender, you have excited our curiosity,' my companion said. 'You must tell us of these wonders.'

'They would seem stupid enough to you,' she answered, with a laugh. 'They are merely a few reminiscences of my early life.'

As we strolled along the pathway which led through the wood we met Copperthorne coming from the opposite direction.

'I was looking for you all,' he said, with an ungainly attempt at geniality. 'I wanted to tell you that it was dinnertime.'

'Our watches told us that,' said John, rather ungraciously as I thought.

'And you have been all rabbiting together?' the secretary continued, as he stalked along beside us.

'Not all,' I answered. 'We met Miss Warrender and the children on our way back.'

'Oh, Miss Warrender came to meet you as you came back!' said he. This quick contortion of my words, together with the sneering way in which he spoke, vexed me so much that I should have made a sharp rejoinder had it not been for the lady's presence.

I happened to turn my eyes towards the governess at the moment, and I saw her glance at the speaker with an angry sparkle in her eyes which showed that she shared my indignation. I was surprised, however, that same night when about ten o'clock I chanced to look out of the window of my study, to see the two of them walking up and down in the moonlight engaged in deep conversation. I don't know how it was, but the sight disturbed me so much that after several fruitless attempts to continue my studies I threw my books aside and gave up work for the night. About eleven I glanced out again, but they were gone, and shortly afterwards I heard the shuffling step of Uncle Jeremy, and the firm heavy footfall of the secretary, as they ascended the staircase which led to their bedrooms upon the upper floor.

IV

John Thurston was never a very observant man, and I believe that before I had been three days under his uncle's roof I knew more of what was going on there than he did. My friend was ardently devoted to chemistry, and spent his days happily among his test-tubes and solutions, perfectly contented so long as he had a congenial companion at hand to whom he could communicate his results. For myself, I have always had a weakness for the study and analysis of human character, and I found much that was interesting in the microcosm in which I lived. Indeed, I became so absorbed in my observations that I fear my studies suffered to a considerable extent.

In the first place, I discovered beyond all doubt that the real master of Dunkelthwaite was not Uncle Jeremy, but Uncle Jeremy's amanuensis. My medical instinct told me that the absorbing love of poetry, which had been nothing more than a harmless eccentricity in the old man's younger days, had now become a complete monomania, which filled his mind to the exclusion of every other subject. Copperthorne, by humouring his employer upon this one point until he had made himself indispensable to him, had succeeded in gaining complete power over him in everything else. He managed his money matters and the affairs of the house unquestioned and uncontrolled. He had sense enough, however, to exert his authority so lightly that it galled no one's neck, and therefore excited no opposition. My friend, busy with his distillations and analyses, was never allowed to realize that he was really a nonentity in the establishment.

I have already expressed my conviction that though Copperthorne had some tender feeling for the governess, she by no means favoured his addresses. After a few days I came to think, however, that there existed besides this unrequited affection some other link which bound the pair together. I have seen him more than once assume an air towards her which can only be described as one of authority. Two or three times also I had observed them pacing the lawn and conversing earnestly in the early hours of the night. I could not guess what mutual understanding existed between them, and the mystery piqued my curiosity.

It is proverbially easy to fall in love in a country house, but my nature has never been a sentimental one, and my judgement was not warped by any such feeling towards Miss Warrender. On the contrary, I set myself to study her as an entomologist might a specimen, critically, but without bias. With this object I used to arrange my studies in such a way as to be free at the times when she took the children out for exercise, so that we had many walks together, and I gained a deeper insight into her character than I should otherwise have done.

She was fairly well read, and had a superficial acquaintance with several languages, as well as a great natural taste for music. Underneath this veneer of culture, however, there was a great dash of the savage in her nature. In the course of her conversation she would every now and again drop some remark which would almost startle me by its primitive reasoning, and by its disregard for the conventionalities of civilization. I could hardly wonder at this, however, when I reflected that she had been a woman before she left the wild tribe which her father ruled.

I remember one instance which struck me as

particularly characteristic, in which her wild original habits suddenly asserted themselves. We were walking along the country road, talking of Germany, in which she had spent some months, when she suddenly stopped short and laid her finger upon her lips. 'Lend me your stick!' she said, in a whisper. I handed it to her, and at once, to my astonishment, she darted lightly and noiselessly through a gap in the hedge, and, bending her body, crept swiftly along under the shelter of a little knoll. I was still looking after her in amazement, when a rabbit rose suddenly in front of her and scuttled away. She hurled the stick after it and struck it, but the creature made good its escape, though trailing one leg behind it.

She came back to me exultant and panting. 'I saw it move among the grass,' she said. 'I hit it.'

'Yes, you hit it. You broke its leg,' I said, somewhat coldly.

'You hurt it,' the little boy cried, ruefully.

'Poor little beast!' she exclaimed, with a sudden change in her whole manner. 'I am sorry I harmed it.' She seemed completely cast down by the incident, and spoke little during the remainder of our walk. For my own part I could not blame her much. It was evidently an outbreak of the old predatory instinct of the savage, though with a somewhat incongruous effect in the case of a fashionably dressed young lady on an English high road.

John Thurston made me peep into her private

sitting-room one day when she was out. She had a thousand little Indian knick-knacks there which showed that she had come well-laden from her native land. Her Oriental love for bright colours had exhibited itself in an amusing fashion. She had gone down to the market town and bought numerous sheets of pink and blue paper, and these she had pinned in patches over the sombre covering which had lined the walls before. She had some tinsel too, which she had put up in the most conspicuous places. The whole effect was ludicrously tawdry and glaring, and yet there seemed to me to be a touch of pathos in this attempt to reproduce the brilliance of the tropics in the cold English dwelling-house.

During the first few days of my visit the curious relationship which existed between Miss Warrender and the secretary had simply excited my curiosity, but as the weeks passed and I became more interested in the beautiful Anglo-Indian a deeper and more personal feeling took possession of me. I puzzled my brains as to what tie could exist between them. Why was it that while she showed every symptom of being averse to his company during the day she would walk about with him alone after night-fall? Could it be that the distaste which she showed for him before others was a blind to conceal her real feelings? Such a supposition seemed to involve a depth of dissimulation in her nature which appeared to be incompatible with her frank eyes and clear-cut proud features. And yet, what other hypothesis could account for, the power which he most certainly exercised over her?

This power showed itself in many ways, but was exerted so quietly and silently that none but a close observer could have known that it existed. I have seen him glance at her with a look so commanding, and, as it seemed to me, so menacing, that next moment I could hardly believe that his white impassive face could be capable of so intense an expression. When he looked at her in this manner she would wince and quiver as though she had been in physical pain. 'Decidedly,' I thought, 'it is fear and not love which produces such effects.'

I was so interested in the question that I spoke to my friend John about it. He was in his little laboratory at the time and was deeply immersed in a series of manipulations and distillations, which ended in the production of an evil-smelling gas, which set us both coughing and choking. I took advantage of our enforced retreat into the fresh air to question him upon one or two points on which I wanted information.

'How long did you say that Miss Warrender had been with your uncle?' I asked.

John looked at me slyly, and shook his acid-stained finger.

'You seem to be wonderfully interested about the daughter of the late lamented Achmet Genghis,' he said.

'Who could help it?' I answered, frankly. 'I

think she is one of the most romantic characters I ever met.'

'Take care of the studies, my boy,' John said, paternally. 'This sort of thing doesn't do before examinations.'

'Don't be ridiculous!' I remonstrated. 'Any one would think that I was in love with Miss Warrender to hear the way in which you talk. I look on her as an interesting psychological problem, nothing more.'

'Quite so – an interesting psychological problem, nothing more.'

John seemed to have some of the vapours of the gas still hanging about his system, for his manner was decidedly irritating.

'To revert to my original question,' I said. 'How long has she been here?'

'About ten weeks.'

'And Copperthorne?'

'Over two years.'

'Do you imagine that they could have known each other before?'

'Impossible!' said John, with decision. 'She came from Germany. I saw the letter from the old merchant, in which he traced her previous life. Coppethorne has always been in Yorkshire except for two years at Cambridge. He had to leave the university under a cloud.'

'What sort of a cloud?'

'Don't know,' John answered. 'They kept it very quiet. I fancy Uncle Jeremy knows. He's very fond of taking rapscallions up and giving them what he calls another start. Some of them will give him a start some of these fine days.'

'And so Copperthorne and Miss Warrender were absolute strangers until the last few weeks?'

'Quite so; and now I think we can go back and analyse the sediment.'

'Never mind the sediment,' I cried, detaining him. 'There's more I want to talk to you about. If these two have only known each other for this short time, how has he managed to gain his power over her?'

John stared at me open-eyed.

'His power?' he said.

'Yes, the power which he exercises over her.'

'My dear Hugh,' my friend said, gravely, 'I'm not in the habit of thus quoting Scripture, but there is one text which occurs irresistibly to my mind, and that is, that "Much-learning hath made thee mad." You've been reading too hard.'

'Do you mean to say,' I cried, 'that you have never observed that there is some secret understanding between your uncle's governess and his amanuensis?'

'Try bromide of potassium,' said John. 'It's very soothing in twenty-grain doses.'

'Try a pair of spectacles,' I retorted, 'you most certainly need them;' with which parting shot I turned on my heel and went off in high dudgeon. I had not gone twenty yards down the gravel walk of the garden before I saw the very couple of whom we had just been speaking. They were some little way off, she leaning against the sundial, he standing in front of her and speaking earnestly, with occasional jerky gesticulations. With his tall, gaunt figure towering above her, and the spasmodic motions of his long arms, he might have been some great bat fluttering over a victim. I remember that that was the simile which rose in my mind at the time, heightened perhaps by the suggestion of shrinking and of fear which seemed to me to lie in every curve of her beautiful figure.

The little picture was such an illustration of the text upon which I had been preaching, that I had half a mind to go back to the laboratory and bring the incredulous John out to witness it. Before I had time to come to a conclusion, however, Copperthorne caught a glimpse of me, and turning away; he strolled slowly in the opposite direction into the shrubbery, his companion walking by his side and cutting at the flowers as she passed with her sunshade.

I went up to my room after this small episode with the intention of pushing on with my studies, but do what I would my mind wandered away from my books in order to speculate upon this mystery.

I had learned from John that Copperthorne's antecedents were not of the best, and yet he had obviously gained enormous power over his almost imbecile employer. I could understand this fact by observing the infinite pains with which he devoted himself to the old man's hobby, and the consummate tact with which he humoured and encouraged his strange poetic whims. But how could I account for the (to me) equally obvious power which he wielded over the governess? She had no whims to be humoured. Mutual love might account for the tie between them, but my instinct as a man of the world and as an observer of human nature told me most conclusively that no such love existed. If not love, it must be fear – a supposition which was favoured by all that I had seen.

What, then, had occurred during these two months to cause this high-spirited, dark-eyed princess to fear the white-faced Englishman with the soft voice and the gentle manner? That was the problem that I set myself to solve with an energy and earnestness which eclipsed my ardour for study, and rendered me superior to the terrors of my approaching examination.

I ventured to approach the subject that same afternon to Miss Warrender, whom I found alone in the library, the two little children having gone to spend the day in the nursery of a neighbouring squire.

'You must be rather lonely when there are no visitors,' I remarked. 'It does not seem to be a very lively part of the country.'

'Children are always good companions,' she answered. 'Nevertheless I shall miss both Mr Thornton and yourself very much when you go.'

'I shall be sorry when the time comes,' I said. 'I never expected to enjoy this visit as I have done; still you won't be quite companionless when we are gone, you'll always have Mr Copperthorne.'

'Yes; we shall always have Mr Copperthorne.' She spoke with a weary intonation.

'He's a pleasant companion,' I remarked; 'quiet, well informed, and amiable. I don't wonder that old Mr Thurston is so fond of him.'

As I spoke in this way I watched my companion intently. There was a slight flush on her dark cheeks, and she drummed her fingers impatiently against the arms of the chair.

'His manner may be a little cold sometimes—' I was continuing, but she interrupted me, turning on me furiously, with an angry glare in her black eyes.

'What do you want to talk to me about him for?' she asked.

'I beg pardon,' I answered, submissively, 'I did not know it was a forbidden subject.'

'I don't wish ever to hear his name,' she cried, passionately. 'I hate it and I hate him. Oh, if I had only some one who loved me – that is, as men love away over the seas in my own land, I know what I should say to him.'

'What would you say?' I asked, astonished at this extraordinary outburst.

She leaned forward until I seemed to feel the quick pants of her warm breath upon my face.

'Kill Copperthorne,' she said. 'That is what I should say to him. Kill Copperthorne. Then you can come and talk of love to me.'

Nothing can describe the intensity of fierceness with which she hissed these words out from between her white teeth.

She looked so venomous as she spoke that I involuntarily shrank away from her. Could this pythoness be the demure young lady who sat every day so primly and quietly at the table of Uncle Jeremy? I had hoped to gain some insight into her character by my leading question, but I had never expected to conjure up such a spirit as this. She must have seen the horror and surprise which was depicted on my face, for her manner changed and she laughed nervously.

'You must really think me mad,' she said. 'You see it is the Indian training breaking out again. We do nothing by halves over there – either loving or hating.'

'And why is it that you hate Mr Copperthorne?' I asked.

'Ah, well,' she answered, in a subdued voice, 'perhaps hate is rather too strong a term after all. Dislike would be better. There are some people you cannot help having an antipathy to, even though you are unable to give any exact reason.'

It was evident that she regretted her recent outburst and was endeavouring to explain it away.

As I saw that she wished to change the conversation, I aided her to do so, and made some remark about a book of Indian prints which she had taken down before I came in, and which still lay upon her lap. Uncle Jeremy's collection was an extensive one, and was particularly rich in works of this class.

'They are not very accurate,' she said, turning over the many-coloured leaves. 'This is good, though,' she continued picking out a picture of a chieftain clad in chain mail with a picturesque turban upon his head. 'This is very good indeed. My father was dressed like that when he rode down on his white charger and led all the warriors of the Dooab to do battle with the Feringhees. My father was chosen out from amongst them all, for they knew that Achmet Genghis Khan was a great priest as well as a great soldier. The people would be led by none but a tried Borka. He is dead now, and of all those who followed his banner there are none who are not scattered or slain, whilst I, his daughter, am a servant in a far land.'

'No doubt you will go back to India some day,' I said, in a somewhat feeble attempt at consolation.

She turned the pages over listlessly for a few moments without answering. Then she gave a sudden little cry of pleasure as she paused at one of the prints.

'Look at this,' she cried, eagerly. 'It is one of our wanderers. He is a Bhuttotee. It is very like.'

The picture which excited her so was one which represented a particularly uninviting-looking native with a small instrument which looked like a miniature pickaxe in one hand,

and a striped handkerchief or roll of linen in the other.

'That handkerchief is his roomal,' she said. 'Of course he wouldn't go about with it openly like that, nor would he bear the sacred axe, but in every other respect he is as he should be. Many a time have I been with such upon the moonless nights when the Lughaees were on ahead and the heedless stranger heard the Pilhaoo away to the left and knew not what it might mean. Ah! that was a life that was worth the living!'

'And what may a roomal be – and the Lughaee and all the rest of it?' I asked.

'Oh, they arc Indian terms,' she answered, with a laugh. 'You would not understand them.'

'But,' I said, 'this picture is marked as Dacoit, and I always thought that a Dacoit was a robber.'

'That is because the English know no better,' she observed. 'Of course, Dacoits are robbers, but they call many people robbers who are not really so. Now this man is a holy man and in all probability a Gooroo.'

She might have given me more information upon Indian manners and customs, for it was a subject upon which she loved to talk; but suddenly as I watched her I saw a change come over her face, and she gazed with a rigid stare at the window behind me. I looked round, and there peering stealthily round the corner at us was the face of the amanuensis. I confess that I

90

was startled myself at the sight, for, with its corpselike pallor, the head might have been one which had been severed from his shoulders. He threw open the sash when he saw that he was observed.

'I'm sorry to interrupt you,' he said, looking in, 'but don't you think, Miss Warrender, that it is a pity to be boxed up on such a fine day in a close room? Won't you come out and take a stroll?'

Though his words were courteous they were uttered in a harsh and almost menacing voice, so as to sound more like a command than a request. The governess rose, and without protest or remark glided away to put on her bonnet. It was another example of Copperthorne's authority over her. As he looked in at me through the open window a mocking smile played about his thin lips, as though he would have liked to have taunted me with this display of his power. With the sun shining in behind him he might have been a demon in a halo. He stood in this manner for a few moments gazing in at me with concentrated malice upon his face. Then I heard his heavy footfall scrunching along the gravel path as he walked round in the direction of the door.

V

For some days after the interview in which Miss Warrender confessed her hatred of the secretary, things ran smoothly at Dunkelthwaite.

91

I had several long conversations with her as we rambled about the woods and fields with the two little children, but I was never able to bring her round to the subject of her outburst in the library, nor did she tell me anything which threw any light at all upon the problem which interested me so deeply. Whenever I made any remark which might lead in that direction she either answered me in a guarded manner or else discovered suddenly that it was high time that the children were back in their nursery, so that I came to despair of ever learning anything from her lips.

During this time I studied spasmodically and irregularly. Occasionally old Uncle Jeremy would shuffle into my room with a roll of manuscript in his hand, and would read me extracts from his great epic poem. Whenever I felt in need of company I used to go a-visiting to John's laboratory, and he in his turn would come to my chamber if he were lonely. Sometimes I used to vary the monotony of my studies by taking my books out into an arbour in the shrubbery and working there during the day. As to Copperthorne, I avoided him as much as possible, and he, for his part, appeared to be by no means anxious to cultivate my acquaintance.

One day about the second week in June, John came to me with a telegram in his hand and a look of considerable disgust upon his face. 'Here's a pretty go!' he cried. 'The governor wants me to go up at once and meet him in London. It's some legal business, I suppose. He was always threatening to set his affairs in order, and now he has got an energetic fit and intends to do it.'

'I suppose you won't be gone long?' I said.

'A week or two perhaps. It's rather a nuisance, just when I was in a fair way towards separating that alkaloid.'

'You'll find it there when you come back,' I said, laughing. 'There's no one here who is likely to separate it in your absence.'

'What bothers me most is leaving you here,' he continued. 'It seems such an inhospitable thing to ask a fellow down to a lonely place like this and then to run away and leave him.'

'Don't you mind about me,' I answered. 'I have too much to do to be lonely. Besides, I have found attractions in this place which I never expected. I don't think any six weeks of my life have ever passed more quickly than the last.'

'Oh, they passed quickly, did they?' said John, and sniggered to himself. I am convinced that he was still under the delusion that I was hopelessly in love with the governess.

He went off that day by the early train, promising to write and tell us his address in town, for he did not know yet at which hotel his father would put up. I little knew what a difference this trifle would make, nor what was to occur before I set eyes upon my friend once more. At the time I was by no means grieved at his departure. It brought the four of us who were left into closer opposition, and seemed to favour the solving of that problem in which I found myself from day to day becoming more interested.

About a quarter of a mile from the house of Dunkelthwaite there is a straggling little village of the same name, consisting of some twenty or thirty slate-roofed cottages, with an ivy-clad church hard by and the inevitable beerhouse. On the afternoon of the very day on which John left us, Miss Warrender and the two children walked down to the post-office there, and I volunteered to accompany them.

Copperthorne would have liked well to have either prevented the excursion or to have gone with us, but fortunately Uncle Jeremy was in the throes of composition, and the services of his secretary were indispensable to him. It was a pleasant walk, I remember, for the road was well shaded by trees, and the birds were singing merrily overhead. We strolled along together, talking of many things, while the little girl and boy ran on, laughing and romping.

Before you get to the post-office you have to pass the beerhouse already mentioned. As we walked down the village street we became conscious that a small knot of people had assembled in front of this building. There were a dozen or so ragged boys and draggle-tailed girls, with a few bonnetless women, and a couple of loungers from the bar – probably as large an assemblage as ever met together in the annals of that quiet neighbourhood. We could not see what it was that was exciting their curiosity, but the children scampered on and quickly returned brimful of information.

'Oh, Miss Warrender,' Johnnie cried, as he dashed up, panting and eager, 'there's a black man there like the ones you tell us stories about!'

'A gipsy, I suppose,' I said.

'No, no,' said Johnnie, with decision; 'he is blacker than that, isn't he, May?'

'Blacker than that,' the little girl echoed.

'I suppose we had better go and see what this wonderful apparition is,' I said.

As I spoke I glanced at my companion. To my surprise, she was very pale, and her great black eyes appeared to be luminous with suppressed excitement.

'Aren't you well?' I asked.

'Oh, yes. Come on!' she cried, eagerly, quickening her step; 'come on!'

It was certainly a curious sight which met our eyes when we joined the little circle of rustics. It reminded me of the description of the opium-eating Malay whom De Quincey saw in the farmhouse in Scotland. In the centre of the circle of homely Yorkshire folk there stood an Oriental wanderer, tall, lithe, and graceful, his linen clothes stained with dust and his brown feet projecting through his rude shoes. It was evident that he had travelled far and long. He had a heavy stick in his hand, on which he leaned, while his dark eyes looked thoughtfully away into space, careless apparently of the throng around him. His picturesque attire, with his coloured turban and swarthy face, had a strange and incongruous effect amongst all the prosaic surroundings.

'Poor fellow!' Miss Warrender said to me, speaking in an excited, gasping voice. 'He is tired and hungry, no doubt, and cannot explain his wants. I will speak to him;' and, going up to the Indian, she said a few words in his native dialect.

Never shall I forget the effect which those few syllables produced. Without a word the wanderer fell straight down upon his face on the dusty road and absolutely grovelled at the feet of my companion. I had read of Eastern forms of abasement when in the presence of a superior, but I could not have imagined that any human being could have expressed such abject humility as was indicated in this man's attitude.

Miss Warrender spoke again in a sharp and commanding voice, on which he sprang to his feet and stood with his hands clasped and his eyes cast down, like a slave in the presence of his mistress. The little crowd, who seemed to think that the sudden prostration had been the prelude to some conjuring feat or acrobatic entertainment, looked on amused and interested.

'Should you mind walking on with the children and posting the letters?' the governess said; 'I should like to have a word with this man.'

I complied with her request, and when I returned in a few minutes the two were still conversing. The Indian appeared to be giving a narrative of his adventures or detailing the causes of his journey, for he spoke rapidly and excitedly, with quivering fingers and gleaming eyes. Miss Warrender listened intently, giving an occasional start or exclamation, which showed how deeply the man's statement interested her.

'I must apologize for detaining you so long in the sun,' she said, turning to me at last. 'We must go home, or we shall be late for dinner.'

With a few parting sentences, which sounded like commands, she left her dusky acquaintance still standing in the village street, and we strolled homewards with the children.

'Well?' I asked, with natural curiosity, when we were out of earshot of the visitors. 'Who is he, and what is he?'

'He comes from the Central Provinces, near the land of the Mahrattas. He is one of us. It has been quite a shock to me to meet a fellow-countryman so unexpectedly; I feel quite upset.'

'It must have been pleasant for you,' I remarked.

'Yes, very pleasant,' she said heartily.

'And why did he fall down like that?'

'Because he knew me to be the daughter of Achmet Genghis Khan,' she said, proudly.

'And what chance has brought him here?'

'Oh, it's a long story,' she said carelessly. 'He has led a wandering life. How dark it is in this avenue, and how the great branches shoot

97

across! If you were to crouch on one of those you could drop down on the back of any one who passed, and they would never know that you were there until they felt your fingers on their throat.'

'What a horrible idea!' I exclaimed.

'Gloomy places always give me gloomy thoughts,' she said, lightly. 'By the way, I want you to do me a favour, Mr Lawrence.'

'What is that?' I asked.

'Don't say anything at the house about this poor compatriot of mine. They might think him a rogue and a vagabond, you know, and order him to be driven from the village.'

'I'm sure Mr Thurston would do nothing so unkind.'

'No; but Mr Copperthorne might.'

'Just as you like,' I said; 'but the children are sure to tell.'

'No, I think not,' she answered.

I don't know how she managed to curb their little prattling tongues, but they certainly preserved silence upon the point, and there was no talk that evening of the strange visitor who had wandered into our little hamlet.

I had a shrewd suspicion that this stranger from the tropics was no chance wanderer, but had come to Dunkelthwaite upon some set errand. Next day I had the best possible evidence that he was still in the vicinity, for I met Miss Warrender coming down the garden walk with a basketful of scraps of bread and of meat in her hand. She was in the habit of taking these leavings to sundry old women in the neighbourhood, so I offered to accompany her.

'Is it old Dame Venables or old Dame Taylforth today?' I asked.

'Neither one nor the other,' she said, with a smile. 'I'll tell you the truth, Mr Lawrence, because you have always been a good friend to me, and I feel I can trust you. These scraps are for my poor countryman. I'll hang the basket here on this branch, and he will get it.'

'Oh, he's still about, then,' I observed.

'Yes, he's still in the neighbourhood.'

'You think he will find it?'

'Oh, trust him for that,' she said. 'You don't blame me for helping him, do you? You would do the same if you lived among Indians and suddenly came upon an Englishman. Come to the hothouse and look at the flowers.'

We walked round to the conservatory together. When we came back the basket was still hanging to the branch, but the contents were gone. She took it down with a laugh and carried it in with her.

It seemed to me that since this interview with her countryman the day before her spirits had become higher and her step freer and more elastic. It may have been imagination, but it appeared to me also that she was not as constrained as usual in the presence of Copperthorne, and that she met his glances more fearlessly, and was less under the influence of his will.

And now I am coming to that part of this statement of mine which describes how I first gained an insight into the relation which existed between those two strange mortals, and learned the terrible truth about Miss Warrender, or of the Princess Achmet Genghis, as I should prefer to call her, for assuredly she was the descendant of the fierce fanatical warrior rather than of her gentle mother.

To me the revelation came as a shock, the effect of which I can never forget. It is possible that in the way in which I have told the story, emphasizing those facts which had a bearing upon her, and omitting those which had not, my readers have already detected the strain which ran in her blood. As for myself, I solemnly aver that up to the last moment I had not the smallest suspicion of the truth. Little did I know what manner of woman this was, whose hand I pressed in friendship, and whose voice was music to my ears. Yet it is my belief, looking back, that she was really well disposed to me, and would not willingly have harmed me.

It was in this manner that the revelation came about. I think that I have mentioned that there was a certain arbour in the shrubbery in which I was accustomed to study during the daytime. One night, about ten o'clock, I found on going to my room that I had left a book on gynaecology in this summer-house, and as I intended to do a couple of hours' work before turning in, I started off with the intention of getting it. Uncle Jeremy and the servants had already gone to bed, so I slipped downstairs very quietly and turned the key gently in the front door. Once in the open air, I hurried rapidly across the lawn, and so into the shrubbery, with the intention of regaining my property and returning as rapidly as possible.

I had hardly passed the little wooden gate and entered the plantation before I heard the sound of talking, and knew that I had chanced to stumble upon one of those nocturnal conclaves which I had observed from my window. The voices were those of the secretary and of the governess, and it was clear to me, from the direction in which they sounded, that they were sitting in the arbour and conversing together without any suspicion of the presence of a third person. I have ever held that eavesdropping, under any circumstances, is a dishonourable practice, and curious as I was to know what passed between these two, I was about to cough or give some other signal of my presence, when suddenly I heard some words of Copperthorne's which brought me to a halt with every faculty overwhelmed with horrified amazement.

'They'll think he died of apoplexy,' were the words which sounded clearly and distinctly through the peaceful air in the incisive tones of the amanuensis.

I stood breathless, listening with all my ears. Every thought of announcing my presence had left me. What was the crime which these ill-assorted conspirators were hatching upon this lovely summer's night?

I heard the deep sweet tones of her voice, but she spoke so rapidly, and in such a subdued manner, that I could not catch the words. I could tell by the intonation that she was under the influence of deep emotion. I drew nearer on tiptoe, with my ears straining to catch every sound. The moon was not up yet, and under the shadows of the trees it was very dark. There was little chance of my being observed.

'Eaten his bread, indeed!' the secretary said, derisively. 'You are not usually so squeamish. You did not think of that in the case of little Ethel.'

'I was mad! I was mad!' she ejaculated in a broken voice. 'I had prayed much to Buddha and to the great Bhowanee, and it seemed to me that in this land of unbelievers it would be a great and glorious thing for me, a lonely woman, to act up to the teachings of my great father. There are few women who are admitted into the secrets of our faith, and it was but by an accident that the honour came upon me. Yet, having once had the path pointed out to me, I have walked straight and fearlessly, and the great Gooroo Ramdeen Singh has said that even in my fourteenth year I was worthy to sit upon the cloth of the Tupounee with the other Bhuttotees. Yet I swear by the sacred pickaxe that I have grieved much over this, for what had the poor child done that she should be sacrificed!'

'I fancy that my having caught you has had more to do with your repentance than the moral aspect of the case,' Copperthorne said, with a sneer. 'I may have had my misgivings before, but it was only when I saw you rising up with the handkerchief in your hand that I knew for certain that we were honoured by the presence of a Princess of the Thugs! An English scaffold would be rather a prosaic end for such a romantic being.'

'And you have used your knowledge ever since to crush all the life out of me,' she said, bitterly. 'You have made my existence a burden to me.'

'A burden to you!' he said, in an altered voice. 'You know what my feelings are towards you. If I have occasionally governed you by the fear of exposure it was only because I found you were insensible to the milder influence of love.'

'Love!' she cried, bitterly. 'How could I love a man who held a shameful death forever before my eyes. But let us come to the point. You promise me my unconditional liberty if I do this one thing for you?'

'Yes,' Copperthorne answered; 'you may go where you will when this is done. I shall forget what I saw here in the shrubbery.'

'You swear it?'

'Yes, I swear it.'

'I would do anything for my freedom,' she said.

'We can never have such a chance again,'

Copperthorne cried. 'Young Thurston is gone, and this friend of his sleeps heavily, and is too stupid to suspect. The will is made out in my favour, and if the old man dies every stick and stone of the great estate will be mine.'

'Why don't you do it yourself, then?' she asked.

'It's not in my line,' he said. 'Besides, I have not got the knack. That roomal, or whatever you call it, leaves no mark. That's the advantage of it.'

'It is an accursed thing to slay one's benefactor.'

'But it is a great thing to serve Bhowanee, the goddess of murder. I know enough of your religion to know that. Would not your father do it if he were here?'

'My father was the greatest of all the Borkas of Jublepore,' she said, proudly. 'He has slain more than there are days in the year.'

'I wouldn't have met him for a thousand pounds,' Copperthorne remarked, with a laugh. 'But what would Achmet Genghis Khan say now if he saw his daughter hesitate with such a chance before her of serving the gods? You have done excellently so far. He may well have smiled when the infant soul of young Ethel was wafted up to this god or ghoul of yours. Perhaps this is not the first sacrifice you have made. How about the daughter of this charitable German merchant? Ah, I see in your face that I am right again! After such deeds you do wrong to hesitate now when there is no danger and all shall be made easy to you. Besides that, the deed will free you from your existence here, which cannot be particularly pleasant with a rope, so to speak, round your neck the whole time. If it is to be done it must be done at once. He might rewrite his will at any moment, for he is fond of the lad, and is as changeable as a weathercock.'

There was a long pause, and a silence so profound that I seemed to hear my own heart throbbing in the darkness.

'When shall it be done?' she asked at last.

'Why not tomorrow night!'

'How am I to get to him?'

'I shall leave his door open,' Copperthorne said. 'He sleeps heavily, and I shall leave a night-light burning, so that you may see your way.'

'And afterwards?'

'Afterwards you will return to your room. In the morning it will be discovered that our poor employer has passed away in his sleep. It will also be found that he has left all his worldly goods as a slight return for the devoted labours of his faithful secretary. Then the services of Miss Warrender the governess being no longer required, she may go back to her beloved country or to anywhere else that she fancies. She can run away with Mr John Lawrence, student of medicine, if she pleases.'

'You insult me,' she said angrily; and then, after a pause, 'You must meet me tomorrow night before I do this.'

'Why so?' he asked.

'Because there may be some last instructions which I may require.'

'Let it be here, then, at twelve,' he said.

'No, not here. It is too near the house. Let us meet under the great oak at the head of the avenue.'

'Where you will,' he answered, sulkily; 'but mind, I'm not going to be with you when you do it.'

'I shall not ask you,' she said, scornfully. 'I think we have said all that needs be said tonight.'

I heard the sound of one or other of them rising to their feet, and though they continued to talk I did not stop to hear more, but crept quietly out from my place of concealment and scudded across the dark lawn and in through the door, which I closed behind me. It was only when I had regained my room and had sunk back into my armchair that I was able to collect my scattered senses and to think over the terrible conversation to which I had listened. Long into the hours of the night I sat motionless, meditating over every word that I had heard and endeavouring to form in my mind some plan of action for the future.

VI

The Thugs! I had heard of the wild fanatics of that name who are found in the central part of India, and whose distorted religion represents murder as being the highest and purest of all the gifts which a mortal can offer to the Creator. I remember, an account of them which I had read in the works of Colonel Meadows Taylor, of their secrecy, their organization, their restlessness, and the terrible power which their homicidal craze has over every other mental or moral faculty. I even recalled now that the roomal – a word which I had heard her mention more than once – was the sacred handkerchief with which they were wont to work their diabolical purpose. She was already a woman when she had left them, and being, according to her own account, the daughter of their principal leader, it was no wonder that the varnish of civilization had not eradicated all her early impressions or prevented the breaking out of occasional fits of fanaticism. In one of these apparently she had put an end to poor Ethel, having carefully prepared an alibi to conceal her crime, and it was Copperthorne's accidental discovery of this murder which gave him his power over his strange associate. Of all deaths, that by hanging is considered among these tribes to be the most impious and degrading, and her knowledge that she had subjected herself to this death by the law of the land was evidently the reason why she had found herself compelled to subject her will and tame her imperious nature when in the presence of the amanuensis.

As to Copperthorne himself, as I thought over what he had done, and what he proposed to do, a great horror and loathing filled my whole soul. Was this his return for the kindness lavished upon him by the poor old man? He had already cozened him into signing away his estates, and now, for fear some prickings of conscience should cause him to change his mind, he had determined to put it out of his power ever to write a codicil. All this was bad enough, but the acme of all seemed to be that, too cowardly to effect his purpose with his own hand, he had made use of this unfortunate woman's horrible conception of religion in order to remove Uncle Jeremy in such a way that no suspicion could possibly fall upon the real culprit. I determined in my mind that, come what might, the amanuensis should not escape from the punishment due to his crimes.

But what was I to do? Had I known my friend's address I should have telegraphed for him in the morning, and he could have been back in Dunkelthwaite before nightfall. Unfortunately John was the worst of correspondents, and though he had been gone for some days we had had no word yet of his whereabouts. There were three maid-servants in the house, but no man, with the exception of old Elijah; nor did I know of any upon whom I could rely in the neighbourhood. This, however, was a small matter, for I knew that in personal strength I was more than a match for the secretary, and I had confidence enough in myself to feel that my resistance alone would prevent any possibility of the plot being carried out.

The question was, what were the best steps for me to take under the circumstances? My first impulse was to wait until morning, and then to quietly go or send to the nearest police-station and summon a couple of constables. I could then hand Copperthorne and his female accomplice over to justice and narrate the conversation which I had overheard. On second thoughts this plan struck me as being a very impracticable one. What grain of evidence had I against them except my story? Which, to people who did not know me, would certainly appear a very wild and improbable one. I could well imagine too the plausible voice and imperturbable manner with which Copperthorne would oppose the accusation, and how he would dilate upon the ill-will which I bore both him and his companion on account of their mutual affection. How easy it would be for him to make a third person believe that I was trumping up a story in the hope of injuring a rival, and how difficult for me to make any one credit that this clerical-looking gentleman and this stylishly-dressed young lady were two beasts of prey who were hunting in couples! I felt that it would be a great mistake for me to show my hand before I was sure of the game.

The alternative was to say nothing and to let things take their course, being always ready to step in when the evidence against the conspirators appeared to be conclusive. This was the course which recommended itself to my young adventurous disposition, and it also appeared to be the one most likely to lead to conclusive results. When at last at early dawn I stretched myself upon my bed I had fully made up my mind to retain my knowledge in my own breast, and to trust to myself entirely for the defeat of the murderous plot which I had overheard.

Old Uncle Jeremy was in high spirits next morning after breakfast, and insisted upon reading aloud a scene from Shelley's 'Cenci,' a work for which he had a profound admiration. Copperthorne sat silent and inscrutable by his side, save when he threw in a suggestion or uttered an exclamation of admiration. Miss Warrender appeared to be lost in thought, and it seemed to me more than once that I saw tears in her dark eyes. It was strange for me to watch the three of them and to think of the real relation in which they stood to each other. My heart warmed towards my little red-faced host with the quaint head-gear and the old-fashioned ways. I vowed to myself that no harm should befall him while I had power to prevent it.

The day wore along slowly and drearily. It was impossible for me to settle down to work, so I wandered restlessly about the corridors to the old-fashioned house and over the garden. Copperthorne was with Uncle Jeremy upstairs, and I saw little of him. Twice when I was striding up and down outside I perceived the governess coming with the children in my direction, but on each occasion I avoided her by hurrying away. I felt that I could not speak to her without showing the intense horror with which she inspired me, and so betraying my knowledge of what had transpired the night before. She noticed that I shunned her, for at luncheon, when my eyes caught hers for a moment, she flashed across a surprised and injured glance, to which, however, I made no response.

The afternoon post brought a letter from John telling us that he was stopping at the Langham. I knew that it was now impossible for him to be of any use to me in the way of sharing the responsibility of whatever might occur, but I nevertheless thought it my duty to telegraph to him and let him know that his presence was desirable. This involved a long walk to the station, but that was useful as helping me to while away the time, and I felt a weight off my mind when I heard the clicking of the needles which told me that my message was flying upon its way.

When I reached the avenue gate on my return from Ingleton I found our old serving-man Elijah standing there, apparently in a violent passion.

'They says as one rat brings others,' he said to me, touching his hat, 'and it seems as it be the same with they darkies.'

He had always disliked the governess on account of what he called her 'uppish ways'.

'What's the matter, then?' I asked.

'It's one o' they furriners a-hidin' and

111

a-prowlin',' said the old man. 'I seed him here among the bushes, and I sent him off wi' a bit o' my mind. Lookin' after the hens as like as not, or maybe wantin' to burn the house and murder us all in our beds. I'll go down to the village, Muster Lawrence, and see what he's after,' and he hurried away in a paroxysm of senile anger.

This little incident made a considerable impression on me, and I thought seriously over it as I walked up the long avenue. It was clear that the wandering Hindoo was still hanging about the premises. He was a factor whom I had forgotten to take into account. If his compatriot enlisted him as an accomplice in her dark plans, it was possible that the three of them might be too many for me. Still it appeared to me to be improbable that she should do so, since she had taken such pains to conceal his presence from Copperthorne.

I was half tempted to take Elijah into my confidence, but on second thoughts I came to the conclusion that a man of his age would be worse than useless as an ally.

About seven o'clock I was going up to my room when I met the secretary, who asked me whether I could tell him where Miss Warrender was. I answered that I had not seen her.

'It's a singular thing,' he said, 'that no one had seen her since dinner-time. The children don't know where she is. I particularly want to speak to her.'

He hurried on with an agitated and disturbed

expression upon his features.

As to me, Miss Warrender's absence did not seem a matter of surprise. No doubt she was out in the shrubbery somewhere, nerving herself for the terrible piece of work which she had undertaken to do. I closed my door behind me and sat down, with a book in my hand, but with my mind too much excited to comprehend the contents. My plan of campaign had been already formed. I determined to be within sight of their trysting-place, to follow them, and to interfere at the moment when my interference would have most effect. I had chosen a thick, knobby stick, dear to my student heart, and with this I knew that I was master of the situation, for I had ascertained that Copperthorne had no firearms.

I do not remember any period of my life when the hours passed so slowly as did those which I spent in my room that night. Far away I heard the mellow tones of the Dunkelthwaite clock as it struck the hours of eight and then of nine, and then, after an interminable pause, of ten. After that it seemed as though time had stopped altogether as I paced my little room, fearing and yet longing for the hour as men will when some great ordeal has to be faced. All things have an end, however, and at last there came pealing through the still night air the first clear stroke which announced the eleventh hour. Then I rose, putting on my soft slippers, I seized my stick and slipped quietly out of my room and down the creaking old-fashioned staircase. I could hear the stertorous snoring of Uncle Jeremy upon the floor above. I managed to feel my way to the door through the darkness, and having opened it passed out into the beautiful starlit night.

I had to be very careful of my movements, because the moon shone so brightly that it was almost as light as day. I hugged the shadow of the house until I reached the garden hedge, and then, crawling down in its shelter, I found myself safe in the shrubbery in which I had been the night before. Through this I made my way, treading very cautiously and gingerly, so that not a stick snapped beneath my feet. In this way I advanced until I found myself among the brushwood at the edge of the plantation and within full view of the great oak-tree which stood at the upper end of the avenue.

There was some one standing under the shadow of the oak. At first I could hardly make out who it was, but presently the figure began to move, and, coming out into a silvery patch where the moon shone down between two branches, looked impatiently to left and to right. Then I saw that it was Copperthorne, who was waiting alone. The governess apparently had not yet kept her appointment.

As I wished to hear as well as to see, I wormed my way along under the dark shadows of the trunks in the direction of the oak. When I stopped I was not more than fifteen paces from the spot where the tall gaunt figure of the amanuensis looked grim and ghastly in the

114

shifting light. He paced about uneasily, now disappearing in the shadow, now reappearing in the silvery patches where the moon broke through the covering above him. It was evident from his movements that he was puzzled and disconcerted at the non-appearance of his accomplice. Finally he stationed himself under a great branch which concealed his figure, while from beneath it he commanded a view of the gravel drive which led down from the house, and along which, no doubt, he expected Miss Warrender to come.

I was still lying in my hiding-place, congratulating myself inwardly at having gained a point from which I could hear all without risk of discovery, when my eye lit suddenly upon something which made my heart rise to my mouth and almost caused me to utter an ejaculation which would have betrayed my presence.

I have said that Copperthorne was standing immediately under one of the great branches of the oak-tree. Beneath this all was plunged in the deepest shadow, but the upper part of the branch itself was silvered over by the light of the moon. As I gazed I became conscious that down this luminous branch something was crawling – a flickering, inchoate something, almost indistinguishable from the branch itself, and yet slowly and steadily writhing its way down it. My eyes, as I looked, became more accustomed to the light, and then this indefinite something took form and substance. It was a human being – a man – the Indian whom I had seen in the village. With his arms and legs twined round the great limb, he was shuffling his way down as silently and almost as rapidly as one of his native snakes.

Before I had time to conjecture the meaning of his presence he was directly over the spot where the secretary stood, his bronzed body showing out hard and clear against the disc of moon behind him. I saw him take something from round his waist, hesitate for a moment, as though judging his distance, and then spring downwards, crashing through the intervening foliage. There was a heavy thud, as of two bodies falling together, and then there rose on the night air a noise as of someone gargling his throat, followed by a succession of croaking sounds, the remembrance of which will haunt me to my dying day.

Whilst this tragedy had been enacted before my eyes its entire unexpectedness and its horror had bereft me of the power of acting in any way. Only those who have been in a similar position can imagine the utter paralysis of mind and body which comes upon a man in such straits, and prevents him from doing the thousand and one things which may be suggested afterwards as having been appropriate to the occasion. When those notes of death, however, reached my ears, I shook off my lethargy and ran forward with a loud cry from my place of concealment. At the sound the young Thug sprang from his victim with a snarl like a wild beast driven from a carcase, and made off down the avenue at such a pace that I felt it to be impossible for me to overtake him. I ran to the secretary and raised his head. His face was purple and horribly distorted. I loosened his shirt-collar and did all I could to restore him, but it was useless. The roomal had done its work, and he was dead.

I have little more to add to this strange tale of mine. If I have been somewhat long-winded in the telling of it, I feel that I owe no apology for that, for I have simply set the successive events down in a plain unvarnished fashion, and the narrative would be incomplete without any one of them. It transpired afterwards that Miss Warrender had caught the 7.20 London train, and was safe in the metropolis before any search could be made for her. As to the messenger of death whom she had left behind to keep her appointment with Copperthorne under the old oak-tree, he was never either heard or seen again. There was a hue and cry over the whole countryside, but nothing came of it. No doubt the fugitive passed the days in sheltered places, and travelled rapidly at night, living on such scraps as can sustain an Oriental, until he was out of danger.

John Thornton returned next day, and I poured all the facts into his astonished ears. He agreed with me that it was best perhaps not to speak of what I knew concerning Copperthorne's plans and the reasons which kept him out so late upon that summer's night. Thus even the county police have never known the full story of that strange tragedy, and they certainly never shall, unless, indeed, the eyes of some of them should chance to fall upon this narrative. Poor Uncle Jeremy mourned the loss of his secretary for months, and many were the verses which he poured forth in the form of epitaphs and of 'In Memoriam' poems. He has been gathered to his fathers himself since then, and the greater part of his estate has, I am glad to say, descended to the rightful heir, his nephew.

There is only one point on which I should like to make a remark. How was it that the wandering Thug came to Dunkelthwaite? This question has never been cleared up; but I have not the slightest doubt in my own mind, nor I think can any one have who considers the facts of the case, that there was no chance about his appearance. The sect in India were a large and powerful body, and when they came to look around for a fresh leader, they naturally bethought them of the beautiful daughter of their late chief. It would be no difficult matter to trace her to Calcutta, to Germany, and finally to Dunkelthwaite. He had come, no doubt, with the message that she was not forgotten in India, and that a warm welcome awaited her if she chose to join her scattered tribesmen. This may seem far-fetched, but it is the opinion which I have always entertained upon the matter.

I began this statement by a quotation from a letter, and I shall end it by one. This was from an old friend, Dr B. C. Haller, a man of encyclopaedic knowledge, and particularly well versed in Indian manners and customs. It is through his kindness that I am able to reproduce the various native words which I heard from time to time from the lips of Miss Warrender, but which I should not have been able to recall to my memory had he not suggested them to me. This is a letter in which he comments upon the matter, which I had mentioned to him in conversation some time previously:

My dear Lawrence, – I promised to write to you *re* Thuggee, but my time has been so occupied that it is only now that I can redeem my pledge. I was much interested in your unique experience, and should much like to have further talk with you upon the subject. I may inform you that it is most unusual for a woman to be initiated into the mysteries of Thuggee, and it arose in this case probably from her having accidentally or by design tasted the sacred goor, which was the sacrifice offered by the gang after each murder. Any one doing this must become an acting Thug, whatever the rank, sex, or condition. Being of noble blood she would then rapidly pass through the different grades of Tilhaee, or scout, Lughaee, or grave-digger, Shumsheea, or holder of the victim's hands, and finally of Bhuttotee, or strangler. In all this she would be instructed by her Gooroo, or spiritual adviser, whom she mentions in your account as having been her own father, who was a Borka, or an expert Thug. Having once attained this position, I do not wonder that her fanatical instincts broke out at times. The Pilhaoo which she mentions in one place was the omen on the left hand, which, if it is followed by the Thibaoo, or omen on the right, was considered to be an indication that all would go well. By the way, you mention that the old coachman saw the Hindoo lurking about among the bushes in the morning. Do you know what he was doing? I am very much mistaken if he was not digging Copperthorne's grave, for it is quite opposed to Thug customs to kill a man without having some receptacle prepared for his body. As far as I know only one English officer in India has ever fallen a victim to the fraternity, and that was Lieutenant Monsell, in 1812. Since then Colonel Sleeman has stamped it out to a great extent, though it is unquestionable that it flourishes far more than the authorities suppose. Truly 'the dark places of the earth are full of cruelty,' and nothing but the Gospel will ever effectually dispel that darkness. You are very welcome to publish these few remarks if they seem to you to throw any light upon your narrative.

Yours very sincerely,

B. C. HALLER.

The Field Bazaar

'I should certainly do it,' said Sherlock Holmes.

I started at the interruption, for my companion had been eating his breakfast with his attention entirely centred upon the paper which was propped up by the coffee pot. Now I looked across at him to find his eyes fastened upon me with the half-amused, half-questioning expression which he usually assumed when he felt that he had made an intellectual point.

'Do what?' I asked.

He smiled as he took his slipper from the mantelpiece and drew from it enough shag tobacco to fill the old clay pipe with which he invariably rounded off his breakfast.

'A most characteristic question of yours, Watson,' said he. 'You will not, I am sure, be offended if I say that any reputation for sharpness which I may possess has been entirely gained by the admirable foil which you have made for me. Have I not heard of debutantes who have insisted upon plainness in their chaperones? There is a certain analogy.'

Our long companionship in the Baker Street rooms had left us on those easy terms of intimacy when much may be said without offence. And yet I acknowledge that I was nettled at his remark.

'I may be very obtuse,' said I, 'but I confess that I am unable to see how you have managed to know that I was . . . I was . . .'

'Asked to help in the Edinburgh University Bazaar.'

'Precisely. The letter has only just come to hand, and I have not spoken to you since.'

'In spite of that,' said Holmes, leaning back in his chair and putting his finger tips together, 'I would even venture to suggest that the object of the bazaar is to enlarge the University cricket field.'

I looked at him in such bewilderment that he vibrated with silent laughter.

'The fact is, my dear Watson, that you are an excellent subject,' said he. 'You are never *blasé*. You respond instantly to any external stimulus. Your mental processes may be slow but they are never obscure, and I found during breakfast that you were easier reading than the leader in the *Times* in front of me.'

'I should be glad to know how you arrived at your conclusions,' said I.

'I fear that my good nature in giving explanations has seriously compromised my reputation,' said Holmes. 'But in this case the train of reasoning is based upon such obvious facts that no credit can be claimed for it. You entered the room with a thoughtful expression, the expression of a man who is debating some point in his mind. In your hand you held a solitary letter.

Now last night you retired in the best of spirits, so it was clear that it was this letter in your hand which had caused the change in you.'

'This is obvious.'

'It is all obvious when it is explained to you. I naturally asked myself what the letter could contain which might have this effect upon you. As you walked you held the flap side of the envelope towards me. and I saw upon it the same shield-shaped device which I have observed upon your old college cricket cap. It was clear, then, that the request came from Edinburgh University – or from some club connected with the University. When you reached the table you laid down the letter beside your plate with the address uppermost, and you walked over to look at the framed photograph upon the left of the mantelpiece.'

It amazed me to see the accuracy with which he had observed my movements. 'What next?' I asked.

'I began by glancing at the address, and I could tell, even at the distance of six feet, that it was an unofficial communication. This I gathered from the use of the word "Doctor" upon the address, to which, as a Bachelor of Medicine, you have no legal claim. I knew that University officials are pedantic in their correct use of titles, and I was thus enabled to say with certainty that your letter was unofficial. When on your return to the table you turned over your letter and allowed me to perceive that the enclosure was a printed one, the idea of a bazaar first occurred to me. I had already weighed the possibility of its being a political communication, but this seemed improbable in the present stagnant conditions of politics.

'When you returned to the table your face still retained its expression and it was evident that your examination of the photograph had not changed the current of your thoughts. In that case it must itself bear upon the subject in question. I turned my attention to the photograph, therefore, and saw at once that it consisted of yourself as a member of the Edinburgh University Eleven, with the pavilion and cricket-field in the background. My small experience of cricket clubs has taught me that next to churches and cavalry ensigns they are the most debt-laden things upon earth. When upon your return to the table I saw you take out your pencil and draw lines upon the envelope, I was convinced that you were endeavouring to realize some projected improvement which was to be brought about by a bazaar. Your face still showed some indecision, so that I was able to break in upon you with my advice that you should assist in so good an object.'

I could not help smiling at the extreme simplicity of his explanation.

'Of course, it was as easy as possible,' said I.

My remark appeared to nettle him.

'I may add,' said he, 'that the particular help which you have been asked to give was that you should write in their album, and that you have already made up your mind that the present incident will be the subject of your article.'

'But how—!' I cried.

'It is as easy as possible,' said he, 'and I leave its solution to your own ingenuity. In the meantime,' he added, raising his paper, 'you will excuse me if I return to this very interesting article upon the trees of Cremona, and the exact reasons for their pre-eminence in the manufacture of violins. It is one of those small outlying problems to which I am sometimes tempted to direct my attention.'

The Story of the Man
with the Watches

There are many who will still bear in mind the singular circumstances which, under the heading of the Rugby Mystery, filled many columns of the daily Press in the spring of the year 1892. Coming as it did at a period of exceptional dullness, it attracted perhaps rather more attention than it deserved, but it offered to the public that mixture of the whimsical and the tragic which is most stimulating to the popular imagination. Interest drooped, however, when, after weeks of fruitless investigation, it was found that no final explanation of the facts was forthcoming, and the tragedy seemed from that time to the present to have finally taken its place in the dark catalogue of inexplicable and unexpiated crimes. A recent communication (the authenticity of which appears to be above question) has, however, thrown some new and clear light upon the matter. Before laying it before the public it would be as well, perhaps, that I should refresh their memories as to the singular facts upon which this commentary is founded. These facts were briefly as follows:

At five o'clock upon the evening of the 18th of March in the year already mentioned a train left Euston Station for Manchester. It was a rainy, squally day, which grew wilder as it progressed, so it was by no means the weather in which anyone would travel who was not driven to do so by necessity. The train, however, is a favourite one among Manchester business men who are returning from town, for it does the journey in four hours and twenty minutes, with only three stoppages upon the way. In spite of the inclement evening it was, therefore, fairly well filled upon the occasion of which I speak. The guard of the train was a tried servant of the company – a man who had worked for twenty-two years without blemish or complaint. His name was John Palmer.

The station clock was upon the stroke of five, and the guard was about to give the customary signal to the engine-driver, when he observed two belated passengers hurrying down the platform. The one was an exceptionally tall man, dressed in a long black overcoat with an astrakhan collar and cuffs. I have already said that the evening was an inclement one, and the tall traveller had the high, warm collar turned up to protect his throat against the bitter March wind. He appeared, as far as the guard could judge by so hurried an inspection, to be a man between fifty and sixty years of age, who had retained a good deal of the vigour and activity of his youth. In one hand he carried a brown leather Gladstone bag. His companion was a lady, tall and erect, walking with a vigorous step which outpaced the gentleman beside her. She wore a long fawn-coloured dust-cloak, a black, close-fitting toque, and a dark veil which concealed the greater part of her face. The two might very well have passed as father and daughter. They walked swiftly down the line of carriages, glancing in at the windows, until the guard, John Palmer, overtook them.

'Now, then, sir, look sharp, the train is going,' said he.

'First-class,' the man answered.

The guard turned the handle of the nearest door. In the carriage, which he had opened, there sat a small man with a cigar in his mouth. His appearance seems to have impressed itself upon the guard's memory, for he was prepared, afterwards, to describe or to identify him. He was a man of thirty-four or thirty-five years of age, dressed in some grey material, sharp nosed, alert, with a ruddy, weather-beaten face, and a small, closely cropped black beard. He glanced up as the door was opened. The tall man paused with his foot upon the step.

'This is a smoking compartment. The lady dislikes smoke,' said he, looking round at the guard.

'All right! Here you are, sir!' said John Palmer. He slammed the door of the smoking carriage, opened that of the next one, which was empty, and thrust the two travellers in. At the same moment he sounded his whistle, and the wheels of the train began to move. The man with the cigar was at the window of his carriage, and said something to the guard as he rolled past him, but the words were lost in the bustle of the departure. Palmer stepped into the guard's van as it came up to him, and thought no more of the incident.

Twelve minutes after its departure the train reached Willesden Junction, where it stopped for a very short interval. An examination of the tickets has made it certain that no one either joined or left it at this time, and no passenger was seen to alight upon the platform. At 5.14 the journey to Manchester was resumed, and Rugby was reached at 6.50, the express being five minutes late.

At Rugby the attention of the station officials was drawn to the fact that the door of one of the first-class carriages was open. An examination of that compartment, and of its neighbour, disclosed a remarkable state of affairs.

The smoking carriage in which the short, red-faced man with the black beard had been seen was now empty. Save for a half-smoked cigar, there was no trace whatever of its recent occupant. The door of this carriage was fastened. In the next compartment, to which attention had been originally drawn, there was no sign either of the gentleman with the astrakhan collar or of the young lady who accompanied him. All three passengers had disappeared. On the other hand, there was found upon the floor of this carriage – the one in which the tall traveller and the lady had been – a young man, fashionably dressed and of elegant appearance. He lay with his knees

129

drawn up, and his head resting against the further door, an elbow upon either seat. A bullet had penetrated his heart, and his death must have been instantaneous. No one had seen such a man enter the train, and no railway ticket was found in his pocket, nor were there any markings upon his linen, nor papers or personal property which might help to identify him. Who he was, whence he had come, and how he had met his end were each as great a mystery as what had occurred to the three people who had started an hour and a half before from Willesden in those two compartments.

I have said that there was no personal property which might help to identify him, but it is true that there was one peculiarity about this unknown young man which was much commented upon at the time. In his pockets were found no fewer than six valuable gold watches, three in the various pockets of his waistcoat, one in his ticket-pocket, one in his breast-pocket, and one small one set in a leather strap and fastened round his left wrist. The obvious explanation that the man was a pick-pocket, and that this was his plunder, was discounted by the fact that all six were of American make, and of a type which is rare in England. Three of them bore the mark of the Rochester Watch-making Company; one was by Mason, of Elmira; one was unmarked; and the small one, which was highly jewelled and ornamented, was from Tiffany, of New York. The other contents of his pocket consisted of an ivory knife with a corkscrew by Rodgers, of Sheffield; a small circular mirror, one-inch in diameter; a re-admission slip to the Lyceum theatre; a silver box full of vesta matches, and a brown leather cigar-case containing two cheroots – also two pounds fourteen shillings in money. It was clear then that whatever motives may have led to his death, robbery was not among them. As already mentioned, there were no markings upon the man's linen, which appeared to be new, and no tailor's name upon his coat. In appearance he was young, short, smooth cheeked, and delicately featured. One of his front teeth was conspicuously stopped with gold.

On the discovery of the tragedy an examination was instantly made of the tickets of all passengers, and the number of the passengers themselves was counted. It was found that only three tickets were unaccounted for, corresponding to the three travellers who were missing. The express was then allowed to proceed, but a new guard was sent with it, and John Palmer was detained as a witness at Rugby. The carriage which included the two compartments in question was uncoupled and sidetracked. Then, on the arrival of Inspector Vane, of Scotland Yard, and of Mr Henderson, a detective in the service of the railway company, an exhaustive inquiry was made into all the circumstances.

That crime had been committed was certain.

The bullet, which appeared to have come from a small pistol or revolver, had been fired from some little distance, as there was no scorching of the clothes. No weapon was found in the compartment (which finally disposed of the theory of suicide), nor was there any sign of the brown leather bag which the guard had seen in the hand of the tall gentleman. A lady's parasol was found upon the rack, but no other trace was to be seen of the travellers in either of the sections. Apart from the crime, the question of how or why three passengers (one of them a lady) could get out of the train, and one other get in during the unbroken run between Willesden and Rugby, was one which excited the utmost curiosity among the general public, and gave rise to much speculation in the London Press.

John Palmer, the guard, was able at the inquest to give some evidence which threw a little light upon the matter. There was a spot between Tring and Cheddington, according to his statement, where, on account of some repairs to the line, the train had for a few minutes slowed down to a pace not exceeding eight or ten miles an hour. At that place it might be possible for a man, or even for an exceptionally active woman, to have left the train without serious injury. It was true that a gang of platelayers was there, and that they had seen nothing, but it was their custom to stand in the middle between the metals, and the open carriage door was upon the far side, so that it was conceivable that someone might have alighted unseen, as the darkness would by that time be drawing in. A steep embankment would instantly screen anyone who sprang out from the observation of the navvies.

The guard also deposed that there was a good deal of movement upon the platform at Willesden Junction, and that though it was certain that no one had either joined or left the train there, it was still quite possible that some of the passengers might have changed unseen from one compartment to another. It was by no means uncommon for a gentleman to finish his cigar in a smoking carriage and then to change to a clearer atmosphere. Supposing that the man with the black beard had done so at Willesden (and the half-smoked cigar upon the floor seemed to favour the supposition), he would naturally go into the nearest section, which would bring him into the company of the two other actors in this drama. Thus the first stage of the affair might be surmised without any great breach of probability. But what the second stage had been, or how the final one had been arrived at, neither the guard nor the experienced detective officers could suggest.

A careful examination of the line between Willesden and Rugby resulted in one discovery which might or might not have a bearing upon the tragedy. Near Tring, at the very place where the train slowed down, there was found at the bottom of the embankment a small pocket Testament, very shabby and worn. It was printed by the Bible Society of London, and bore an inscription: 'From John to Alice. Jan. 13th. 1856', upon the fly-leaf. Underneath was written: 'James. July 4th, 1859', and beneath that again: 'Edward, Nov. 1st, 1869', all the entries being in the same handwriting. This was the only clue, if it could be called a clue, which the police obtained, and the coroner's verdict of, 'Murder by a person or persons unknown' was the unsatisfactory ending of a singular case. Advertisement, rewards, and inquiries proved equally fruitless, and nothing could be found which was solid enough to form the basis for a profitable investigation.

It would be a mistake, however, to suppose that no theories were formed to account for the facts. On the contrary, the Press, both in England and in America, teemed with suggestions and suppositions, most of which were obviously absurd. The fact that the watches were of American make, and some peculiarities in connection with the gold stopping of his front tooth, appeared to indicate that the deceased was a citizen of the United States, though his linen, clothes, and boots were undoubtedly of British manufacture. It was surmised, by some, that he was concealed under the seat, and that, being discovered, he was for some reason, possibly because he had overheard their guilty secrets, put to death by his fellow passengers. When coupled with generalities as to the ferocity and cunning of anarchical and other secret societies, this theory sounded as plausible as any.

The fact that he should be without a ticket would be consistent with the idea of concealment, and it was well known that women played a prominent part in the Nihilistic propaganda. On the other hand, it was clear, from the guard's statement, that the man must have been hidden there *before* the others arrived, and how unlikely the coincidence that conspirators should stray exactly into the very compartment in which a spy was already concealed! Besides, this explanation ignored the man in the smoking carriage, and gave no reason at all for his simultaneous disappearance. The police had little difficulty in showing that such a theory would not cover the facts, but they were unprepared in the absence of evidence to advance any alternative explanation.

There was a letter in the *Daily Gazette*, over the signature of a well-known criminal investigator, which gave rise to considerable discussion at the time. He had formed a hypothesis which had at least ingenuity to recommend it, and I cannot do better than append it in his own words.

'Whatever may be the truth,' said he, 'it must depend upon some bizarre and rare combination of events, so we need have no hesitation in postulating such events in our explanation. In the absence of data we must abandon the analytic or scientific method of investigation, and must approach it in the synthetic fashion. In a word, instead of taking known events and deducing from them what has occurred, we must build up a fanciful explanation if it will only be consistent with known events. We can then test this explanation by any fresh facts which may arise. If they all fit into their places, the probability is that we are upon the right track, and with each fresh fact this probability increases in a geometrical progression until the evidence becomes final and convincing.

'Now, there is one most remarkable and suggestive fact which has not met with the attention which it deserves. There is a local train running through Harrow and King's Langley, which is timed in such a way that the express must have overtaken it at or about the period when it eased down its speed to eight miles an hour on account of the repairs of the line. The two trains would at that time be travelling in the same direction at a similar rate of speed and upon parallel lines. It is within everyone's experience how, under such circumstances, the occupant of each carriage can see very plainly the passengers in the other carriages opposite to him. The lamps of the express had been lit at Willesden, so that each compartment was brightly illuminated, and most visible to an observer from outside.

'Now, the sequence of events as I reconstruct them would be after this fashion. This young man with the abnormal number of watches was alone in the carriage of the slow train. His ticket, with his papers and gloves and other things, was, we will suppose, on the seat beside him. He was probably an American, and also probably a man of weak intellect. The excessive wearing of jewellery is an early symptom in some forms of mania.

'As he sat watching the carriages of the express which were (on account of the state of the line) going at the same pace as himself, he suddenly saw some people in it whom he knew. We will suppose for the sake of our theory that these people were a woman whom he loved and a man whom he hated – and who in return hated him. The young man was excitable and impulsive. He opened the door of his carriage, stepped from the footboard of the local train to the footboard of the express, opened the other door, and made his way into the presence of these two people. The feat (on the supposition that the trains were going at the same pace) is by no means so perilous as it might appear.

'Having now got our young man without his ticket into the carriage in which the elder man and the young woman are travelling, it is not difficult to imagine that a violent scene ensued. It is possible that the pair were also Americans, which is the more probable as the man carried a weapon – an unusual thing in England. If our supposition of incipient mania is correct, the young man is likely to have assaulted the other. As the upshot of the quarrel the elder man shot the intruder, and then made his escape from the carriage, taking the young lady with him.

We will suppose that all this happened very rapidly, and that the train was still going at so slow a pace that it was not difficult for them to leave it. A woman might leave a train going at eight miles an hour. As a matter of fact, we know that this woman *did* do so.

'And now we have to fit in the man in the smoking carriage. Presuming that we have, up to this point, reconstructed the tragedy correctly, we shall find nothing in this other man to cause us to reconsider our conclusions. According to my theory, this man saw the young fellow cross from one train to the other, saw him open the door, heard the pistol-shot, saw the two fugitives spring out on to the line, realized that murder had been done, and sprang out himself in pursuit. Why he has never been heard of since – whether he met his own death in the pursuit, or whether, as is more likely, he was made to realize that it was not a case for his interference – is a detail which we have at present no means of explaining. I acknowledge that there are some difficulties in the way. At first sight, it might seem improbable that at such a moment a murderer would burden himself in his flight with a brown leather bag. My answer is that he was well aware that if the bag were found his identity would be established. It was absolutely necessary for him to take it with him. My theory stands or falls upon one point, and I call upon the railway company to make strict inquiry as to whether a ticket was found unclaimed in the local train through

138

Harrow and King's Langley upon the 18th of March. If such a ticket were found my case is proved. If not, my theory may still be the correct one, for it is conceivable either that he travelled without a ticket or that his ticket was lost.'

To this elaborate and plausible hypothesis the answer of the police and of the company was, first, that no such ticket was found; secondly, that the slow train would never run parallel to the express; and, thirdly, that the local train had been stationary in King's Langley Station when the express, going at fifty miles an hour, had flashed past it. So perished the only satisfying explanation, and five years have elapsed without supplying a new one. Now, at last, there comes a statement which covers all the facts, and which must be regarded as authentic. It took the shape of a letter dated from New York, and addressed to the same criminal investigator whose theory I have quoted. It is given here in extenso, with the exception of the two opening paragraphs, which are personal in their nature:

'You'll excuse me if I am not very free with names. There's less reason now than there was five years ago when mother was still living. But for all that, I had rather cover up our tracks all I can. But I owe you an explanation, for if your idea of it was wrong, it was a mighty ingenious one all the same. I'll have to go back a little so as you may understand all about it.

'My people came from Bucks., England, and

emigrated to the States in the early fifties. They settled in Rochester, in the State of New York, where my father ran a large dry goods store. There were only two sons; myself, James, and my brother, Edward. I was ten years older than my brother, and after my father died I sort of took the place of a father to him, as an elder brother would. He was a bright, spirited boy, and just one of the most beautiful creatures that ever lived. But there was always a soft spot in him, and it was like mold in cheese, for it spread and spread, and nothing that you could do would stop it. Mother saw it just as clearly as I did, but she went on spoiling him all the same, for he had such a way with him that you could refuse him nothing. I did all I could to hold him in, and he hated me for my pains.

'At last he fairly got his head, and nothing that we could do would stop him. He got off into New York, and went rapidly from bad to worse. At first he was only fast, and then he was criminal; and then, at the end of a year or two, he was one of the most notorious young crooks in the city. He had formed a friendship with Sparrow MacCoy, who was at the head of his profession as a bunco-steerer, green-goodsman, and general rascal. They took to card-sharping, and frequented some of the best hotels in New York. My brother was an excellent actor (he might have made an honest name for himself if he had chosen), and he would take the parts of a young Englishman of title, of a simple lad from the West, or of a

140

college undergraduate, whichever suited Sparrow MacCoy's purpose. And then one day he dressed himself as a girl, and he carried it off so well, and made himself such a valuable decoy, that it was their favorite game afterwards. They had made it right with Tammany and with the police, so it seemed as if nothing could ever stop them, for those were in the days before the Lexow Commission, and if you only had a pull, you could do pretty nearly anything you wanted.

'And nothing would have stopped them if they had only stuck to cards and New York, but they must needs come up Rochester way, and forge a name upon a check. It was my brother that did it, though everyone knew that it was under the influence of Sparrow MacCoy. I bought up that check, and a pretty sum it cost me. Then I went to my brother, laid it before him on the table, and swore to him that I would prosecute if he did not clear out of the country. At first he simply laughed. I could not prosecute, he said, without breaking our mother's heart, and he knew that I would not do that. I made him understand, however, that our mother's heart was being broken in any case, and that I had set firm on the point that I would rather see him in a Rochester gaol than in a New York hotel. So at last he gave in, and he made me a solemn promise that he would see Sparrow MacCoy no more, that he would go to Europe, and that he would turn his hand to any honest trade that I helped him to get. I

141

took him down right away to an old family friend, Joe Willson, who is an exporter of American watches and clocks, and I got him to give Edward an agency in London, with a small salary and a 5 per cent commission on all business. His manner and appearance were so good that he won the old man over at once, and within a week he was sent off to London with a case full of samples.

'It seemed to me that this business of the check had really given my brother a fright, and that there was some chance of his settling down into an honest line of life. My mother had spoken with him, and what she said had touched him, for she had always been the best of mothers to him, and he had been the great sorrow of her life. But I knew that this man Sparrow MacCoy had a great influence over Edward, and my chance of keeping the lad straight lay in breaking the connection between them. I had a friend in the New York detective force, and through him I kept a watch upon MacCoy. When within a fortnight of my brother's sailing I heard that MacCoy had taken a berth in the *Etruria*, I was as certain as if he had told me that he was going over to England for the purpose of coaxing Edward back again into the ways that he had left. In an instant I had resolved to go also, and to put my influence against MacCoy's. I knew it was a losing fight, but I thought, and my mother thought, that it was my duty. We passed the last night together in prayer for my success, and she gave me her own Testament that my father had given her on the day of their marriage in the Old Country, so that I might always wear it next my heart.

'I was a fellow-traveller, on the steamship, with Sparrow MacCoy, and at least I had the satisfaction of spoiling his little game for the voyage. The very first night I went into the smoking-room, and found him at the head of a card table, with half-a-dozen young fellows who were carrying their full purses and their empty skulls over to Europe. He was settling down for his harvest, and a rich one it would have been. But I soon changed all that.

' "Gentlemen," said I, "are you aware whom you are playing with?"

' "What's that to you? You mind your own business!" said he, with an oath.

' "Who is it, anyway?" asked one of the dudes.

' "He's Sparrow MacCoy, the most notorious card-sharper in the States."

'Up he jumped with a bottle in his hand, but he remembered that he was under the flag of the effete Old Country, where law and order run, and Tammany has no pull. Gaol and the gallows wait for violence and murder, and there's no slipping out by the back door on board an ocean liner.

' "Prove your words, you—!" said he.

' "I will!" said I. "If you will turn up your right shirt-sleeve to the shoulder, I will either prove my words or I will eat them."

'He turned white and said not a word. You see, I knew something of his ways, and I was aware that part of the mechanism which he and all such sharpers use consists of an elastic down the arm with a clip just above the wrist. It is by means of this clip that they withdraw from their hands the cards which they do not want, while they substitute other cards from another hiding-place. I reckoned on it being there, and it was. He cursed me, slunk out of the saloon, and was hardly seen again during the voyage. For once, at any rate, I got level with Mister Sparrow MacCoy.

'But he soon had his revenge upon me, for when it came to influencing my brother he outweighed me every time. Edward had kept himself straight in London for the first few weeks, and he had done some business with his American watches, until this villain came across his path once more. I did my best, but the best was little enough. The next thing I heard there had been a scandal at one of the Northumberland Avenue hotels; a traveller had been fleeced of a large sum by two confederate card-sharpers, and the matter was in the hands of Scotland Yard. The first I learned of it was in the evening paper, and I was at once certain that my brother and MacCoy were back at their old games. I hurried at once to Edward's lodgings. They told me that he and a tall gentleman (whom I recognized as MacCoy) had gone off together, and that he had left the lodgings and taken his things with him. The landlady had heard them give several directions to the cabman, ending with Euston Station, and she had accidentally overheard the tall gentleman saying something about Manchester. She believed that that was their destination.

'A glance at the time-table showed me that the most likely train was at five, though there was another at 4.35 which they might have caught. I had only time to get the later one, but found no sign of them either at the depot or in the train. They must have gone on by the earlier one, so I determined to follow them to Manchester and search for them in the hotels there. One last appeal to my brother by all that he owed to my mother might even now be the salvation of him. My nerves were overstrung, and I lit a cigar to steady them. At that moment, just as the train was moving off, the door of my compartment was flung open, and there were MacCoy and my brother on the platform.

'They were both disguised, and with good reason, for they knew that the London police were after them. MacCoy had a great astrakhan collar drawn up, so that only his eyes and nose were showing. My brother was dressed like a woman, with a black veil half down his face, but of course it did not deceive me for an instant, nor would it have done so even if I had not known that he had often used such a dress before. I started up, and as I did so MacCoy recognized me. He said something, the conductor slammed the door, and they

145

were shown into the next compartment. I tried to stop the train so as to follow them, but the wheels were already moving, and it was too late.

'When we stopped at Willesden, I instantly changed my carriage. It appears that I was not seen to do so, which is not surprising, as the station was crowded with people. MacCoy, of course, was expecting me, and he had spent the time between Euston and Willesden in saying all he could to harden my brother's heart and set him against me. That is what I fancy, for I had never found him so impossible to soften or to move. I tried this way and I tried that; I pictured his future in an English gaol; I described the sorrow of his mother when I came back with the news; I said everything to touch his heart, but all to no purpose. He sat there with a fixed sneer upon his handsome face, while every now and then Sparrow MacCoy would throw in a taunt at me, or some word of encouragement to hold my brother to his resolutions.

' "Why don't you run a Sunday-school?" he would say to me, and then, in the same breath; "He thinks you have no will of your own. He thinks you are just the baby brother and that he can lead you where he likes. He's only just finding out that you are a man as well as he."

'It was those words of his which set me talking bitterly. We had left Willesden, you understand, for all this took some time. My temper got the better of me, and for the first

146

time in my life I let my brother see the rough side of me. Perhaps it would have been better had I done so earlier and more often.

' "A man!" said I. "Well, I'm glad to have your friend's assurance of it, for no one would suspect it to see you like a boarding-school missy. I don't suppose in all this country there is a more contemptible-looking creature than you are as you sit there with that Dolly pinafore upon you." He coloured up at that, for he was a vain man, and he winced from ridicule.

' "It's only a dust-cloak," said he, and he slipped it off. "One has to throw the coppers off one's scent, and I had no other way to do it." He took his toque off with the veil attached, and he put both it and the cloak into his brown bag. "Anyway, I don't need to wear it until the conductor comes round," said he.

' "Nor then, either," said I, and taking the bag I slung it with all my force out of the window, "Now," said I, "you'll never make a Mary Jane of yourself while I can help it. If nothing but that disguise stands between you and a gaol, then to gaol you shall go."

'That was the way to manage him. I felt my advantage at once. His supple nature was one which yielded to roughness far more readily than to entreaty. He flushed with shame, and his eyes filled with tears. But MacCoy saw my advantage also, and was determined that I should not pursue it.

' "He's my pard, and you shall not bully him," he cried.

' "He's my brother, and you shall not ruin him," said I. "I believe a spell of prison is the very best way of keeping you apart, and you shall have it, or it will be no fault of mine."

' "Oh, you would squeal, would you?" he cried, and in an instant he whipped out his revolver. I sprang for his hand, but saw that I was too late, and jumped aside. At the same instant he fired, and the bullet which would have struck me passed through the heart of my unfortunate brother.

'He dropped without a groan upon the floor of the compartment, and MacCoy and I, equally horrified, knelt at each side of him, trying to bring back some signs of life. MacCoy still held the loaded revolver in his hand, but his anger against me and my resentment towards him had both for that moment been swallowed up in this sudden tragedy. It was he who first realized the situation. The train was for some reason going very slowly at the moment, and he saw his opportunity for escape. In an instant he had the door open, but I was as quick as he, and jumping upon him the two of us fell off the foot-board and rolled in each other's arms down a steep embankment. At the bottom I struck my head against a stone, and I remembered nothing more. When I came to myself I was lying among some low bushes, not far from the railroad track, and somebody was bathing my head with a wet handkerchief. It was Sparrow MacCoy.

' "I guess I couldn't leave you," said he. "I

didn't want to have the blood of two of you on my hands in one day. You loved your brother, I've no doubt; but you didn't love him a cent more than I loved him, though you'll say that I took a queer way to show it. Anyhow, it seems a mighty empty world now that he is gone, and I don't care a continental whether you give me over to the hangman or not."

'He had turned his ankle in the fall, and there we sat, he with his useless foot, and I with my throbbing head, and we talked and talked until gradually my bitterness began to soften and to turn into something like sympathy. What was the use of revenging his death upon a man who was as much stricken by that death as I was? And then, as my wits gradually returned, I began to realize also that I could do nothing against MacCoy which would not recoil upon my mother and myself. How could we convict him without a full account of my brother's career being made public – the very thing which of all others we had to avoid? It was really as much our interest as his to cover the matter up, and from being an avenger of crime I found myself changed to a conspirator against Justice. The place in which we found ourselves was one of those pheasant preserves which are so common in the Old Country, and as we groped our way through it I found myself consulting the slayer of my brother as to how far it would be possible to hush it up.

'I soon realized from what he said that unless

there were some papers of which we knew nothing in my brother's pockets, there was really no possible means by which the police could identify him or learn how he had got there. His ticket was in MacCoy's pocket and so was the ticket for some baggage which they had left at the depot. Like most Americans, he had found it cheaper and easier to buy an outfit in London than to bring one from New York, so that all his linen and clothes were new and unmarked. The bag, containing the dust cloak, which I had thrown out of the window, may have fallen among some bramble patch where it is still concealed, or may have been carried off by some tramp, or may have come into the possession of the police, who kept the incident to themselves. Anyhow, I have seen nothing about it in the London papers. As to the watches, they were a selection from those which had been intrusted to him for business purposes. It may have been for the same business purposes that he was taking them to Manchester, but – well, it's too late to enter into that.

'I don't blame the police for being at fault, I don't see how it could have been otherwise. There was just one little clue that they might have followed up, but it was a small one. I mean that small circular mirror which was found in my brother's pocket. It isn't a very common thing for a young man to carry about with him, is it? But a gambler might have told you what such a mirror may mean to a card-sharper. If you sit back a little from the table, and lay the mirror, face upwards, upon your lap, you can see, as you deal, every card that you give to your adversary. It is not hard to say whether you see a man or raise him when you know his cards as well as your own. It was as much a part of a sharper's outfit as the elastic clip upon Sparrow McCoy's arm. Taking that, in connection with the recent frauds at the hotels, the police might have got hold of one end of the string.

'I don't think there is much more for me to explain. We got to a village called Amersham that night in the character of two gentlemen upon a walking tour, and afterwards we made our way quietly to London, whence MacCoy went on to Cairo and I returned to New York. My mother died six months afterwards, and I am glad to say that to the day of her death she never knew what had happened. She was always under the delusion that Edward was earning an honest living in London, and I never had the heart to tell her the truth. He never wrote, but then, he never did write at any time, so that made no difference. His name was the last upon her lips.

'There's just one other thing that I have to ask you, sir, and I should take it as a kind return for all this explanation, if you could do it for me. You remember that Testament that was picked up. I always carried it in my inside pocket, and it must have come out in my fall. I value it very highly, for it was the family book with my birth and my brother's marked by my father in the beginning of it. I wish you would apply at the proper place and have it sent to me. It can be of no possible value to anyone else. If you address it to X, Bassano's Library, Broadway, New York, it is sure to come to hand.'

The Story of the Lost Special

The confession of Herbert de Lernac, now lying under sentence of death at Marseilles, has thrown a light upon one of the most inexplicable crimes of the century – an incident which is, I believe, absolutely unprecedented in the criminal annals of any country. Although there is a reluctance to discuss the matter in official circles, and little information has been given to the Press, there are still indications that the statement of this arch-criminal is corroborated by the facts, and that we have at last found a solution for a most astounding business. As the matter is eight years old, and as its importance was somewhat obscured by a political crisis which was engaging the public attention at the time, it may be as well to state the facts as far as we have been able to ascertain them. They are collated from the Liverpool papers of that date, from the proceedings at the inquest upon John Slater, the engine-driver, and from the records of the London and West Coast Railway Company, which have been courteously put at my disposal. Briefly, they are as follows.

On the 3rd of June, 1890, a gentleman, who gave his name as Monsieur Louis Caratal, desired an interview with Mr James Bland, the superintendent of the Central London and West Coast Station in Liverpool. He was a small man, middle-aged and dark, with a stoop which was so marked that it suggested some deformity of the spine. He was accompanied by a friend, a man of imposing physique, whose deferential manner and constant attention suggested that his position was one of dependence. This friend or companion, whose name did not transpire, was certainly a foreigner, and probably, from his swarthy complexion, either a Spaniard or a South American. One peculiarity was observed in him. He carried in his left hand a small black leather despatch-box, and it was noticed by a sharp-eyed clerk in the Central office that this box was fastened to his wrist by a strap. No importance was attached to the fact at the time, but subsequent events endowed it with some significance. Monsieur Caratal was shown up to Mr Bland's office, while his companion remained outside.

Monsieur Caratal's business was quickly dispatched. He had arrived that afternoon from Central America. Affairs of the utmost importance demanded that he should be in Paris without the loss of an unnecessary hour. He had missed the London express. A special must be provided. Money was of no importance. Time was everything. If the company would speed him on his way, they might make their own terms.

Mr Bland struck the electric bell, summoned

Mr Potter Hood, the traffic manager, and had the matter arranged in five minutes. The train would start in three-quarters of an hour. It would take that time to insure that the line should be clear. The powerful engine called Rochdale (No. 247 on the company's register) was attached to two carriages, with a guard's van behind. The first carriage was solely for the purpose of decreasing the inconvenience arising from the oscillation. The second was divided, as usual, into four compartments, a first-class smoking, a second-class, and a second-class smoking. The first compartment, which was the nearest to the engine, was the one allotted to the travellers. The other three were empty. The guard of the special train was James McPherson, who had been some years in the service of the company. The stoker, William Smith, was a new hand.

Monsieur Caratal, upon leaving the superintendent's office, rejoined his companion, and both of them manifested extreme impatience to be off. Having paid the money asked, which amounted to fifty pounds five shillings, at the usual special rate of five shillings a mile, they demanded to be shown the carriage, and at once took their seats in it, although they were assured that the better part of an hour must elapse before the line could be cleared. In the meantime a singular coincidence had occurred in the office which Monsieur Caratal had just quitted.

A request for a special is not a very uncommon circumstance in a rich commercial centre, but that two should be required upon the same afternoon was most unusual. It so happened, however, that Mr Bland had hardly dismissed the first traveller before a second entered with a similar request. This was a Mr Horace Moore, a gentlemanly man of military appearance, who alleged that the sudden serious illness of his wife in London made it absolutely imperative that he should not lose an instant in starting upon the journey. His distress and anxiety were so evident that Mr Bland did all that was possible to meet his wishes. A second special was out of the question, as the ordinary local service was already somewhat deranged by the first. There was the alternative, however, that Mr Moore should share the expense of Monsieur Caratal's train, and should travel in the other empty first-class compartment, if Monsieur Caratal objected to having him in the one which he occupied. It was difficult to see any objection to such an arrangement, and yet Monsieur Caratal, upon the suggestion being made to him by Mr Potter Hood, absolutely refused to consider it for an instant. The train was his, he said, and he would insist upon the exclusive use of it. All argument failed to overcome his ungracious objections, and finally the plan had to be abandoned. Mr Horace Moore left the station in great distress, after learning that his only course was to take the ordinary slow train which leaves Liverpool at six o'clock. At four thirty-one exactly by the station clock the special train, containing the crippled Monsieur Caratal and his gigantic companion, steamed out of the Liverpool station. The line was at that time clear, and there should have been no stoppage before Manchester.

The trains of the London and West Coast Railway run over the lines of another company as far as this town, which should have been reached by the special rather before six o'clock. At a quarter after six considerable surprise and some consternation were caused amongst the officials at Liverpool by the receipt of a telegram from Manchester to say that it had not yet arrived. An inquiry directed to St Helens, which is a third of the way between the two cities, elicited the following reply:

TO JAMES BLAND, SUPERINTENDENT, CENTRAL L. & W. C. LIVERPOOL. – SPECIAL PASSED HERE AT 4.52, WELL UP TO TIME. – DOWSER, ST HELENS.

This telegram was received at 6.40. At 6.50 a second message was received from Manchester:

NO SIGN OF SPECIAL AS ADVISED BY YOU.

And then ten minutes later a third, more bewildering:

PRESUME SOME MISTAKE AS TO PROPOSED RUNNING OF SPECIAL. LOCAL TRAIN FROM ST HELENS TIMED TO FOLLOW IT HAS JUST ARRIVED

AND HAS SEEN NOTHING OF IT. KINDLY WIRE ADVICES. – MANCHESTER.

The matter was assuming a most amazing aspect, although in some respects the last telegram was a relief to the authorities at Liverpool. If an accident had occurred to the special, it seemed hardly possible that the local train could have passed down the same line without observing it. And yet, what was the alternative? Where could the train be? Had it possibly been sidetracked for some reason in order to allow the slower train to go past? Such an explanation was possible if some small repair had to be effected. A telegram was dispatched to each of the stations between St Helens and Manchester, and the superintendent and traffic manager waited in the utmost suspense at the instrument for the series of replies which would enable them to say for certain what had become of the missing train. The answers came back in the order of questions, which was the order of the stations beginning at the St Helens end:

SPECIAL PASSED HERE FIVE O'CLOCK. – COLLINS GREEN.
SPECIAL PASSED HERE SIX PAST FIVE. – EARLESTOWN.
SPECIAL PASSED HERE 5.10. – NEWTON.
SPECIAL PASSED HERE 5.20. – KENYON JUNCTION.
NO SPECIAL TRAIN HAS PASSED HERE. – BARTON MOSS.

158

The two officials stared at each other in amazement.

'This is unique in my thirty years of experience,' said Mr Bland.

'Absolutely unprecedented and inexplicable, sir. The special has gone wrong between Kenyon Junction and Barton Moss.'

'And yet there is no siding, as far as my memory serves me, between the two stations. The special must have run off the metals.'

'But how could the four-fifty parliamentary pass over the same line without observing it?'

'There's no alternative, Mr Hood. It *must* be so. Possibly the local train may have observed something which may throw some light upon the matter. We will wire to Manchester for some information, and to Kenyon Junction with instructions that the line be examined instantly as far as Barton Moss.'

The answer from Manchester came within a few minutes:

NO NEWS OF MISSING SPECIAL. DRIVER AND GUARD OF SLOW TRAIN POSITIVE THAT NO ACCIDENT BETWEEN KENYON JUNCTION AND BARTON MOSS. LINE QUITE CLEAR, AND NO SIGN OF ANYTHING UNUSUAL. – MANCHESTER.

'That driver and guard will have to go,' said Mr Bland, grimly. 'There has been a wreck and they have missed it. The special has obviously run off the metals without disturbing the line – how it could have done so passes my

159

comprehension – but so it must be, and we shall have a wire from Kenyon or Barton Moss presently to say that they have found her at the bottom of an embankment.'

But Mr Bland's prophecy was not destined to be fulfilled. A half-hour passed, and then there arrived the following message from the stationmaster of Kenyon Junction:

THERE ARE NO TRACES OF THE MISSING SPECIAL. IT IS QUITE CERTAIN THAT SHE PASSED HERE, AND THAT SHE DID NOT ARRIVE AT BARTON MOSS. WE HAVE DETACHED ENGINE FROM GOODS TRAIN, AND I HAVE MYSELF RIDDEN DOWN THE LINE, BUT ALL IS CLEAR, AND THERE IS NO SIGN OF ANY ACCIDENT.

Mr Bland tore his hair in his perplexity.

'This is rank lunacy, Hood!' he cried. 'Does a train vanish into thin air in England in broad daylight? The thing is preposterous. An engine, a tender, two carriages, a van, five human beings – and all lost on a straight line of railway! Unless we get something positive within the next hour I'll take Inspector Collins, and go down myself.'

And then at last something positive did occur. It took the shape of another telegram from Kenyon Junction.

'Regret to report that the dead body of John Slater, driver of the special train, has just been found among the gorse bushes at a point two and a quarter miles from the junction. Had fallen from his engine, pitched down the embankment, and rolled among bushes. Injuries to his head, from the fall, appear to be cause of death. Ground has now been carefully examined, and there is no trace of the missing train.'

The country was, as has already been stated, in the throes of a political crisis, and the attention of the public was further distracted by the important and sensational developments in Paris, where a huge scandal threatened to destroy the Government and to wreck the reputations of many of the leading men in France. The papers were full of these events, and the singular disappearance of the special train attracted less attention than would have been the case in more peaceful times. The grotesque nature of the event helped to detract from its importance, for the papers were disinclined to believe the facts as reported to them. More than one of the London journals treated the matter as an ingenious hoax, until the coroner's inquest upon the unfortunate driver (an inquest which elicited nothing of importance) convinced them of the tragedy of the incident.

Mr Bland, accompanied by Inspector Collins, the senior detective officer in the service of the company, went down to Kenyon Junction the same evening, and their research lasted throughout the following day, but was attended with purely negative results. Not only was no trace found of the missing train, but no conjecture could be put forward which could possibly explain the facts. At the same time, Inspector Collins's official report (which lies before me as I write) served to show that the possibilities were more numerous than might have been expected.

'In the stretch of railway between these two points,' said he, 'the country is dotted with ironworks and collieries. Of these, some are being worked and some have been abandoned. There are no fewer than twelve which have small gauge lines which run trolly-cars down to the main line. These can, of course, be disregarded. Besides these, however, there are seven which have or have had proper lines running down and connecting with points to the main line, so as to convey their produce from the mouth of the mine to the great centres of distribution. In every case these lines are only a few miles in length. Out of the seven, four belong to collieries which are worked out, or at least to shafts which are no longer used. These are the Redgauntlet, Hero, Slough of Despond, and Heartsease mines, the latter having ten years ago been one of the principal mines in Lancashire. These four side lines may be eliminated from our inquiry, for, to prevent possible accidents, the rails nearest to the main line have been taken up, and there is no longer any connection. There remain three other side lines leading (a) to the Carnstock Iron Works; (b) to the Big Ben Colliery; (c) to the Perseverance Colliery.

'Of these the Big Ben line is not more than a

quarter of a mile long, and ends at a dead wall of coal waiting removal from the mouth of the mine. Nothing had been seen or heard there of any special. The Carnstock Iron Works line was blocked all day upon the 3rd of June by sixteen truckloads of hematite. It is a single line, and nothing could have passed. As to the Perseverance line, it is a large double line, which does a considerable traffic, for the output of the mine is very large. On the 3rd of June this traffic proceeded as usual; hundreds of men, including a gang of railway platelayers, were working along the two miles and a quarter which constitute the total length of the line, and it is inconceivable that an unexpected train could have come down there without attracting universal attention. It may be remarked in conclusion that this branch line is nearer to St Helens than the point at which the engine-driver was discovered, so that we have every reason to believe that the train was past that point before misfortune overtook her.

'As to John Slater, there is no clue to be gathered from his appearance or injuries. We can only say that, as far as we can see, he met his end by falling off his engine, though why he fell, or what became of the engine after his fall, is a question upon which I do not feel qualified to offer an opinion.' In conclusion, the inspector offered his resignation to the Board, being much nettled by an accusation of incompetence in the London papers.

A month elapsed, during which both the

police and the company prosecuted their inquiries without the slightest success. A reward was offered and a pardon promised in case of crime, but they were both unclaimed. Every day the public opened their papers with the conviction that so grotesque a mystery would at last be solved, but week after week passed by, and a solution remained as far off as ever. In broad daylight, upon a June afternoon in the most thickly inhabited portion of England, a train with its occupants had disappeared as completely as if some master of subtle chemistry had volatilized it into gas. Indeed, among the various conjectures which were put forward in the public Press there were some which seriously asserted that supernatural, or, at least, preternatural, agencies had been at work, and that the deformed Monsieur Caratal was probably a person who was better known under a less polite name. Others fixed upon his swarthy companion as being the author of the mischief, but what it was exactly which he had done could never be clearly formulated in words.

Amongst the many suggestions put forward by various newspapers or private individuals, there were one or two which were feasible enough to attract the attention of the public. One which appeared in the *Times*, over the signature of an amateur reasoner of some celebrity at that date, attempted to deal with the matter in a critical and semi-scientific manner. An extract must suffice, although the curious can see the whole letter in the issue of the 3rd of July.

'It is one of the elementary principles of practical reasoning,' he remarked, 'that when the impossible has been eliminated the residuum, *however improbable*, must contain the truth. It is certain that the train left Kenyon Junction. It is certain that it did not reach Barton Moss. It is in the highest degree unlikely, but still possible, that it may have taken one of the seven available side lines. It is obviously impossible for a train to run where there are no rails, and, therefore, we may reduce our improbables to the three open lines, namely, the Carnstock Iron Works, the Big Ben and the Perseverance. Is there a secret society of colliers, and English *camorra*, which is capable of destroying both train and passengers? It is improbable, but it is not impossible. I confess that I am unable to suggest any other solution. I should certainly advise the company to direct all their energies towards the observation of those three lines, and of the workmen at the end of them. A careful supervision of the pawnbrokers' shops of the district might possibly bring some suggestive facts to light.'

The suggestion coming from a recognized authority upon such matters created considerable interest, and a fierce opposition from those who considered such a statement to be a preposterous libel upon an honest and deserving set of men. The only answer to this criticism was a challenge to the objectors to lay any more feasible explanation before the public. In reply to this two others were forthcoming (*Times*, July 7th and 9th). The first suggested that the train might have run off the metals and by lying submerged in the Lancashire and Staffordshire Canal, which runs parallel to the railway for some hundreds of yards. This suggestion was thrown out of court by the published depth of the canal, which was entirely insufficient to conceal so large an object. The second correspondent wrote calling attention to the bag which appeared to be the sole luggage which the travellers had brought with them, and suggesting that some novel explosive of immense and pulverizing power might have been concealed in it. The obvious absurdity, however, of supposing that the whole train might be blown to dust while the metals remained uninjured reduced any such explanation to a farce. The investigation had drifted into this hopeless position when a new and most unexpected incident occurred, which raised hopes never destined to be fulfilled.

This was nothing less than the receipt by Mrs McPherson of a letter from her husband, James McPherson, who had been the guard of the missing train. The letter, which was dated July 5th, 1890, was dispatched from New York, and came to hand upon July 14th. Some doubts were expressed as to its genuine character, but

Mrs McPherson was positive as to the writing, and the fact that it contained a remittance of a hundred dollars in five-dollar notes was enough in itself to discount the idea of a hoax. No address was given in the letter, which ran in this way:

'MY DEAR WIFE, – I have been thinking a great deal, and I find it very hard to give you up. The same with Lizzie. I try to fight against it, but it will always come back to me. I send you some money which will change into twenty English pounds. This should be enough to bring both Lizzie and you across the Atlantic, and you will find the Hamburg boats which stop at Southampton very good boats, and cheaper than Liverpool. If you could come here and stop at the Johnston House I would try and send you word how to meet, but things are very difficult with me at present, and I am not very happy, finding it hard to give you both up. So no more at present, from your loving husband,

JAMES MCPHERSON.'

For a time it was confidently anticipated that this letter would lead to the clearing up of the whole matter, the more so as it was ascertained that a passenger who bore a close resemblance to the missing guard had travelled from Southampton under the name of Summers in the Hamburg and New York liner *Vistula*, which started upon the 7th of June. Mrs

McPherson and her sister Lizzie Dolton went across to New York as directed, and stayed for three weeks at the Johnston House, without hearing anything from the missing man. It is probable that some injudicious comments in the Press may have warned him that the police were using them as a bait. However this may be, it is certain that he neither wrote nor came, and the women were eventually compelled to return to Liverpool.

And so the matter stood, and has continued to stand up to the present year of 1898. Incredible as it may seem, nothing has transpired during these eight years which has shed the least light upon the extraordinary disappearance of the special train which contained Monsieur Caratal and his companion. Careful inquiries into the antecedents of the two travellers have only established the fact that Monsieur Caratal was well known as a financier and political agent in Central America, and that during his voyage to Europe he had betrayed extraordinary anxiety to reach Paris. His companion, whose name was entered upon the passenger lists as Eduardo Gomez, was a man whose record was a violent one, and whose reputation was that of a bravo and a bully. There was evidence to show, however, that he was honestly devoted to the interests of Monsieur Caratal, and that the latter, being a man of puny physique, employed the other as a guard and protector. It may be added that no information came from Paris as to what the objects of Monsieur Caratal's hurried journey may have been. This comprises all the facts of the case up to the publication in the Marseilles papers of the recent confession of Herbert de Lernac, now under sentence of death for the murder of a merchant named Bonvalot. This statement may be literally translated as follows:

'It is not out of mere pride or boasting that I give this information, for, if that were my object, I could tell a dozen actions of mine which are quite as splendid; but I do it in order that certain gentlemen in Paris may understand that I, who am able here to tell about the fate of Monsieur Caratal, can also tell in whose interest and at whose request the deed was done, unless the reprieve which I am awaiting comes to me very quickly. Take warning, messieurs, before it is too late! You know Herbert de Lernac, and you are aware that his deeds are as ready as his words. Hasten then, or you are lost!

'At present I shall mention no names – if you only heard the names, what would you not think! – but I shall merely tell you how cleverly I did it. I was true to my employers then, and no doubt they will be true to me now. I hope so, and until I am convinced that they have betrayed me, these names, which would convulse Europe, shall not be divulged. But on that day . . . well, I say no more!

'In a word, then, there was a famous trial in Paris, in the year 1890, in connection with a monstrous scandal in politics and finance. How monstrous that scandal was can never be known

169

save by such confidential agents as myself. The honour and careers of many of the chief men in France were at stake. You have seen a group of nine-pins standing, all so rigid, and prim, and unbending. Then there comes the ball from faraway and pop, pop – there are your nine-pins on the floor. Well, imagine some of the greatest men in France as these nine-pins, and then this Monsieur Caratal was the ball which could be seen coming from far away. If he arrived, then it was pop, pop, pop for all of them. It was determined that he should not arrive.

'I do not accuse them all of being conscious of what was to happen. There were, as I have said, great financial as well as political interests at stake, and a syndicate was formed to manage the business. Some subscribed to the syndicate who hardly understood what were its objects. But others understood very well, and they can rely upon it that I have not forgotten their names. They had ample warning that Monsieur Caratal was coming long before he left South America, and they knew that the evidence which he held would certainly mean ruin to all of them. The syndicate had the command of an unlimited amount of money – absolutely unlimited, you understand. They looked round for an agent who was capable of wielding this gigantic power, The man chosen must be inventive, resolute, adaptive – a man in a million. They chose Herbert de Lernac, and I admit that they were right.

'My duties were to choose my subordinates,

to use freely the power which money gives, and to make certain that Monsieur Caratal should never arrive in Paris. With characteristic energy I set about my commission within an hour of receiving my instructions, and the steps which I took were the very best for the purpose which could possibly be devised.

'A man whom I could trust was dispatched instantly to South America to travel home with Monsieur Caratal. Had he arrived in time the ship would never have reached Liverpool; but, alas, it had already started before my agent could reach it. I fitted out a small armed brig to intercept it, but again I was unfortunate. Like all great organizers I was, however, prepared for failure, and had a series of alternatives prepared, one or the other of which must succeed. You must not underrate the difficulties of my undertaking, or imagine that a mere commonplace assassination would meet the case. We must destroy not only Monsieur Caratal, but Monsieur Caratal's documents, and Monsieur Caratal's companions also, if we had reason to believe that he had communicated his secrets to them. And you must remember that they were on the alert, and keenly suspicious of any such attempt. It was a task which was in every way worthy of me, for I am always most masterful where another would be appalled.

'I was all ready for Monsieur Caratal's reception in Liverpool, and I was the more eager because I had reason to believe that he had made arrangements by which he would have a considerable guard from the moment that he arrived in London. Anything which was to be done must be done between the moment of his setting foot upon the Liverpool quay and that of his arrival at the London and West Coast terminus in London. We prepared six plans, each more elaborate than the last; which plan would be used would depend upon his own movements. Do what he would, we were ready for him. If he had stayed in Liverpool, we were ready. If he took an ordinary train, an express, or a special, all was ready. Everything had been foreseen and provided for.

'You may imagine that I could not do all this myself. What could I know of the English railway lines? But money can procure willing agents all the world over, and I soon had one of the acutest brains in England to assist me. I will mention no names, but it would be unjust to claim all the credit for myself. My English ally was worthy of such an alliance. He knew the London and West Coast line thoroughly, and he had the command of a band of workers who were trustworthy and intelligent. The idea was his, and my own judgement was only required in the details. We bought over several officials, amongst whom the most important was James McPherson, whom we had ascertained to be the guard most likely to be employed upon a special train. Smith, the stoker, was also in our employ. John Slater, the engine-driver, had been approached, but had been found to be obstinate and dangerous, so we desisted. We had no

172

certainty Monsieur Caratal would take a special, but we thought it very probable, for it was of the utmost importance to him that he should reach Paris without delay. It was for this contingency, therefore, that we made special preparations – preparations which were complete down to the last detail long before his steamer had sighted the shores of England. You will be amused to learn that there was one of my agents in the pilot-boat which brought that steamer to its moorings.

'The moment that Caratal arrived in Liverpool we knew that he suspected danger and was on his guard. He had brought with him as an escort a dangerous fellow, named Gomez, a man who carried weapons, and was prepared to use them. This fellow carried Caratal's confidential papers for him, and was ready to protect either them or his master. The probability was that Caratal had taken him into his counsels, and that to remove Caratal without removing Gomez would be a mere waste of energy. It was necessary that they should be involved in a common fate, and our plans to that end were much facilitated by their request for a special train. On that special train you will understand that two out of the three servants of the company were really in our employ, at a price which would make them independent for a lifetime. I do not go as far as to say that the English are more honest than any other nation, but I have found them more expensive to buy.

'I have already spoken of my English agent –

who is a man with a considerable future before him, unless some complaint of the throat carries him off before his time. He had charge of all arrangements at Liverpool, whilst I was stationed at the inn at Kenyon, where I awaited a cipher signal to act. When the special was arranged for, my agent instantly telegraphed to me and warned me how soon I should have everything ready. He himself under the name of Horace Moore applied immediately for a special also, in the hope that he would be sent down with Monsieur Caratal, which might under certain circumstances have been helpful to us. If, for example, our great *coup* had failed, it would then have become the duty of my agent to have shot them both and destroyed their papers. Caratal was on his guard, however, and refused to admit any other traveller. My agent then left the station, returned by another entrance, entered the guard's van on the side farthest from the platform, and travelled down with McPherson, the guard.

'In the meantime you will be interested to know what my own movements were. Everything had been prepared for days before, and only the finishing touches were needed. The side line which we had chosen had once joined the main line, but it had been disconnected. We had only to replace a few rails to connect it once more. These rails had been laid down as far as could be done without danger of attracting attention, and now it was merely a case of completing a juncture with the line, and arranging the points as they had been before. The sleepers had never been removed, and the rails, fish-plates, and rivets were all ready, for we had taken them from a siding on the abandoned portion of the line. With my small but competent band of workers, we had everything ready long before the special arrived. When it did arrive, it ran off upon the small side line so easily that the jolting of the points appears to have been entirely unnoticed by the two travellers.

'Our plan had been that Smith the stoker should chloroform John Slater the driver, so that he should vanish with the others. In this respect, and in this respect only, our plans miscarried – I expect the criminal folly of McPherson in writing home to his wife. Our stoker did his business so clumsily that Slater in his struggles fell off the engine, and though fortune was with us so far that he broke his neck in the fall, still he remained as a blot upon that which would otherwise have been one of those complete masterpieces which are only to be contemplated in silent admiration. The criminal expert will find in John Slater the one flaw in all our admirable combinations. A man who has had as many triumphs as I can afford to be frank, and I therefore lay my finger upon John Slater, and I proclaim him to be a flaw.

'But now I have got our special train upon the small line two kilometres, or rather more than one mile in length, which leads, or rather used to lead, the the abandoned Heartsease mine, once one of the largest coal mines in England. You will ask how it is that no one saw the train upon this unused line. I answer that along its entire length it runs through a deep cutting, and that, unless someone had been on the edge of that cutting, he could not have seen it. There *was* someone on the edge of that cutting. I was there. And now I will tell you what I saw.

'My assistant had remained at the points in order that he might superintend the switching off of the train. He had four armed men with him, so that if the train ran off the line – we thought it probable, because the points were very rusty – we might still have resources to fall back upon. Having once seen it safely on the side line, he handed over the responsibility to me. I was waiting at a point which overlooks the mouth of the mine, and I was also armed, as were my two companions. Come what might, you see, I was always ready.

'The moment that the train was fairly on the side line, Smith, the stoker, slowed-down the engine, and then, having turned it on to the fullest speed again, he and McPherson, with my English lieutenant, sprang off before it was too late. It may be that it was this slowing-down which first attracted the attention of the travellers, but the train was running at full speed again before their heads appeared at the open window. It makes me smile to think how bewildered they must have been. Picture to yourself your own feelings if, on looking out of your luxurious carriage, you suddenly perceived that the lines upon which you ran were rusted and corroded, red and yellow with disuse and decay! What a catch must have come in their breaths as in a second it flashed upon them that it was not Manchester but Death which was waiting for them at the end of that sinister line. But the train was running with frantic speed, rolling and rocking over the rotten line, while the wheels made a frightful screaming sound upon the rusted surface. I was close to them, and could see their faces. Caratal was praying, I think – there was something like a rosary dangling out of his hand. The other roared like a bull who smells the blood of the slaughter-house. He saw us standing on the bank, and he beckoned to us like a madman. Then he tore at his wrist and threw his despatch-box out of the window in our direction. Of course, his meaning was obvious. Here was the evidence, and they would promise to be silent if their lives were spared. It would have been very agreeable if we could have done so, but business is business. Besides, the train was now as much beyond our control as theirs.

'He ceased howling when the train rattled round the curve and they saw the black mouth of the mine yawning before them. We had removed the boards which had covered it, and we had cleared the square entrance. The rails had formerly run very close to the shaft for the convenience of loading the coal, and we had only to add two or three lengths of rail in order to lead to the very brink of the shaft. In fact, as

177

the lengths would not quite fit, our line projected about three feet over the edge. We saw the two heads at the window: Caratal below, Gomez above; but they had both been struck silent by what they saw. And yet they could not withdraw their heads. The sight seemed to have paralyzed them.

'I had wondered how the train running at a great speed would take the pit into which I had guided it, and I was much interested in watching it. One of my colleagues thought that it would actually jump it, and indeed it was not very far from doing so. Fortunately, however, it fell short, and the buffers of the engine struck the other lip of the shaft with a tremendous crash. The funnel flew off into the air. The tender, carriages, and van were all mashed into one jumble, which, with the remains of the engine, choked for a minute or so the mouth of the pit. Then something gave way in the middle, and the whole mass of green iron, smoking coals, brass fittings, wheels, woodwork, and cushions all crumbled together and crashed down into the mine. We heard the rattle, rattle, rattle, as the *débris* struck against the walls, and then quite a long time afterwards there came a deep roar as the remains of the train struck the bottom. The boiler may have burst, for a sharp crash came after the roar, and then a dense cloud of steam and smoke swirled up out of the black depths, falling in a spray as thick as rain all round us. Then the vapour shredded off into thin wisps, which floated away

178

in the summer sunshine, and all was quiet again in the Heartsease mine.

'And now, having carried out our plans so successfully, it only remained to leave no trace behind us. Our little band of workers at the other end had already ripped up the rails and disconnected the side line, replacing everything as it had been before. We were equally busy at the mine. The funnel and other fragments were thrown in, the shaft was planked over as it used to be, and the lines which led to it were torn up and taken away. Then, without flurry, but without delay, we all made our way out of the country, most of us to Paris, my English colleague to Manchester, and McPherson to Southampton, whence he emigrated to America. Let the English papers of that date tell how thoroughly we had done our work, and how completely we had thrown the cleverest of their detectives off our track.

'You will remember that Gomez threw his bag of papers out of the window, and I need not say that I secured that bag and brought them to my employers. It may interest my employers now, however, to learn that out of that bag I took one or two little papers as a souvenir of the occasion. I have no wish to publish these papers; but, still, it is every man for himself in this world, and what else can I do if my friends will not come to my aid when I want them? Messieurs, you may believe that Herbert de Lernac is quite as formidable when he is against you as when he is with you, and that he is not a man to go to the guillotine until he has seen that every one of you is *en route* for New Caledonia. For your own sake, if not for mine, make haste. Monsieur de. —, and General —, and Baron — (you can fill up the blanks for yourselves as you read this). I promise you that in the next edition there will be no blanks to fill.

'P.S. – As I look over my statement there is only one omission which I can see. It concerns the unfortunate man McPherson, who was foolish enough to write to his wife and to make an appointment with her in New York. It can be imagined that when interests like ours were at stake, we could not leave them to the chance of whether a man in that class of life would or would not give away his secrets to a woman. Having once broken his oath by writing to his wife, we could not trust him any more. We took steps therefore to insure that he should not see his wife. I have sometimes thought that it would be a kindness to write to her and to assure her that there is no impediment to her marrying again.'

The Adventure of the Tall Man

I

The Plot

A girl calls on Sherlock Holmes in great distress. A murder has been committed in her village – her uncle has been found shot in his bedroom, apparently through the open window. Her lover has been arrested. He is suspected on several grounds.

(1) He has had a violent quarrel with the old man, who has threatened to alter his will, which is in the girl's favour, if she ever speaks to her lover again.

(2) A revolver has been found in his house, with his initials scratched on the butt, and one chamber discharged. The bullet found in the dead man's body fits this revolver.

(3) He possesses a light ladder, the only one in the village, and there are the marks of the foot of such a ladder on the soil below the bedroom window, while similar soil (fresh) has been found on the feet of the ladder.

His only reply is that he never possessed a revolver, and that it has been discovered in a drawer of the hatstand in his hall, where it would be easy for anyone to place it. As for the mould on the ladder (which he has not used for a month) he has no explanation whatever.

Notwithstanding these damning proofs, however, the girl persists in believing her lover to be perfectly innocent, while she suspects another man, who has also been making love to her, though she has no evidence whatever against him, except that she feels by instinct that he is a villain who would stick at nothing.

Sherlock and Watson go down to the village and inspect the spot, together with the detective in charge of the case. The marks of the ladder attract Holmes's special attention. He ponders – looks about him – inquires if there is any place where anything bulky could be concealed. There is – a disused well, which has not been searched because apparently nothing is missing. Sherlock, however, insists on the well being explored. A village boy consents to be lowered into it, with a candle. Before he goes down Holmes whispers something in his ear – he appears surprised. The boy is lowered and, on his signal, pulled up again. He brings to the surface *a pair of stilts*!

'Good Lord!' cries the detective, 'who on earth could have expected this?' – 'I did,' replies Holmes. – 'But why?' – 'Because the marks on the garden soil were made by two perpendicular poles – the feet of a ladder, which is on the slope, would have made depressions slanting towards the wall.'

(N.B. The soil was a strip beside a gravel path on which the stilts left no impression.)

182

This discovery lessened the weight of the evidence of the ladder, though the other evidence remained.

The next step was to trace the user of the stilts, if possible. But he had been too wary, and after two days nothing had been discovered. At the inquest the young man was found guilty of murder. But Holmes is convinced of his innocence. In these circumstances, and as a last hope, he resolves on a sensational stratagem.

He goes up to London, and, returning on the evening of the day when the old man is buried, he and Watson and the detective go to the cottage of the man whom the girl suspects, taking with them a man whom Holmes has brought from London, who has a disguise which makes him the living image of the murdered man, wizened body, grey shrivelled face, skull-cap, and all. They have also with them the pair of stilts. On reaching the cottage, the disguised man mounts the stilts and stalks up the path towards the man's open bedroom window, at the same time crying out his name in a ghastly sepulchral voice. The man, who is already half mad with guilty terrors, rushes to the window and beholds in the moonlight the terrific spectacle of his victim stalking towards him. He reels back with a scream as the apparition, advancing to the window, calls in the same unearthly voice – 'As you came for me, I have come for you!' When the party rush upstairs into his room he darts to them, clinging to them, gasping, and, pointing to the window, where the dead man's face is glaring in, shrieks out, 'Save me! My God! He has come for me as I came for him.'

Collapsing after this dramatic scene, he makes a full confession. He has marked the revolver, and concealed it where it was found – he has also smeared the ladder-foot with soil from the old man's garden. His object was to put his rival out of the way, in the hope of gaining possession of the girl and her money.

II

The Completed Adventure

On a blustery afternoon towards the end of the summer of 1900, I returned to Baker Street from a short stroll in the park to find Sherlock Holmes as I had left him earlier that day. He lay stretched out upon the sofa with his eyes half closed, the fumes of the shag in his blackened clay rising gently to the ceiling.

Finding my companion too absorbed for conversation, I moved the heap of crumpled newspapers which had overflowed into my armchair and settled back to pursue the latest copy of the *British Medical Journal*. Presently the solitude was broken by the ring of the downstairs bell and the stately tread of Mrs Hudson in answer.

'Holmes,' said I, glancing at my companion 'who can that be?'

'A client, undoubtedly,' he answered, 'and from that persistent ringing I'd say it must be an urgent matter.'

His eyes sparkled, and he rubbed his hands together in a fit of excited satisfaction. We heard a hurried step upon the stair and in a moment, an impatient knock at our door. Holmes reached out and turned the reading lamp away from himself and towards the vacant chair in which our visitor must sit.

'Come in!' he called.

The woman who entered was young, some two-and-twenty at the outside. She was dressed in a neat, fashionable attire, but I immediately noted that she carried with her the look of a person who is weighed down with an immense anxiety. Her eyes darted about in the manner of a frightened animal, as she looked first at Holmes, then at me.

'I am Sherlock Holmes, and this is my friend and colleague, Doctor Watson.'

'I must apologize,' she blurted forth, 'for disturbing you at this hour without an appointment, but I need your help desperately.'

'Pray sit down and compose yourself,' said Holmes as he looked her over in the minute and yet abstract fashion which was peculiar to him. 'Why have you come all the way from Yorkshire by train to consult me?'

'Mr Holmes,' she cried, 'you know me?'

'Not at all; it was merely a deduction. I observe the second half of a return ticket protruding from your glove. The turf which adheres to your umbrella tip and the lower part of your skirt is quite distinctive to Yorkshire.'

'Why, it is quite simple when you explain it.'

'Quite so,' Holmes answered, a little nettled.

'But now, I am sure that you can help me.'

'I can but try. Pray state the essential facts of your problem.'

So saying, my friend leaned back on the sofa, brows drawn, fingertips together, and awaited her story.

'My name,' she began, 'is Emila Pratt. I live – or rather lived, with my uncle, Sir Charles Goodlin, in his lodge near Sheffield, Yorkshire, ever since my father died four years ago. I can not say my life was an unhappy one – that is until a few months ago. At that time I met Arthur Morley. He was only a clerk in our local bank but we fell in love immediately. My uncle was shocked and when Arthur came to ask for my hand, they had a violent quarrel. Uncle Charles, thinking Arthur was only after the fortune which was bequeathed to me in the advent of his death, threatened to alter his will if we ever so much as spoke again and he even had the bank discharge Arthur. Then, last night, as Uncle sat in bed on the second floor, someone reached in the window and shot him. When the police came and the servants told them of uncle's argument with Arthur they searched his house. In the hall hat-stand they found a revolver with "A M" scratched on the handle. One chamber was discharged and the bullet found in my uncle's body fits this revolver.'

'Dear me,' said Holmes, 'that makes things look quite badly for your young man. What has he to say in his defence?'

'Arthur swears he never owned a revolver in his life. The hat-stand was in the hallway where anyone could have gotten to it.'

'A possible explanation. Is there any more?'

'Yes, Arthur possesses a light ladder, the police found fresh soil adhering to the rungs and bottom of the supports. Directly beneath my uncle's window they found two holes where the murderer rested a ladder. Since Arthur has not used his ladder for a month, he can find no possible explanation.'

'Could the ladder have been removed for a time and then returned?'

'No, Mr Holmes. It was chained to the garden wall.'

With this damning disclosure, our client broke down and sobbed freely into her handkerchief. Holmes leaned forward and laid his thin fingers upon her shoulder, using the almost hypnotic power of soothing which he possessed. The agitated features relaxed, and her sunken frame slowly drew up.

'You must compose yourself,' Holmes began, 'if we are to help your young man.'

'Do you think you can free Arthur, Mr Holmes?'

'Ah, I do not have enough data as yet. I cannot tell. Perhaps you yourself have some suspicion as to who is the murderer?'

'Yes, I do. I am just as sure Jack Morgan is the murderer as I am Arthur is innocent. Yet, I have no proof of any kind against him – I just feel by instinct that he is guilty. I know for sure

187

that he is a good-for-nothing. Why, he even had the audacity to try to make me run away with him to be married.'

'Well, he can't be arrested for that. However, we will investigate him further when we reach Sheffield. At the moment he is our prime suspect. Is that all, Miss Pratt?'

'Yes, Mr Holmes, except to thank you from the bottom of my heart for what you are doing.'

'Thanks will be in order if I free your young Mr Morley. Understand, however, if I uncover new evidence against him I shall inform the police immediately.'

'I understand perfectly. Are you leaving now?'

'No, not at once. I am now closing a case and when I receive word the criminal has been apprehended Doctor Watson and I shall hasten to Sheffield.'

'Very well. Goodbye, gentlemen.'

When Emila Pratt went out the door, she seemed to have gained new strangth. After ·she had gone, Holmes turned to me.

'What do you think, Watson?'

'It looks quite bad for Morley. And you have nothing to go on but a woman's suspicions.'

'A woman's intuition,' he corrected. 'I have found that it can be relied upon greatly. However, we shall see.'

The rest of that evening Holmes lectured on the similarities and differences of the ancient Cornish dialect to the Gaelic tongue. Presently a commissionaire arrived with a message addressed to my friend.

'Aha,' he cried with delight, 'Wilson has been caught. Now we can turn our attention to Miss Pratt's case.'

He shot out his long, thin arm and picked out the *Bradshaw*.

'If we hurry we can catch the 1.30 from St Pancras.'

We dashed down the stairs and clambered into a hansom Holmes had engaged previously. Arriving at the station we reached the train with but a moment to spare. Already the warning whistle could be heard and almost as we stepped aboard, the train shuttled out of the station. In a few moments we were comfortably settled in a first class carriage, speeding through the night.

It was one of Holmes characteristics that he could command sleep at will. Unfortunately he could resist it at will also, and often have I had to remonstrate with him on the harm he must be doing himself when, deeply engrossed in one of his strange or baffling problems, he would go for several consecutive days and nights without one wink of sleep. He put the shades over the lamps, leaned back in his corner, and in less than two minutes his regular breathing told me he was fast asleep. Not being blessed with the same gift myself, I lay back in my corner for some time nodding to the rhythmical throb of the express as it hurled itself forward in the darkness. Now and then as we shot through some brilliantly illuminated station or past a line of flaming furnaces, I caught for an instant a glimpse of Holmes' figure coiled up snugly in the far corner with his head sunk upon his breast.

We arrived in Sheffield early that morning and engaged a hansom to drive us to the Goodlin Lodge, a few miles outside the city, stopping only to see the Inspector in charge of the case. At the mention of Holmes' name, he was ready to render every service and at my friend's request he accompanied us to the scene of the tragedy.

Inspector Baynes uncovered a strip of soil beside a gravel path which ran around the house.

'Here,' he said, 'are the marks made by Morley's ladder.'

Holmes knelt down and, as I had seen him do so many times, whipped a large round magnifying glass from his pocket. He slowly scrutinized the soil and the pathway. Drawing himself erect he nonchalantly gazed at the ground, the sky, the house, and the surrounding terrain.

'Is there any place in this vicinity where a long thin object might be hidden?' he asked.

'A long thin object? Why I don't see the connection, but off-hand I can think of only one place. On the opposite side of the house there is a disused well.'

'Did you search it?'

'Why should we search it? There is nothing missing from the house, I fail to see—.'

'You are not the only one, Watson. Come – let us look at it.'

The inspector led the way around the house

and we came upon the well, partially boarded over and certainly abandoned for a long time. Holmes produced a half-crown and persuaded Tommy, a village boy who was an interested spectator, to permit himself to be lowered into the well. Before he went down, Holmes leaned close and whispered into his ear. The boy uttered a cry of amazement but nodded his head that he understood. We slowly lowered Tommy into the dark well and watched the light from the lantern he carried play about the walls and floor. In a few seconds he tugged at the rope – the signal to pull him to the surface. Up he came, and with him came two long thin poles – a pair of stilts.

'Good Lord,' cried Baynes, 'who on earth could have expected this?'

'I did,' replied Holmes. 'The marks in the garden were by two perpendicular poles – the feet of a ladder, which would be on a slope, would have made depressions slanting towards the wall. If you remember the pathway is made of gravel – the stilts left no impressions on that.'

'Well, Mr Holmes,' the Inspector said, 'this discovery certainly lessens the weight of the ladder, but there is still the motive and the revolver.'

'True, and we shall attack those in time. But now – the next step is to trace the user of these stilts, if possible.'

The next two days were spent in a fruitless search for that information. Holmes located the London manufacturer who had fashioned the stilts, but there the trail ended – the buyer had been too wary. Meanwhile, an inquest had been held, and young Morley was now officially charged with murder. Holmes paced about our rooms at the local inn.

'I am convinced of Morley's innocence, Watson. But how can I prove it? While waiting for word from London, I investigated Miss Pratt's suspect, Jack Morgan. Her suspicions are well founded, for he has a bad reputation about this vicinity. Even so, there is nothing against him – he has no police record. In the eyes of the police he does not even have a motive. One thing – I saw him at the bar yesterday and it is evident that he is half mad with guilty terrors in spite of the nonchalant air he shows. Halloa! I have it! Our last hope, Watson. It is certainly a sensational plan, but if it succeeds, young Morley shall go free. I am leaving for London immediately, but should return tomorrow evening.

The next day Sir Charles was buried in the family plot at the local cemetery. Miss Pratt, already grief-stricken, began to despair that Holmes could not help her. That evening, however, he returned in high spirits, accompanied by a mysterious Mr Fairchild. Holmes, Fairchild, the Inspector, and myself set off for Jack Morgan's cottage. At my friend's request Baynes carried the stilts which we had found the first day. As we reached the cottage Fairchild parted company.

'You know what to do,' said Holmes.

'Right,' he answered. 'Give me about ten minutes and I'll be ready.'

'Give Mr Fairchild the stilts, Inspector.'

'Very well, Mr Holmes. But I hold you responsible for them – they are evidence, you know.'

Fairchild took the stilts and silently crept off into the bushes.

'Come here, where we can watch the action,' whispered Holmes. 'Be ready to move when necessary.'

'Holmes,' I began, what—.'

'Patience, Watson, patience. Watch the upper window.'

In a few minutes there was a rustle of leaves and out of the protective cover of the trees came a ghastly spectre, mounted on stilts.

'Holmes,' I cried, 'that's Sir Charles!'

'It's a ghost,' cried the Inspector.

'Quiet,' cautioned Holmes, 'or you'll ruin the effect. That is Fairchild, a very able actor as you can see. He wears a disguise that transforms him into the living image of Sir Charles. But listen . . .'

The figure stalked up the garden path towards Morgan's open bedroom window. Suddenly it cried out his name in a ghastly sepulchral voice. Morgan rushed to the window and beheld the spectre coming towards him.

'As you came for me, I have come for you,' it moaned.

The terrified man reeled back from the window and a horrifying scream rent the air.

With Holmes leading the way, we rushed to the door, and bursting through, climbed the stairs to Morgan's bedroom. He turned, and seeing us, darted forward and threw himself to our feet. Clinging to Holmes' hand, he pointed at the dead man's face in the window.

'Save me, save me! My God! He has come for me as I came for him.'

'The only way to save yourself is to confess,' cried Holmes.

'I confess – I killed him. I smeared Morley's ladder with soil – I scratched his initials on the revolver and hid it in his house.'

'Why did you do it?'

'To rid myself of Morley. With him out of the way I could gain Emila Pratt and the money she would receive after Goodlin's death.'

After this damning admission, Morgan collapsed.

'Wonderful!' cried the Inspector. 'Wonderful!'

'You must obtain the release of young Morley as soon as possible,' said Holmes. 'I confess that I think you owe him an apology. Miss Pratt and he will probably be married after these unpleasantries are over. When we have finished at the police station, Watson, I think that something nutritious at the Inn would not be out of place. And at 2.10 there is a morning express that will enable us to reach Baker Street in time for breakfast.'

The Painful Predicament
of Sherlock Holmes

A fantasy in about one tenth of an Act

The play takes place in Sherlock Holmes's
Baker Street Apartments somewhere about
the date of the day before yesterday

Characters:
Gwendolyn Cobb
Sherlock Holmes
Billy
Two Valuable Assistants

*(Sherlock Holmes is discovered seated on the floor
before the fire smoking. The fire is at L. There is a
table C with various things on it, an arm chair right of
it. A high upholstered stool is at its left. Firelight from
fire at L. Moonlight from window up C and up L)*

*(Strange lights from door R and from door up R
when it is open. After the curtain is up and the
firelight on, there is a* PAUSE*)*

*(Sudden loud ringing at front door bell outside at R
in distance, continuing impatiently. After time for
opening of door, loud talking and protestations*

*heard outside R in distance, Gwendolyn pouring
forth a steady stream in a high key insisting that she
must see Mr Holmes, that it is very important, a
matter of life and death, etc., Billy trying to tell her
she cannot come up and shouting louder and louder
in his efforts to make her hear. This continues a
moment and then suddenly grows louder as the two
come running up the stairs and approach the door;
Billy leading and the voice after him)*

*(Enter Billy at door up R, very excited. He pulls
the door shut after him, and holds it while he turns
to speak to Holmes)*

BILLY

I beg your pardon, sir –

*(The door is pulled from outside and Billy turns
to hold it, but turns again quickly to Holmes)
(Same business)*

I beg your pardon, sir – If you please, sir! –
It's a young lady 'as just came in, an' says she
must see you – she's 'ere now, sir, a-tryin' to
pull the door open – but I don't like 'er eye,
sir! . . . I don't like it at all, sir!

*(Holmes rises and moves up L C. Turns up
lamp. Lights on)*

'Er eye is certainly bad, sir! An' she – she
don't seem to be able to leave off talkin' long

enough fer me to tell 'er as 'ow she can't see you, sir!

(*Holmes moves towards C carrying pipe in left hand and watches Billy and the door with interest*)

I tried to tell 'er as you give orders not to see no one. I shouted it out tremendous – but she was talkin' so loud it never got to 'er – so I run up to warn you – an' she come runnin' after me – an' – an' –

(*Door suddenly pulled upon from outside while Billy is talking to Holmes*)

An' . . . an' 'ere she is, sir!

(*Enter Gwendolyn Cobb at door up R with unrestricted enthusiasm*)

GWENDOLYN

(*Entering joyously*)

Oh! There you are! This is Mr Holmes, I know! Oh – I've heard so much about you! You really can't imagine! (*going toward Holmes*) And I've simply longed to see you myself and see if . . . oh, do shake hands with me. (*they shake hands*) Isn't it wonderful to realize I'm shaking hands with Sherlock Holmes! It's simply ripping! To think that

I've lived to see this day! (*looks at him*) Of course, I suppose you're the real one – detectives have so many disguises and things that it might be you were only pretending – but still, why should you?

(*He motions her to seat, she does not pause an instant for any business*)

Oh, thank you. Yes – I will sit down.

(*She moves down C to R C to chair at R of table and sits on arm of it*)

(*Holmes motions Billy to go*)

(*Exit Billy*)

(*Holmes goes down C standing near table*)

Because I came to ask you advice about something! Oh, yes, it wasn't just curiosity that brought me here – I'm in a dreadful predicament – that's what you like, isn't it? – predicaments! Well, this is one – it is a lolla! It's simply awful! You've no idea! I don't suppose you ever had such a frightful affair to unravel. It isn't a murder or anything like that – it's a thousand times worse! Oh – millions of times worse. There are worse things than murder – aren't there, Mr Holmes?

(*Holmes nods again to indicate that he thinks so too*)

Oh, how nice of you to agree with me about it – few would do it so soon. But you can fathom my inmost soul – I feel that you are doing it now – and it gives me strength to go on – indeed it does, Mr Holmes! Just your presence and your sympathy encourages me! (*looking at him admiringly*) And it's really you. And there's the fire.

(*Gwendolyn jumps up and runs to it, going around the table*)

(*Holmes moves to R of table, a little above it, and stands regarding her*)

I suppose it's a real fire, isn't it? You know one can never tell in these days when everything seems to be adulterated – you don't know what you're getting, do you?

(*Holmes shakes head emphatically*)

No, you don't! There you go again agreeing with me. How nice of you! It's inspiring! (*looking at him in rapture*) And it's so perfectly ripping to see you there before my eyes! But you're not smoking. Oh, I do wish you'd smoke. I always think of you that way! It doesn't seem right! Do smoke!

(*Holmes lights pipe*)

Where's the tobacco? (*looking on mantel, takes jar*) Here! (*smells*) Is it true you smoke that terrible shag tobacco? What is it like? (*drops jar*) Oh, I'm so sorry! (*steps back and breaks violin*) Oh! Isn't that too bad!

(*Stamps about on violin trying to extricate herself. Continues talking and apologizing all the while. Suddenly sits on lounge to get loose from violin and breaks the bow which lies across the arm of lounge*)

Oh, dear me! I'm so sorry! Mercy, what was that?

(*Takes out broken violin bow*)

I'm afraid you won't want me to come again – if I go on like this! Oh! (*springs to her feet*) What have you got there cooking over that lamp – I would so like a cup of tea!

(*Goes up C to retort, etc.*)

But I suppose – (*smells of things*) No – it isn't tea! What a funny thing you're boiling in it! It looks like a soap bubble with a handle! I'm going to see what – (*takes up retort and instantly drops it on floor*) Oh! it was hot! Why didn't you tell me it was hot! (*gesturing excitedly*) How could I know – I've never

200

been here before – one can't know every-thing about things, alone and unprotected . . .

(*Backing up in her excitement upsets lamp, etc. which goes over with a crash*)

(*Lights off, firelights again. Moonlight from window. Red light from door, Red light from R, L, etc., etc.*)

There goes something else! It does seem to me that you have more loose truck lying about – oh – I see! It's to trap people! What a splendid idea! They break the glass and you have them. (*moving toward him admiringly*) And you can tell from the kind of glass they break where they were born and why they murdered the man! Oh, it's perfectly thrilling! Now I suppose you know just from the few little things I've done since I've been here exactly what sort of a person I am – do you?

(*Holmes nods quietly. He lights a candle*)

(*Lights on*)

Oh, how wonderful! Everything seems won-derful! All the things about here . . . only it's so . . . oh! (*goes up R C*) Why that looks just like a friend of mine!

(*Turning up papers on wall*)

And there's another! What a handsome man! But what has he got all those lines running across his face for? I should think it would hurt – and here's oh, this is beautiful! (*tears it off*) You must let me keep this – it looks so much like a young man I know.

(*The other sketches fall down*)

Oh, dear, there go the rest of them. But you've got plenty more, haven't you? (*looks about*) See that lady's foot? Why do you have such an ugly foot hung up here! It isn't nice at all!

(*Pulls it down. Other sketches hung up fall with it*)

I'll send you a pretty water-colour of cows drinking at a stream – it'll look so much better! Mercy – did that man's fingers grow together like that? How it must have hurt . . . What did you do for him? I suppose Dr Watson attended to him – oh, if I could only see him! And I want him to help you about this dreadful affair of mine! (*goes down towards left of table*) It needs you both! And if Dr Watson wasn't with you it wouldn't seem as if you were detecting at all. It's a terrible thing – I'm in such trouble.

(*Holmes motions her to sit*)

(She is sitting on stool L of table. Holmes remains standing)

Oh thank you. I suppose I'd better tell you about it now – and then you can talk it over with Dr Watson and ask him what his idea is, and then it'll turn out that he was wrong and you knew all the time . . . oh – that's so wonderful – it gives me that delicious crawly, creepy feeling as if mice were running up and down my spine – oh! (*facing towards front*) Oh! . . .

(Holmes has edged round on the upper side of table and as she shudders, etc. he quietly takes a handkerchief out of her dress or pocket and moves quietly to R side of table and sits. Puffing occasionally and listening to her. He examines the handkerchief while she is not looking, using a magnifying glass, etc.)

Now this is what I came to ask you about – I'm sure you've never had such a painful case to attend to – because it affects two human souls . . . not bodies . . . pah . . . what are bodies . . . merely mud . . . But souls . . . they are immortal – they live forever . . . His name is Levi Lichenstein. He's what they call a Yankee. Of course you know, without my telling you, that we adore each other! Oh, Mr Holmes, we adore each other. It couldn't be expressed in words! Poets couldn't do it! . . . What are poets?

Pooh! (*snaps fingers*) We adore each other. Do I need to say more?

(*Holmes shakes head*)

No! Of course I don't . . . ah, how you understand! It's perfectly wonderful! Now listen – I want to tell you my troubles.

(*Holmes quietly scribbles on a pad of paper*)

That's right – take down what I say. Every word is important. He's in jail! Put that down! It's outrageous. And my own father did it. I'm not ashamed of it – but if – (*affected*) if – Oh, my God! (*grabs for handkerchief to weep but is unable to find it*) There! (*springs to her feet*) It's been stolen. I *knew* I should lose something if I came here . . . where the air seems simply charged with thugs and pickpockets.

(*Holmes rises and politely passes her handkerchief to her and sits again as before*)

Oh, thank you! (*sits*) My father put him there! (*she sobs*)

(*Holmes rings bell on table*)

(*Gwendolyn gives a convulsive sob on ringing of bell. But she goes right on talking, not paying any attention to the business and going on excitedly through her sobs and eye-wipings)*

(Enter Billy at door up R Holmes motions him. He comes down R back of Holmes.

Holmes hands him the paper he has been scribbling upon and motions him off)

(Exit Billy up R)

Oh, Mr Holmes – think of one's own father being the one to bring disgrace upon one! Think of one's own father doing these cruel and shameful things. But it's always one's own father – he is the one out of the world who jumps headlong at the chance to be heartless and cruel and – and –

(Three heavy and resounding thuds heard in distance, as if someone were pounding a heavy beam on the floor)

(Gwendolyn springs to her feet with a scream)

(MELODRAMATIC MUSIC)

Oh! . . . There it is . . . those awful three knocks! Something is going to happen. Is there any danger – do tell me . . .

(Holmes scribbles on piece of paper)

Oh, don't keep me in this dreadful suspense

– I have dreamt of those three awful knocks
. . . but why should they come to me? Oh,
heaven . . . you're not going to let them . . .

(*Holmes pushes the paper across to her. She
snatches it up and reads it in a loud voice*)

'Plumbers – in – the – house.'

(*Stop music*)

Oh, I see! Plumbers! (*she sits again*) And you
knew it . . . you could tell it was the plumbers
without once leaving your chair! Oh, how
wonderful . . . do you know, Levi is a little
that way. He really is, Mr Holmes. That's the
reason I adore him so! Perhaps he can see too
much! Do you think there's any danger of
that? . . . Oh, Mr Holmes – tell me – do you
think we'll be happy together? Oh – I'm sure
you know – and you will tell me, won't you?

(*Holmes scribbles on piece of paper*)

It's perfectly clear to you without even seeing
him. I know it is – and so much depends
upon it . . . when two souls seem drawn to
each other. Tell me . . . I can bear anything
. . . and I'd so like to know if we shall be
happy together or not.

(*Holmes pushes piece of paper towards her.*

She picks it up, quickly and reads it in a slow, loud, distinct voice)

'Has – he – ever – spoken – to – you?' Oh, yes! Indeed he has . . . He once told me . . .

(MELODRAMATIC MUSIC)

Oh, heavens . . . And he's in jail. He'll never speak again. I haven't told you yet . . . take down all these things . . . my father put him there. Yes – my own father! Levi has lent a friend of mine some money – a mere pittance – scarcely as much as that – say half a pittance. My friend gave him a mortgage on some furniture his grandmother had left to him and when he couldn't pay, the furniture came to Levi. Then they found another will and it left all this furniture to a distant aunt out in America and the lawyers issued a writ of replevin and then Levi sued out a habeas corpus and signed a bond so that he was responsible – and my father went on this bond – and the furniture was taken back! Levi had to get another bond, and while he was swearing it the distant aunt arrived from America and had him arrested for obtaining a habeas corpus under false pretences and he brought suit against her for defamation of character – and he was right – she said the most *frightful things*. Why, (*rising*) she stood there – in the office of his own barristers and spoke of him as a reprobate and a right angle triable!

(*Raises voice in excitement and moves about L C wildly*)

That miserable woman – with painted face and horrible American accent actually accused him of having *falsified some of the furniture.* And my father hearing that we loved each other, swore out a warrant and he is in jail! (*screams, etc.*)

(*Enter two uniformed men up L C followed by Billy. They stop an instant up R looking at Gwendolyn. In the height of her excitement she sees them and stops dead with a wild moan. They go down to her at once and get her quickly off at door up R. She goes without resistance*)

BILLY

It was the *right* Asylum, sir!

(*Exit at door up R*)

(*Holmes rises. Takes an injection of cocaine. Lights pipe with candle which he then blows out*)

(*Lights off except red light of fire, etc.*)

(Holmes goes to lounge at L before fire, and sinks down upon it, leaning back on the cushions)

(LIGHTS GRADUALLY OFF)

DARK CURTAIN

(STOP MUSIC)

The Case of the Man who was Wanted

During the late autumn of 'ninety-five a fortunate chance enabled me to take some part in another of my friend Sherlock Holmes's fascinating cases.

My wife not having been well for some time, I had at last persuaded her to take a holiday in Switzerland in the company of her old school friend Kate Whitney, whose name may be remembered in connection with the strange case I have already chronicled under the title of 'The Man with the Twisted Lip'. My practice had grown much, and I had been working very hard for many months and never felt in more need myself of a rest and a holiday. Unfortunately I dared not absent myself for a long enough period to warrant a visit to the Alps. I promised my wife, however, that I would get a week or ten days' holiday in somehow, and it was only on this understanding that she consented to the Swiss tour I was so anxious for her to take. One of my best patients was in a very critical state at the time, and it was not until August was gone that he passed the crisis and began to recover. Feeling then that I could leave my practice with a good conscience in the hands of a *locum tenens*, I began to wonder where and how I should best find the rest and change I needed.

Almost at once the idea came to my mind that I would hunt up my old friend Sherlock Holmes, of whom I had seen nothing for several months. If he had no important inquiry in hand, I would do my uttermost to persuade him to join me.

Within half an hour of coming to this resolution I was standing in the doorway of the familiar old room in Baker Street.

Holmes was stretched upon the couch with his back towards me, the familiar dressing gown and old brier pipe as much in evidence as of yore.

'Come in, Watson,' he cried, without glancing round. 'Come in and tell me what good wind blows you here?'

'What an ear you have, Holmes,' I said. 'I don't think that I could have recognized your tread so easily.'

'Nor I yours,' said he, 'if you hadn't come up my badly lighted staircase taking the steps two at a time with all the familiarity of an old fellow lodger; even then I might not have been sure who it was, but when you stumbled over the new mat outside the door which has been there for nearly three months, you needed no further announcement.'

Holmes pulled out two or three cushions from the pile he was lying on and threw them across into the armchair. 'Sit down, Watson, and make yourself comfortable; you'll find cigarettes in a box behind the clock.'

As I proceeded to comply, Holmes glanced whimsically across at me. 'I'm afraid I shall have to disappoint you, my boy,' he said. 'I had a wire only half an hour ago which will prevent me from joining in any little trip you may have been about to propose.'

'Really, Holmes,' I said, 'don't you think this is going a little *too* far? I begin to fear you are a fraud and pretend to discover things by observation, when all the time you really do it by pure out-and-out clairvoyance!'

Holmes chuckled. 'Knowing you as I do it's absurdly simple,' said he. 'Your surgery hours are from five to seven, yet at six o'clock you walk smiling into my rooms. Therefore you must have a *locum* in. You are looking well, though tired, so the obvious reason is that you are having, or about to have, a holiday. The clinical thermometer, peeping out of your pocket, proclaims that you have been on your rounds today, hence it's pretty evident that your real holiday begins tomorrow. When, under these circumstances, you come hurrying into my rooms – which, by the way, Watson, you haven't visited for nearly three months – with a new Bradshaw timetable of excursion bookings bulging out of your coat pocket, then it's more than probable you have come with the idea of suggesting some joint expedition.'

It's all perfectly true,' I said, and explained to him, in a few words, my plans. 'And I'm more disappointed than I can tell you,' I concluded, 'that you are not able to fall in with my little scheme.'

Holmes picked up a telegram from the table and looked at it thoughtfully. 'If only the inquiry this refers to promised to be of anything like the interest of some we have gone into together, nothing would have delighted me more than to have persuaded you to throw your lot in with mine for a time; but really I'm afraid to do so, for it sounds a particularly commonplace affair,' and he crumpled the paper into a ball and tossed it over to me.

I smoothed it out and read: 'To Holmes, 221B Baker Street, London, S.W. Please come to Sheffield at once to inquire into case of forgery. Jervis, Manager British Consolidated Bank.'

'I've wired back to say I shall go up to Sheffield by the one-thirty a.m. express from St Pancras,' said Holmes. 'I can't go sooner as I have an interesting little appointment to fulfil tonight down in the East End, which should give me the last information I need to trace home a daring robbery from the British Museum to its instigator – who possesses one of the oldest titles and finest houses in the country, along with a most insatiable greed, almost mania, for collecting ancient documents. Before discussing the Sheffield affair any further, however, we had perhaps better see what the evening paper has to say about it,' continued Holmes, as his boy entered with the

213

Evening News, Standard, Globe and *Star*. 'Ah, this must be it,' he said, pointing to a paragraph headed 'Daring Forger's Remarkable Exploits in Sheffield'.

Whilst going to press we have been informed that a series of most cleverly forged cheques have been successfully used to swindle the Sheffield banks out of a sum which cannot be less than six thousand pounds. The full extent of the fraud has not yet been ascertained, and the managers of the different banks concerned, who have been interviewed by our Sheffield correspondent, are very reticent.

It appears that a gentleman named Mr Jabez Booth, who resides at Broomhill, Sheffield, and has been an employee since January, 1881, at the British Consolidated Bank in Sheffield, yesterday succeeded in cashing quite a number of cleverly forged cheques at twelve of the principal banks in the city and absconding with the proceeds.

The crime appears to have been a strikingly deliberate and well thought-out one. Mr Booth had, of course, in his position in one of the principal banks in Sheffield, excellent opportunities of studying the various signatures which he forged, and he greatly facilitated his chances of easily and successfully obtaining cash for the cheques by opening banking accounts last year at each of the twelve banks at which he presented the forged cheques, and by this means becoming personally known at each.

He still further disarmed suspicion by crossing each of the forged cheques and paying them into his account, while, at the same time, he drew and cashed a cheque of his own for about half the amount of the forged cheque paid in.

It was not until early this morning, Thursday, that the fraud was discovered, which means that the rascal has had some twenty hours in which to make good his escape. In spite of this we have little doubt but that he will soon be laid by the heels, for we are informed that the finest detectives from Scotland Yard are already upon his track, and it is also whispered that Mr Sherlock Holmes, the well-known and almost world-famed criminal expert of Baker Street, has been asked to assist in hunting down this daring forger.

'Then there follows a lengthy description of the fellow, which I needn't read but will keep for future use,' said Holmes, folding the paper and looking across at me. 'It seems to have been a pretty smart affair. This Booth may not be easily caught, for though he hasn't had a long time in which to make his escape we mustn't lose sight of the fact that he's had twelve months in which to plan how he would do the vanishing trick when the time came. Well! What do you say, Watson? Some of the little problems we have gone into in the past should have at least have taught us that the most interesting cases do not always present the most bizarre features at the outset.'

' "So far from it, on the contrary, quite the reverse," to quote Sam Weller,' I replied. 'Personally nothing would be more to my taste than to join you.'

'Then we'll consider it settled,' said my friend. 'And now I must go and attend to that other little matter of business I spoke to you about. Remember,' he said, as we parted, 'one-thirty at St Pancras.'

I was on the platform in good time, but it was not until the hands of the great station clock indicated the very moment due for our departure, and the porters were beginning to slam the carriage doors noisily, that I caught the familiar sight of Holmes's tall figure.

'Ah! here you are Watson,' he cried cheerily. 'I fear you must have thought I was going to be too late. I've had a very busy evening and no time to waste; however, I've succeeded in putting into practice Phileas Fogg's theory that "a well-used minimum suffices for everything", and here I am.'

'About the last thing I should expect of you,' I said as we settled down into two opposite corners of an otherwise empty first-class carriage, 'would be that you should do such an unmethodical thing as to miss a train. The only thing which would surprise me more, in fact, would be to see you at the station ten minutes before time.'

216

'I should consider that the greatest evil of the two,' said Holmes sententiously. 'But now we must sleep; we have every prospect of a heavy day.'

It was one of Holmes's characteristics that he could command sleep at will; unfortunately he could resist it at will also, and often have I had to remonstrate with him on the harm he must be doing himself, when, deeply engrossed in one of his strange or baffling problems, he would go for several consecutive days and nights without one wink of sleep.

He put the shades over the lamps, leaned back in his corner, and in less than two minutes his regular breathing told me he was fast asleep. Not being blessed with the same gift myself, I lay back in my corner for some time, nodding to the rhythmical throb of the express as it hurled itself forward through the darkness. Now and again as we shot through some brilliantly illuminated station or past a line of flaming furnaces, I caught for an instant a glimpse of Holmes's figure coiled up snugly in the far corner with his head sunk upon his breast.

It was not until after we had passed Nottingham that I really fell asleep and, when a more than usually violent lurch of the train over some points woke me again, it was broad daylight, and Holmes was sitting up, busy with a Bradshaw and boat timetable. As I moved, he glanced across at me.

'If I'm not mistaken, Watson, that was the Dore and Totley tunnel through which we have

217

just come, and if so we shall be in Sheffield in a few minutes. As you see I've not been wasting my time altogether, but studying my Bradshaw, which, by the way, Watson, is the most useful book published, without exception, to anyone of my calling.'

'How can it possibly help you now?' I asked in some surprise.

'Well it may or may not,' said Holmes thoughtfully. 'But in any case it's well to have at one's fingertips all knowledge which may be of use. It's quite probable that this Jabez Booth may have decided to leave the country and, if this supposition is correct, he would undoubtedly time his little escapade in conformity with information contained in this useful volume. Now I learn from this *Sheffield Telegraph* which I obtained at Leicester, by the way, when you were fast asleep, that Mr Booth cashed the last of his forged cheques at the North British Bank in Saville Street at precisely two fifteen p.m. on Wednesday last. He made the round of the various banks he visited in a hansom, and it would take him about three minutes only to get from this bank to the G.C. station. From what I gather of the order in which the different banks were visited, he made a circuit, finishing at the nearest point to the G.C. station, at which he could arrive at about two eighteen. Now I find that at two twenty-two a boat express would leave Sheffield G.C., due in Liverpool at four-twenty, and in connection with it the White Star liner *Empress*

Queen should have sailed from Liverpool docks at six thirty for New York. Or again, at two forty-five a boat train would leave Sheffield for Hull, at which town it was due at four thirty in time to make a connection with the Holland steam packet, Comet, sailing at six thirty for Amsterdam.

'Here we are provided with two not unlikely means of escape, the former being the most probable; but both worth bearing in mind.'

Holmes had scarcely finished speaking when the train drew up.

'Nearly five past four,' I remarked.

'Yes,' said Holmes, 'we are exactly one and a half minutes behind time. And now I propose a good breakfast and a cup of strong coffee, for we have at least a couple of hours to spare.'

After breakfast we visited first the police station where we learned that no further developments had taken place in the matter we had come to investigate. Mr Lestrade of Scotland Yard had arrived the previous evening and had taken the case in hand officially.

We obtained the address of Mr Jervis, the manager of the bank at which Booth had been an employee, and also that of his landlady at Broomhill.

A hansom landed us at Mr Jervis's house at Fulwood at seven thirty. Holmes insisted upon my accompanying him, and we were both shown into a spacious drawing room and asked to wait until the banker could see us.

Mr Jervis, a stout, florid gentleman of about fifty, came puffing into the room in a very short time. An atmosphere of prosperity seemed to envelop, if not actually to emanate from him.

'Pardon me for keeping you waiting, gentlemen,' he said, 'but the hour is an early one.'

'Indeed, Mr Jervis,' said Holmes, 'no apology is needed unless it be on our part. It is, however, necessary that I should ask you a few questions concerning this affair of Mr Booth, before I can proceed in the matter, and that must be our excuse for paying you such an untimely visit.'

'I shall be most happy to answer your questions as far as it lies in my power to do so,' said the banker, his fat fingers playing with a bunch of seals at the end of his massive gold watch chain.

'When did Mr Booth first enter your bank?' said Holmes.

'In January, 1881.'

'Do you know where he lived when he first came to Sheffield?'

'He took lodgings at Ashgate Road, and has, I believe, lived there ever since.'

'Do you know anything of his history or life before he came to you?'

'Very little I fear; beyond that his parents were both dead, and that he came to us with the best testimonials from one of the Leeds branches of our bank, I know nothing.'

'Did you find him quick and reliable?'

'He was one of the best and smartest men I have ever had in my employ.'

'Do you know whether he was conversant with any other language besides English?'

'I feel pretty sure he wasn't. We have one clerk who attends to any foreign correspondence we may have, and I know that Booth has repeatedly passed letters and papers on to him.'

'With your experience of banking matters, Mr Jervis, how long a time do you think he might reasonably have calculated would elapse between the presentation of the forged cheques and their detection?'

'Well that would depend very largely upon circumstances,' said Mr Jervis. 'In the case of a single cheque it might be a week or two, unless the amounts were so large as to call for special inquiry, in which case it would probably never be cashed at all until such inquiry had been made. In the present case, when there were a dozen forged cheques, it was most unlikely that some one of them should not be detected within twenty-four hours and so lead to the discovery of the fraud. No sane person would dare to presume upon the crime remaining undetected for a longer period than that.'

'Thanks,' said Holmes, rising. 'Those were the chief points I wished to speak to you about. I will communicate to you any news of importance I may have.'

'I am deeply obliged to you, Mr Holmes. The case is naturally causing us great anxiety. We leave it entirely to your discretion to take whatever steps you may consider best. Oh, by the way, I sent instructions to Booth's landlady to disturb nothing in his rooms until you had had an opportunity of examining them.'

'That was a very wise thing to do,' said Holmes, 'and may be the means of helping us materially.'

'I am also instructed by my company,' said the banker, as he bowed us politely out, 'to ask you to make a note of any expenses incurred, which they will of course immediately defray.'

A few moments later we were ringing the bell of the house in Ashgate Road, Broomhill, at which Mr Booth had been a lodger for over seven years. It was answered by a maid who informed us that Mrs Purnell was engaged with a gentleman upstairs. When we explained our errand she showed us at once up to Mr Booth's rooms, on the first floor, where we found Mrs Purnell, a plump, voluble, little lady of about forty, in conversation with Mr Lestrade, who appeared to be just concluding his examination of the rooms.

'Good morning, Holmes,' said the detective, with a very self-satisfied air. 'You arrive on the scene a little too late; I fancy I have already got all the information needed to catch our man!'

'I'm delighted to hear it,' said Holmes dryly, 'and must indeed congratulate you, if this is actually the case. Perhaps after I've made a little tour of inspection we can compare notes.'

'Just as you please,' said Lestrade, with the

air of one who can afford to be gracious. 'Candidly I think you will be wasting time, and so would you if you knew what I've discovered.'

'Still I must ask you to humour my little whim,' said Holmes, leaning against the mantelpiece and whistling softly as he looked round the room.

After a moment he turned to Mrs Purnell. 'The furniture of this room belongs, of course, to you?'

Mrs Purnell assented.

'The picture that was taken down from the mantelpiece last Wednesday morning,' continued Holmes, 'that belonged to Mr Booth, I presume?'

I followed Holmes's glance across to where an unfaded patch on the wallpaper clearly indicated that a picture had recently been hanging. Well as I knew my friend's methods of reasoning, however, I did not realize for a moment that the little bits of spiderweb which had been behind the picture, and were still clinging to the wall, had told him that the picture could only have been taken down immediately before Mrs Purnell had received orders to disturb nothing in the room; otherwise her brush, evidently busy enough elsewhere, would not have spared them.

The good lady stared at Sherlock Holmes in open-mouthed astonishment. 'Mr Booth took it down himself on Wednesday morning,' she said. 'It was a picture he had painted himself, and he thought no end of it. He wrapped it up and took it out with him, remarking that he was going to give it to a friend. I was very much surprised at the time, for I knew he valued it very much; in fact he once told me that he wouldn't part with it for anything. Of course, it's easy to see now why he got rid of it.'

'Yes,' said Holmes. 'It wasn't a large picture, I see. Was it a water-colour?'

'Yes, a painting of a stretch of moorland, with three or four large rocks arranged like a big table on a bare hilltop. Druidicals, Mr Booth called them, or something like that.'

'Did Mr Booth do much painting, then?' enquired Holmes.

'None, whilst he's been here, sir. He has told me he used to do a good deal as a lad, but he had given it up.'

Holmes's eyes were glancing round the room again, and an exclamation of surprise escaped him as they encountered a photo standing on the piano.

'Surely that's a photograph of Mr Booth,' he said. 'It exactly resembles the description I have of him?'

'Yes,' said Mrs Purnell, 'and a very good one it is too.'

'How long has it been taken?' said Holmes picking it up.

'Oh, only a few weeks, sir. I was here when the boy from the photographer's brought them up. Mr Booth opened the packet whilst I was in the room. There were only two photos, that one and another which he gave to me.'

'You interest me exceedingly,' said Holmes. 'This striped lounge suit he is wearing. Is it the same he had on when he left Wednesday morning?'

'Yes, he was dressed just like that, as far as I can remember.'

'Do you recollect anything of importance that Mr Booth said to you last Wednesday before he went out?'

'Not very much, I'm afraid, sir. When I took his cup of chocolate up to his bedroom, he said—'

'One moment,' interrupted Holmes. 'Did Mr Booth usually have a cup of chocolate in the morning?'

'Oh, yes, sir, summer and winter alike. He was very particular about it and would ring for it as soon as he waked. I believe he'd rather have gone without his breakfast almost than have missed his cup of chocolate. Well, as I was saying, sir, I took it up to him myself on Wednesday morning, and he made some remark about the weather and then, just as I was leaving the room, he said, "Oh, by the way, Mrs Purnell, I shall be going away tonight for a couple of weeks. I've packed my bag and will call for it this afternoon." '

'No doubt you were very much surprised at this sudden announcement?' queried Holmes.

'Not very much, sir. Ever since he's had this auditing work to do for the branch banks there's been no knowing when he would be away. Of course, he'd never been off for two weeks at a stretch, except at holiday times, but he had so often been away for a few days at a time that I had got used to his popping off with hardly a moment's notice.'

'Let me see, how long has he had this extra work at the bank – several months, hasn't he?'

'More. It was about last Christmas, I believe, when they gave it to him.'

'Oh, yes, of course,' said Holmes carelessly, 'and this work naturally took him from home a good deal?'

'Yes, indeed, and it seemed to quite tire him, so much evening and night work too, you see, sir. It was enough to knock him out, for he was always such a very quiet, retiring gentleman and hardly ever used to go out in the evenings before.'

'Has Mr Booth left many of his possessions behind him?' asked Holmes.

'Very few, indeed, and what he has are mostly old useless things. But he's a most honest thief, sir,' said Mrs Purnell paradoxically, 'and paid me his rent, before he went out on Wednesday morning, right up to next Saturday, because he wouldn't be back by then.'

'That was good of him,' said Holmes, smiling thoughtfully. 'By the way, do you happen to know if he gave away any other treasures, before he left?'

'Well not *just* before, but during the last few months he's taken away most of his books and sold them I think, a few at a time. He had rather a fancy for old books and has told me that some editions he had were worth quite a lot.'

During this conversation, Lestrade had been sitting drumming his fingers impatiently on the table. Now he got up. 'Really, I fear I shall have to leave you to this gossip,' he said. 'I must go and wire instructions for the arrest of Mr Booth. If only you would have looked before at this old blotter, which I found in the wastebasket, you would have saved yourself a good deal of unnecessary trouble, Mr Holmes,' and he triumphantly slapped down a sheet of well-used blotting paper on the table.

Holmes picked it up and held it in front of a mirror over the sideboard. Looking over his shoulder I could plainly read the reflected impression of a note written in Mr Booth's handwriting, of which Holmes had procured samples.

It was to a booking agency in Liverpool, giving instructions to them to book a first-class private cabin and passage on board the *Empress Queen* from Liverpool to New York. Parts of the note were slightly obliterated by other impressions, but it went on to say that a cheque was enclosed to pay for tickets, etc., and it was signed J. Booth.

Holmes stood silently scrutinizing the paper for several minutes.

It was a well-used sheet, but fortunately the impression of the note was well in the centre, and hardly obliterated at all by the other marks and blots, which were all round the outer circumference of the paper. In one corner the address of the Liverpool booking agency was plainly decipherable, the paper evidently having been used to blot the envelope with also.

'My dear Lestrade, you have indeed been more fortunate than I had imagined,' said Holmes at length, handing the paper back to him. 'May I ask what steps you propose to take next?'

'I shall cable at once to the New York police to arrest the fellow as soon as he arrives,' said Lestrade, 'but first I must make quite certain the boat doesn't touch at Queenstown or anywhere and give him a chance of slipping through our fingers.'

'It doesn't,' said Holmes quietly. 'I had already looked to see as I thought it not unlikely, at first, that Mr Booth might have intended to sail by the *Empress Queen*.'

Lestrade gave me a wink for which I would dearly have liked to have knocked him down, for I could see that he disbelieved my friend. I felt a keen pang of disappointment that Holmes's foresight should have been eclipsed in this way by what, after all, was mere good luck on Lestrade's part.

Holmes had turned to Mrs Purnell and was thanking her.

'Don't mention it, sir,' she said. 'Mr Booth deserves to be caught, though I must say he's always been a gentleman to me. I only wish

I could have given you some more useful information.'

'On the contrary,' said Holmes, 'I can assure you that what you have told us has been of the utmost importance and will very materially help us. It's just occurred to me, by the way, to wonder if you could possibly put up my friend Dr Watson and myself for a few days, until we have had time to look into this little matter?'

'Certainly, sir, I shall be most happy.'

'Good,' said Holmes. 'Then you may expect us back to dinner about seven.'

When we got outside, Lestrade at once announced his intention of going to the police office and arranging for the necessary orders for Booth's detention and arrest to be cabled to the head of the New York police; Holmes retained an enigmatical silence as to what he purposed to do but expressed his determination to remain at Broomhill and make a few further inquiries. He insisted, however, upon going alone.

'Remember, Watson, you are here for a rest and holiday and I can assure you that if you did remain with me you would only find my programme a dull one. Therefore, I insist upon your finding some more entertaining way of spending the remainder of the day.'

Past experience told me that it was quite useless to remonstrate or argue with Holmes when once his mind was made up, so I consented with the best grace I could, and leaving Holmes, drove off in the hansom, which he assured me he would not require further.

I passed a few hours in the art gallery and museum and then, after lunch, had a brisk walk out on the Manchester Road and enjoyed the fresh air and moorland scenery, returning to Ashgate Road at seven with better appetite than I had been blessed with for months.

Holmes had not returned, and it was nearly half past seven before he came in. I could see at once that he was in one of his most reticent moods, and all my inquiries failed to elicit any particulars of how he had passed his time or what he thought about the case.

The whole evening he remained coiled up in an easy chair puffing at his pipe and hardly a word could I get from him.

His inscrutable countenance and persistent silence gave me no clue whatever as to his thought on the inquiry he had in hand, although I could see his whole mind was concentrated upon it.

Next morning, just as we had finished breakfast, the maid entered with a note. 'From Mr Jervis, sir; there's no answer,' she said.

Holmes tore open the envelope and scanned the note hurriedly and, as he did so, I noticed a flush of annoyance spread over his usually pale face.

'Confound his impudence,' he muttered. 'Read that, Watson. I don't ever remember to have been treated so badly in a case before.'

The note was a brief one:

The Cedars, Fulwood.
September sixth

Mr Jervis, on behalf of the directors of the British Consolidated Bank, begs to thank Mr Sherlock Holmes for his prompt attention and valued services in the matter concerning the fraud and disappearance of their ex-employee, Mr Jabez Booth.

Mr Lestrade, of Scotland Yard, informs he that he has succeeded in tracking the individual in question who will be arrested shortly. Under these circumstances they feel it unnecessary to take up any more of Mr Holmes's valuable time.

'Rather cool, eh, Watson? I'm much mistaken if they don't have cause to regret their action when it's too late. After this I shall certainly refuse to act for them any further in the case, even if they ask me to do so. In a way I'm sorry because the matter presented some distinctly interesting features and is by no means the simple affair our friend Lestrade thinks.'

'Why, don't you think he is on the right scent?' I exclaimed.

'Wait and see, Watson,' said Holmes mysteriously. 'Mr Booth hasn't been caught yet, remember.' And that was all I could get out of him.

One result of the summary way in which the banker had dispensed with my friend's services was that Holmes and I spent a most restful and enjoyable week in the small village of Hathersage, on the edge of the Derbyshire moors, and returned to London feeling better for our long moorland rambles.

Holmes having very little work in hand at the time, and my wife not yet having returned from her Swiss holiday, I prevailed upon him, though not without considerable difficulty, to pass the next few weeks with me instead of returning to his rooms at Baker Street.

Of course, we watched the development of the Sheffield forgery case with the keenest interest. Somehow the particulars of Lestrade's discoveries got into the papers, and the day after we left Sheffield they were full of the exciting chase of Mr Booth, the man wanted for the Sheffield Bank frauds.

They spoke of 'the guilty man restlessly pacing the deck of the *Empress Queen*, as she ploughed her way majestically across the solitary wastes of the Atlantic, all unconscious that the inexorable hand of justice could stretch over the ocean and was already waiting to seize him on his arrival in the New World.' And Holmes after reading these sensational paragraphs would always lay down the paper with one of his enigmatical smiles.

At last the day on which the *Empress Queen* was due at New York arrived, and I could not help but notice that even Holmes's usually inscrutable face wore a look of suppressed excitement as he unfolded the evening paper. But our surprise was doomed to be prolonged

232

still further. There was a brief paragraph to say that the *Empress Queen* had arrived off Long Island at six a.m. after a good passage. There was, however, a case of cholera on board, and the New York authorities had consequently been compelled to put the boat in quarantine, and none of the passengers or crew would be allowed to leave her for a period of twelve days.

Two days later there was a full column in the papers stating that it had been definitely ascertained that Mr Booth was really on board the *Empress Queen*. He had been identified and spoken to by one of the sanitary inspectors who had had to visit the boat. He was being kept under close observation, and there was no possible chance of his escaping. Mr Lestrade of Scotland Yard, by whom Booth had been so cleverly tracked down and his escape forestalled, had taken passage on the *Oceania*, due in New York on the tenth, and would personally arrest Mr Booth when he was allowed to land.

Never before or since have I seen my friend Holmes so astonished as when he had finished reading this announcement. I could see that he was thoroughly mystified, though why he should be so was quite a puzzle to me. All day he sat coiled up in an easy chair, with his brows drawn down into two hard lines and his eyes half closed as he puffed away at his oldest brier in silence.

'Watson,' he said once, glancing across at me. 'It's perhaps a good thing that I was asked to drop that Sheffield case. As things are turning out I fancy I should only have made a fool of myself.'

'Why?' I asked.

'Because I began by assuming that somebody else wasn't one – and now it looks as though I had been mistaken.'

For the next few days Holmes seemed quite depressed, for nothing annoyed him more than to feel that he had made any mistake in his deductions or got onto a false line of reasoning.

At last the fatal tenth of September, the day on which Booth was to be arrested, arrived. Eagerly but in vain we scanned the evening papers. The morning of the eleventh came and still brought no news of the arrest, but in the evening papers of that day there was a short paragraph hinting that the criminal had escaped again.

For several days the papers were full of the most conflicting rumours and conjectures as to what had actually taken place, but all were agreed in affirming that Mr Lestrade was on his way home alone and would be back in Liverpool on the seventeenth or eighteenth.

On the evening of the last named day Holmes and I sat smoking in his Baker Street rooms, when his boy came in to announce that Mr Lestrade of Scotland Yard was below and would like the favour of a few minutes' conversation.

'Show him up, show him up,' said Holmes, rubbing his hands together with an excitement quite unusual to him.

Lestrade entered the room and sat down in the seat to which Holmes waved him, with a most dejected air.

'It's not often I'm at fault, Mr Holmes,' he began, 'but in this Sheffield business I've been beaten hollow.'

'Dear me,' said Holmes pleasantly, 'you surely don't mean to tell me that you haven't got your man yet.'

'I do,' said Lestrade. 'What's more, I don't think he ever will be caught!'

'Don't despair so soon,' said Holmes encouragingly. 'After you have told us all that's already happened, it's just within the bounds of possibility that I may be able to help you with some little suggestions.'

Thus encouraged Lestrade began his strange story to which we both listened with breathless interest.

'It's quite unnecessary for me to dwell upon incidents which are already familiar,' he said. 'You know of the discovery I made in Sheffield which, of course, convinced me that the man I wanted had sailed for New York on the *Empress Queen*. I was in a fever of impatience for his arrest, and when I heard that the boat he had taken passage on had been placed in quarantine, I set off at once in order that I might actually lay hands upon him myself. Never have five days seemed so long.

'We reached New York on the evening of the ninth, and I rushed off at once to the head of the New York police and from him learned that there was no doubt whatever that Mr Jabez Booth was indeed on board the *Empress Queen*. One of the sanitary inspectors who had had to visit the boat had not only seen but actually spoken to him. The man exactly answered the description of Booth which had appeared in the papers. One of the New York detectives had been sent on board to make a few inquiries and to inform the captain privately of the pending arrest. He found that Mr Jabez Booth had actually had the audacity to book his passage and travel under his real name without even attempting to disguise himself in any way. He had a private first-class cabin, and the purser declared that he had been suspicious of the man from the first. He had kept himself shut up in his cabin nearly all the time, posing as an eccentric semi-invalid person who must not be disturbed on any account. Most of his meals had been sent down to his cabin, and he had been seen on deck but seldom and hardly ever dined with the rest of the passengers. It was quite evident that he had been trying to keep out of sight, and to attract as little attention as possible. The stewards and some of the passengers who were approached on the subject later were all agreed that this was the case.

'It was decided that during the time the boat was in quarantine nothing should be said to Booth to arouse his suspicions but that the pursers, steward and captain, who were the only persons in the secret, should between them keep him under observation until the tenth, the day on which passengers would be allowed to leave the boat. On that day he should be arrested.'

Here we were interrupted by Holmes's boy who came in with a telegram. Holmes glanced at it with a faint smile.

'No answer,' he said, slipping it in his waistcoat pocket. 'Pray continue your very interesting story, Lestrade.'

'Well, on the afternoon of the tenth, accompanied by the New York chief inspector of police and detective Forsyth,' resumed Lestrade, 'I went on board the *Empress Queen* half an hour before she was due to come up to the landing stage to allow passengers to disembark.

'The purser informed us that Mr Booth had been on deck and that he had been in conversation with him about fifteen minutes before our arrival. He had then gone down to his cabin and the purser, making some excuse to go down also, had actually seen him enter it. He had been standing near the top of the companionway since then and was sure Booth had not come up on deck again since.

' "At last," I muttered to myself, as we all went down below, led by the purser who took us straight to Booth's cabin. We knocked but, getting no answer, tried the door and found it locked. The purser assured us, however, that this was nothing unusual. Mr Booth had had his cabin door locked a good deal and, often, even his meals had been left on a tray outside. We held a hurried consultation and, as time was short, decided to force the door. Two good blows with a heavy hammer broke it from the hinges, and we all rushed in. You can picture the astonishment when we found the cabin empty. We searched it thoroughly, and Booth was certainly not there.'

'One moment,' interrupted Holmes. 'The key of the door – was it on the inside of the lock or not?'

'It was nowhere to be seen,' said Lestrade. 'I was getting frantic, for by this time I could feel the vibration of the engines and hear the first churning sound of the screw as the great boat began to slide slowly down towards the landing stage.

'We were at our wits' end; Mr Booth must be hiding somewhere on board, but there was now no time to make a proper search for him, and in a very few minutes passengers would be leaving the boat. At last the captain promised us that, under the circumstances, only one landing gangway should be run out and, in company with the purser and stewards, I should stand by it with a complete list of passengers ticking off each one as he or she left. By this means it would be quite impossible for Booth to escape us even if he attempted some disguise, for no person whatever would be allowed to cross the gangway until identified by the purser or one of the stewards.

'I was delighted with the arrangement, for there was now no way by which Booth could give me the slip.

'One by one the passengers crossed the gang-way and joined the jostling crowd on the landing stage and each one was identified and his or her name crossed off my list. There were one hundred and ninety-three first-class passengers on board the *Empress Queen*, including Booth, and, when one hundred and ninety-two had disembarked, his was the only name which remained!

'You can scarcely realize what a fever of impatience we were in,' said Lestrade, mopping his brow at the very recollection, 'nor how interminable the time seemed as we slowly but carefully ticked off one by one the whole of the three hundred and twenty-four second-class passengers and the three hundred and ten steerage from my list. Every passenger except Mr Booth crossed that gangway, but he certainly did not do so. There was no possible room for doubt on that point.

'He must therefore be still on the boat, we agreed, but I was getting panic-stricken and wondered if there were any possibility of his getting smuggled off in some of the luggage which the great cranes were now beginning to swing up onto the pier.

'I hinted my fear to detective Forsyth, and he at once arranged that every trunk or box in which there was any chance for a man to hide should be opened and examined by the customs officers.

'It was a tedious business, but they didn't shirk it, and at the end of two hours were able to assure us that by no possibility could Booth have been smuggled off the boat in this way.

'This left only one possible solution to the

mystery. He *must* be still in hiding somewhere on board. We had had the boat kept under the closest observation ever since she came up to the landing stage, and now the superintendent of police lent us a staff of twenty men and, with the consent of the captain and the assistance of the pursers and stewards etc., the *Empress Queen* was searched and re-searched from stem to stern. We didn't leave unexamined a place in which a cat could have hidden, but the missing man wasn't there. Of that I'm certain – and there you have the whole mystery in a nutshell, Mr Holmes. Mr Booth certainly *was* on board the *Empress Queen* up to, and at, eleven o'clock on the morning of the tenth, and although he could not by any possibility have left it, we are nevertheless face to face with the fact that he wasn't there at five o'clock in the afternoon.'

Lestrade's face as he concluded his curious and mysterious narrative, bore a look of the most hopeless bewilderment I ever saw, and I fancy my own must have pretty well matched it, but Holmes threw himself back in his easy chair, with his long thin legs stuck straight out in front of him, his whole frame literally shaking with silent laughter. 'What conclusions have you come to?' he gasped at length. 'What steps do you propose to take next?'

'I've no idea. Who could know what to do? The whole thing is impossible, perfectly impossible; it's an insoluble mystery. I came to you to see if you could, by any chance, suggest some entirely fresh line of inquiry upon which I might begin to work.'

'Well,' said Holmes, cocking his eye mischievously at the bewildered Lestrade, 'I can give you Booth's present address, if it will be of any use to you?'

'His what!' cried Lestrade.

'His present address,' repeated Holmes quietly. 'But before I do so, my dear Lestrade, I must make one stipulation. Mr Jervis has treated me very shabbily in the matter, and I don't desire that my name shall be associated with it any further. Whatever you do you must not hint the source from which any information I may give you has come. You promise?'

'Yes,' murmured Lestrade, who was in a state of bewildered excitement.

Holmes tore a leaf from his pocket book and scribbled on it: Mr A. Winter, c/o Mrs Thackary, Glossop Road, Broomhill, Sheffield.

'You will find there the present name and address of the man you are in search of,' he said, handing the paper across to Lestrade. 'I should strongly advise you to lose no time in getting hold of him, for though the wire I received a short time ago – which unfortunately interrupted your most interesting narrative – was to tell me that Mr Winter had arrived back home again after a temporary absence, still it's more than probable that he will leave there, for good, at an early date. I can't say how soon – not for a few days I should think.'

Lestrade rose. 'Mr Holmes, you're a brick,'

he said, with more real feeling than I have ever seen him show before. 'You've saved my reputation in this job just when I was beginning to look like a perfect fool, and now you're forcing me to take all the credit, when I don't deserve one atom. As to how you've found this out, it's as great a mystery to me as Booth's disappearance was.'

'Well, as to that,' said Holmes airily, 'I can't be sure of all the facts myself, for of course I've never looked properly into the case. But they are pretty easy to conjecture, and I shall be most happy to give you my idea of Booth's trip to New York on some future occasion when you have more time to spare.

'By the way,' called out Holmes, as Lestrade was leaving the room, 'I shouldn't be surprised if you find Mr Jabez Booth, alias Mr Archibald Winter, a slight acquaintance of yours, for he would undoubtedly be a fellow passenger of yours, on your homeward journey from America. He reached Sheffield a few hours before you arrived in London and, as he has certainly just returned from New York, like yourself, it's evident you must have crossed on the same boat. He would be wearing smoked glasses and have a heavy dark moustache.'

'Ah!' said Lestrade, 'there *was* a man called Winter on board who answered to that description. I believe it must have been he, and I'll lose no more time,' and Lestrade hurried off.

'Well, Watson, my boy, you look nearly as

bewildered as our friend Lestrade,' said Holmes, leaning back in his chair and looking roguishly across at me, as he lighted his old brier pipe.

'I must confess that none of the problems you have had to solve in the past seemed more inexplicable to me than Lestrade's account of Booth's disappearance from the *Empress Queen*.'

'Yes, that part of the story is decidedly neat,' chuckled Holmes, 'but I'll tell you how I got at the solution of the mystery. I see you are ready to listen.

'The first thing to do in any case is to gauge the intelligence and cunning of the criminal. Now, Mr Booth was undoubtedly a clever man. Mr Jervis himself, you remember, assured us as much. The fact that he opened banking accounts in preparation for the crime twelve months before he committed it proves it to have been a long-premeditated one. I began the case, therefore, with the knowledge that I had a clever man to catch, who had had twelve months in which to plan his escape.

'My first real clues came from Mrs Purnell,' said Holmes. 'Most important were her remarks about Booth's auditing work which kept him from home so many days and nights, often consecutively. I felt certain at once, and inquiry confirmed, that Mr Booth had had no such extra work at all. Why then had he invented lies to explain these absences to his landlady? Probably because they were in some way connected, either with the crime or with his plans for escaping after he had committed it. It was inconceivable that so much mysterious outdoor occupation could be directly connected with the forgery, and I at once deduced that this time had been spent by Booth in paving the way for his escape.

'Almost at once the idea that he had been living a double life occurred to me, his intention doubtless being to quietly drop one individuality after committing the crime and permanently take up the other – a far safer and less clumsy expedient than the usual one of assuming a new disguise just at the very moment when everybody is expecting and looking for you to do so.

'Then there were the interesting facts relating to Booth's picture and books. I tried to put myself in his place. He valued these possessions highly; they were light and portable, and there was really no reason whatever why he should part with them. Doubtless, then, he had taken them away by degrees and put them someplace where he could lay hands on them again. If I could find out where this place was, I felt sure there would be every chance I could catch him when he attempted to recover them.

'The picture couldn't have gone far for he had taken it out with him on the very day of the crime . . . I needn't bore you with details . . . I was two hours making inquiries before I found the house at which he had called and left it – which was none other than Mrs Thackary's in Glossop Road.

'I made a pretext for calling there and found

Mrs T. one of the most easy mortals in the world to pump. In less than half an hour I knew that she had a boarder named Winter, that he professed to be a commercial traveller and was from home most of the time. His description resembled Booth's save that he had a moustache, wore glasses.

'As I've often tried to impress upon you before, Watson, details are the most important things of all, and it gave me a real thrill of pleasure to learn that Mr Winter had a cup of chocolate brought up to his bedroom every morning. A gentleman called on the Wednesday morning and left a parcel, saying it was a picture he had promised for Mr Winter, and asking Mrs Thackary to give it to Winter when he returned. Mr Winter had taken the rooms the previous December. He had a good many books which he had brought in from time to time. All these facts taken in conjunction made me certain that I was on the right scent. Winter and Booth were one and the same person, and as soon as Booth had put all his pursuers off the track he would return, as Winter, and repossess his treasures.

'The newly taken photo and the old blotter with its tell-tale note were too obviously intentional means of drawing the police onto Booth's track. The blotter, I could see almost at once, was a fraud, for not only would it be almost impossible to use one in the ordinary way so much without the central part becoming undecipherable, but I could see where it had been touched up.

'I concluded therefore that Booth, alias Winter, never actually intended to sail on the *Empress Queen*, but in that I underestimated his ingenuity. Evidently he booked *two* berths on the boat, one in his real, and one in his assumed name, and managed very cleverly to successfully keep up the two characters throughout the voyage, appearing first as one individual and then as the other. Most of the time he posed as Winter, and for this purpose Booth became the eccentric semi-invalid passenger who remained locked up in his cabin for such a large part of his time. This, of course, would answer his purpose well; his eccentricity would only draw attention to his presence on board and so make him one of the best-known passengers on the boat, although he showed so little of himself.

'I had left instructions with Mrs Thackary to send me a wire as soon as Winter returned. When Booth had led his pursuers to New York, and there thrown them off the scent, he had nothing more to do but to take the first boat back. Very naturally it chanced to be the same as that on which our friend Lestrade returned, and that was how Mrs Thackary's wire arrived at the opportune moment it did.'

THE 'COSMOPOLITAN' EDITOR'S NOTE: We are aware that there are several inconsistencies in this story. We have not tried to correct them. The story is published exactly as it was found except for minor changes in spelling and punctuation.

Some Personalia About Sherlock Holmes

At the request of the Editor I have spent some days in looking over an old letter-box in which from time to time I have placed letters referring directly or indirectly to the notorious Mr Holmes. I wish now that I had been more careful in preserving the references to this gentleman and his little problems. A great many have been lost or mislaid. His biographer has been fortunate enough to find readers in many lands, and the reading has elicited the same sort of response, though in many cases that response has been in a tongue difficult to comprehend. Very often my distant correspondent could neither spell my own name nor that of my imaginary hero! Many such letters have been from Russians. Where the Russian letters have been in the vernacular I have been compelled, I am afraid, to take them as read, but when they have been in English they have been among the most curious in my collection. There was one young lady who began all her epistles with the words 'Good Lord'. Another had a large amount of guile underlying her simplicity. Writing from Warsaw she stated that she had been bedridden for two years, and that my novels had been her only, etc., etc. So touched was I by this flattering statement that I at once prepared an autographed parcel of them to complete the fair invalid's collection. By good luck, however, I met a brother author upon the same day to whom I recounted the touching incident. With a cynical smile he drew an identical letter out of his pocket. His novels also had been for two years her only, etc., etc. I do not know how many more the lady had written to, but if, as I imagine, her correspondence had extended to several countries, she must have amassed a rather interesting library.

The young Russian's habit of addressing me as 'Good Lord' had an even stranger parallel at home, which links it up with the subject of this article. Shortly after I received a knighthood I had a bill from a tradesman which was quite correct and businesslike in every detail save that it was made out to Sir Sherlock Holmes. I hope that I can stand a joke as well as my neighbours, but this particular piece of humour seemed rather misapplied, and I wrote sharply upon the subject. In response to my letter there arrived at my hotel a very repentant clerk, who expressed his sorrow at the incident, but kept on repeating the phrase, 'I assure you, sir, that it was *bonâ fide*.' 'What do you mean by *bonâ fide*?' I asked. 'Well, sir, my mates in the shop told me that you had been knighted, and that when a man was knighted he changed his name, and that you had taken that one.' I need not say that my annoyance vanished, and that I laughed as heartily as his pals were probably doing round the corner.

There are certain problems which are continually recurring in these Sherlock Holmes letters. One of them has exercised men's minds in the most out-of-the-way places, from Labrador to Tibet; indeed, if a matter needs thought it is just the men in these outlying stations who have the time and solitude for it. I dare say I have had twenty letters upon the one point alone. It arises in 'The Adventure of the Priory School', where Holmes, glancing at the track of a bicycle, says, 'It is evidently going from us, not towards us.' He did not give his reasoning, which my correspondents resent, and all assert that the deduction is impossible. As a matter of fact it is simple enough upon soft undulating ground such as the moor in question. The weight of the rider falls most upon the hind wheel, and in soft soil it makes a perceptibly deeper track. Where the machine goes up a slope this hind mark would be very much deeper; where it goes down a slope rapidly it would be hardly deeper at all. Thus the depth of the mark of the hind wheel would show which way the bike was travelling.

One of the quaintest proofs of Holmes's reality to many people is that I have frequently received autograph books by post, asking me to procure his signature. When it was announced that he was retiring from practice and intended to keep bees on the South Downs I had several letters offering to help him in his project. Two of them lie before me as I write. One says: 'Will Mr Sherlock Holmes require a housekeeper for his country cottage at Christmas? I know someone who loves a quiet country life, and bees especially – an old-fashioned, quiet woman.' The other, which is addressed to Holmes himself, says: 'I see by some of the morning papers that you are about to retire and take up beekeeping. If correct I shall be pleased to render you service by giving any advice you may require. I trust you will read this letter in the same spirit in which it is written, for I make this offer in return for many pleasant hours.' Many other letters have reached me in which I have been implored to put my correspondents in touch with Mr Holmes, in order that he might elucidate some point in their private affairs.

Occasionally I have been so far confused with my own character that I have been asked to take up professional work upon these lines. I had, I remember, one offer, in the case of an aristocratic murder trial in Poland some years ago, to go across and look into the matter upon my own terms. I need not say that I would not do such a thing for money, since I am diffident as to how far my own services would be of any value; but I have several times as an amateur been happy to have been of some assistance to people in distress. I can say, though I touch wood as I say it, that I have never entirely failed in any attempt which I have made to reduce Holmes's methods to practical use, save in one instance to which I allude later. For the case of Mr Edalji I can claim little credit, for it did not take any elaborate deduction to come to the conclusion that a man who is practically blind did not make a journey at night which involved crossing a main line of railway, and would have tested a trained athlete had he been called upon to do it in the time. The man was obviously innocent, and it is a disgrace to this country that he has never received a penny of compensation for the three years which he spent in jail. A more complex case is that of Oscar Slater, who is still working out his sentence as a convict. I have examined the evidence carefully, including the supplementary evidence given at the very limited and unsatisfactory commission appointed to inquire into the matter, and I have not the faintest doubt that the man is innocent. When the judge asked him at the trial whether he had anything to say why the sentence of death for the murder of Miss Gilchrist should not be pronounced upon him, he cried aloud, 'My Lord, I did not know there was such a woman in the world.' I am convinced that this was the literal truth. However, it is proverbially impossible to prove a negative, so there the matter must stand until the people of Scotland insist upon a real investigation into all the circumstances which surround this deplorable case.

A few of the problems which have come my way have been very similar to some which I had invented for the exhibition of the reasoning of Mr Holmes. I might perhaps quote one in which that gentleman's method of thought was copied with complete success. The case was as follows. A gentleman had disappeared. He had drawn a bank balance of forty pounds, which was known to be on him. It was feared that he had been murdered for the sake of the money. He had last been heard of stopping at a large hotel in London, having come from the country that day. In the evening he went to a music-hall performance, came out of it about ten o'clock, returned to his hotel, changed his evening clothes, which were found in his room next day, and disappeared utterly. No one saw him leave the hotel, but a man occupying a neighbouring room declared that he had heard him moving during the night. A week had elapsed at the time that I was consulted, but the police had discovered nothing. Where was the man?

These were the whole of the facts as communicated to me by his relatives in the country. Endeavouring to see the matter through the eyes of Mr Holmes, I answered by return of post that he was evidently either in Glasgow or in Edinburgh. I proved later that he had as a fact gone to Edinburgh, though in the week that had passed he had moved to another part of Scotland.

There I should leave the matter, for, as Dr Watson has often shown, a solution explained is a mystery spoiled. However, at this stage the reader can lay down the magazine and show how simple it all is by working out the problem for himself. He has all the data which were ever given to me. For the sake of those, however, who have no turn for such conundrums I will try to indicate the links which make the chain. The one advantage which I possessed was that I was familiar with the routine of London hotels – though, I fancy, it differs little from that of hotels elsewhere.

The first thing was to look at the facts and separate what was certain from what was conjecture. It was *all* certain except the statement of the person who heard the missing man in the night. How could he tell such a sound from any other sound in a large hotel? That point could be disregarded if it traversed the general conclusions. The first clear deduction was that the man had meant to disappear. Why else should he draw all his money? He had got out of the hotel during the night. But there is a night porter in all hotels, and it is impossible to get out without his knowledge when the door is once shut. The door is shut after the theatre-goers return – say at twelve o'clock. Therefore the man left the hotel before twelve o'clock. He had come from the music-hall at ten, had changed his clothes, and had departed with his bag. No one had seen him do so. The inference is that he had done it at the moment when the hall was full of the returning guests, which is from eleven to eleven-thirty. After that hour, even if the door were still open, there are few people coming and going; so that he with his bag would certainly have been seen.

Having got so far upon firm ground we now ask ourselves why a man who desires to hide himself should go out at such an hour. If he intended to conceal himself in London he need never have gone to the hotel at all. Clearly, then, he was going to catch a train which would carry him away. But a man who is deposited by a train in any provincial station during the night is likely to be noticed, and he might be sure that when the alarm was raised and his description given some guard or porter would remember him. Therefore his destination would be some large town, which he would reach in daylight hours, as a terminus, where all his fellow-passengers would disembark and where he would lose himself in the crowd. When one turns up the timetable and sees that the great Scotch expresses bound for Edinburgh and Glasgow start about midnight, the goal is reached. As for his dress-suit, the fact that he abandoned it proved that he intended to adopt a line of life where there were no social amenities. This deduction also proved to be correct.

I quote such a case in order to show that the general lines of reasoning advocated by Holmes have a real practical application to life. In another case where a girl had become engaged to a young foreigner who suddenly disappeared I was able by a similar process of deduction to show her very clearly both whither he had gone and how unworthy he was of her affections. On the other hand, these semi-scientific methods are occasionally laboured and slow as compared with the results of the rough-and-ready practical man. Lest I should seem to have been throwing bouquets either to myself or to Mr Holmes, let me state that on the occasion of a burglary of the village inn, within a stone-throw of my house, the village constable, with no theories at all, had seized the culprit, while I had got no farther than that he was a left-handed man with nails in his boots.

The unusual or dramatic effects which leads to the invocation of Mr Holmes in fiction are, of course, great aids to him in reaching a conclusion. It is the cases where there is nothing to get hold of which is the deadly one. I heard of such a one in America which would certainly have presented a formidable problem. A gentleman of blameless life, starting off for a Sunday evening walk with his family, suddenly observed that he had forgotten his stick. He went back into the house, the door of which was still open, and he left his people waiting for him outside. He never reappeared, and from that day to this there has been no clue as to what befell him. This was certainly one of the strangest cases of which I have ever heard in real life.

Another very singular case came within my own observation. It was sent to me by an eminent publisher. This gentleman had in his employment a head of department whose name we shall take as Musgrave. He was a hard-working person with no special feature in his character. Mr Musgrave died, and several years after his death a letter was received addressed to him, care of his employers. It bore the postmark of a tourist resort in the West of Canada, and had the note 'Conf[1] films' upon the outside of the envelope, with the words 'Report Sy' in one corner. The publishers naturally opened the envelope, as they had no note of the dead man's relatives. Inside were two blank sheets of paper. The letter, I may add, was registered. The publisher, being unable to make anything of this, sent it on to me, and I submitted the blank sheets to every possible chemical and heat test, with no result whatever. Beyond the fact that the writing appeared to be that of a woman, there is nothing to add to this account. The matter was, and remains, an insoluble mystery. How the correspondent could have something so secret to say to Mr Musgrave and yet not be aware that this person had been dead for several years is very hard to understand – or why blank sheets should be so carefully registered through the post. I may add that I did not trust the sheets to my own chemical tests, but had the best expert advice, without getting any result. Considered as a case it was a failure – and a very tantalizing one.

Mr Sherlock Holmes has always been a fair mark for practical jokers, and I have had numerous bogus cases of various degrees of ingenuity, marked cards, mysterious warnings, cipher messages, and other curious communications. Upon one occasion, as I was entering the hall to take part in an amateur billiard competition, I was handed a small packet which had been left for me. Upon opening it I found a piece of ordinary green chalk such as is used in billiards. I was amused by the incident, and I put the chalk into my waistcoat pocket and used it during the game. Afterwards I continued to use it until one day, some months later, as I rubbed the tip of my cue, the face of the chalk crumpled in, and I found it was hollow. From the recess thus exposed I drew out a small slip of paper with the words, 'From Arsène Lupin to Sherlock Holmes.' Imagine the state of mind of the joker who took such trouble to accomplish such a result!

One of the mysteries submitted to Mr Holmes was rather upon the psychic plane, and therefore beyond his powers. The facts as alleged are most remarkable, though I have no proof of their truth save that the lady wrote earnestly and gave both her name and address. The person, whom we will call Mrs Seagrave, had been given a curious secondhand ring, snake-shaped, and of dull gold. This she took from her fingers at night. One night she slept in it, and had a fearsome dream in which she seemed to be pushing off some furious creature which fastened its teeth into her arm. On awakening the pain in the arm continued, and next day the imprint of a double set of teeth appeared upon her arm, with one tooth of the lower jaw missing. The marks were in the shape of blue-black bruises which had not broken the skin. 'I do not know,' says my correspondent, 'what made me think the ring had anything to do with the matter, but I took a dislike to the thing and did not wear it for some months, when, being on a visit, I took to wearing it again.' To make a long story short, the same thing happened, and the lady settled the matter for ever by dropping her ring into the hottest corner of the kitchen-range. This curious story, which I believe to be genuine, may not be as supernatural as it seems. It is well known that in some subjects a strong mental impression does produce a physical effect. Thus a very vivid nightmare-dream with the impression of a bite might conceivably produce the mark of a bite. Such cases are well attested in medical annals. The second incident would, of course, arise by unconscious suggestion from the first. None the less, it is a very interesting little problem, whether psychic or material.

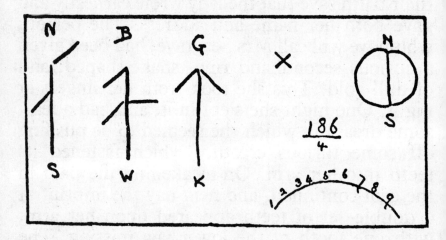

Buried treasures are naturally among the problems which have come to Mr Holmes. One genuine case was accompanied by the diagram here reproduced. It refers to an Indiaman who was wrecked upon the South African coast in the year 1782. If I were a younger man I should be seriously inclined to go personally and look into that matter. The ship contained a remarkable treasure, including, I believe, the gold crown regalia of Delhi. It is surmised that they buried these near the coast and that this chart is a note of the spot. Each Indiaman in those days had its own semaphore code, and it is conjectured that the three marks upon the left are signals from a three-armed semaphore. Some record of their meaning might perhaps even now be found in the old papers of the India Office. The circle upon the right gives the compass bearings. The larger semicircle may be the curved edge of a reef or of a rock. The figures above are the indications how to reach the X which marks the treasure. Possibly they may give the bearings as 186 feet from the 4 upon the semicircle. The scene of the wreck is a lonely part of the country, but I shall be surprised if sooner or later someone does not seriously set to work to solve the mystery.

One last word before I close these jottings about my imaginary character. It is not given to every man to see the child of his brain endowed with life through the genius of a great sympathetic artist, but that was my good fortune when Mr Gillette turned his mind and his great talents to putting Holmes upon the stage. I cannot end my remarks more fittingly than by my thanks to the man who changed a creature of thin air into an absolutely convincing human being.

The Case of the
Inferior Sleuth

Two poems on the Holmes-Dupin-Lecoq Controversy

To Sir ARTHUR CONAN DOYLE
By Arthur Guitermann

Gentle Sir Conan, I'll venture that few have been
Half as prodigiously lucky as you have been.
Fortune, the flirt! has been wondrously kind to
    you,
Ever beneficent, sweet, and refined to you.
Doomed though you seemed – one might swear
    without perjury –
Doomed to the practice of physic and surgery,
Yet, growing weary of pills and physicianing,
Off to the Arctic you packed, expeditioning.
Roving and dreaming, Ambition that heady sin,
Gave you a spirit too restless for medicine;
That, I presume, as Romance is the quest of us,
Made you an Author – the same as the rest of
    us.
Ah, but the rest of us clamor distressfully,
'How do you manage the game so successfully?
Tell us, disclose to us how under Heaven you

Squeeze from the inkpot so splendid a revenue!'
Then, when you'd published your volume that
  vindicates
England's South African raid (or the
  Syndicate's),
Pleading that Britain's extreme bellicosity
Wasn't (as most of us think) an atrocity –
Straightway they gave you a cross with a chain
  to it –
(Oh, what an honour! I could not attain to it,
Not if I lived to the age of Methusalem!) –
Made you a Knight of St John of Jerusalem!
Faith! as a teller of tales you've the trick
  with you!
Still there's a bone I've been longing to pick
  with you:
Holmes is your hero of drama and serial;
All of us know where you dug the material
Whence he was moulded – 'tis almost a
  platitude;
Yet your detective, in shameless ingratitude –
Sherlock your sleuthhound with motives
  ulterior
Sneers at Poe's 'Dupin' as 'very inferior!'
Labels Gaboriau's clever 'Lecoq', indeed,
Merely 'a bungler', a creature to mock, indeed!
This, when your plots and your methods in
  story owe
More than a trifle to Poe and Gaboriau,
Sets all the Muses of Helicon sorrowing.
Borrow, Sir Knight, but be decent in borrowing!
Still let us own that your bent is a cheery one,
Little you've written to bore or to weary one,

Plenty that's slovenly, nothing with harm in it,
Much with abundance of vigour and charm
   in it.
Give me detectives with brains analytical
Rather than weaklings with morals mephitical –
Stories of battles and man's intrepidity
Rather than wails of neurotic morbidity!
Give me adventures and fierce dinotheriums
Rather than Hewlett's ecstatic deliriums!
Frankly, Sir Conan, some hours I've eased with
   you
And, on the whole, I am pretty well pleased
   with you.

To an Undiscerning Critic
By A. Conan Doyle

Sure there are times when one cries with acidity,
'Where are the limits of human stupidity?'
Here is a critic who says as a platitude
That I am guilty because 'in gratitude
Sherlock, the sleuth-hound, with motives
   ulterior,
Sneers at Poe's Dupin as very "inferior".'
Have you not learned, my esteemed
   commentator,
That the created is not the creator?
As the creator I've praised to satiety
Poe's Monsieur Dupin, his skill and variety,
And have admitted that in my detective work
I owe to my model a deal of selective work.
But is it not on the verge of inanity

To put down to me my creation's crude vanity?
He, the created, would scoff and would sneer,
Where I, the creator, would bow and revere.'
So please grip this fact with your cerebral
    tentacle:
The doll and its maker are never identical.

The Crown Diamond

An Evening with Sherlock Holmes

A Play in One Act

Characters:

Mr Sherlock Holmes	*The famous detective*
Dr Watson	*His friend*
Billy	*Page to Mr Holmes*
Col Sebastian Moran	*An intellectual criminal*
Sam Merton	*A boxer*

SCENE: *Mr Holmes's room in Baker Street.*

It presents the usual features, but there is a deep bow window to it, and across there is drawn a curtain running upon a brass rod fastened across 8 feet above the ground, and enclosing recess of the window.

Enter WATSON *and* BILLY.

WATSON: Well, Billy, when will he be back?
BILLY: I'm sure I couldn't say, Sir.
WATSON: When did you see him last?

BILLY:	I really couldn't tell you.
WATSON:	What, you couldn't tell me?
BILLY:	No, Sir. There was a clergyman looked in yesterday, and there was an old bookmaker, and there was a workman.
WATSON:	Well?
BILLY:	But I'm not sure they weren't *all* Mister Holmes. You see, he's very hot on a chase just now.
WATSON:	Oh!
BILLY:	He neither eats nor sleeps. Well, you've lived with him same as me. You now what he's like when he's after someone.
WATSON:	Yes, I know.
BILLY:	He's a responsibility, Sir, that he is. It's a real worry to me sometimes. When I asked him if he would order dinner, he said 'Yes, I'll have chops and mashed potatoes at 7.30 the day after tomorrow.' 'Won't you eat before then, Sir?' I asked. 'I haven't time, Billy, I'm busy,' said he. He gets thinner and paler, and his eyes get brighter. It's awful to see him.
WATSON:	Tut, tut, this will never do. I must certainly stop and see him.
BILLY:	Yes, Sir, it will ease my mind.
WATSON:	But what is he after?
BILLY:	It's this case of the Crown Diamond.

WATSON:	What, the hundred thousand pound burglary?
BILLY:	Yes, Sir. They must get it back, Sir. Why, we had the Prime Minister and the Home Secretary both sitting on that very sofa. Mr Holmes promised he'd do his very best for them. Quite nice he was to them. Put them at their ease in a moment.
WATSON:	Dear me! I've read about it in the paper. But I say, Billy, what have you been doing to the room? What's this curtain?
BILLY:	I don't know, Sir. Mr Holmes had it put there three days ago. But we've got something funny behind it.
WATSON:	Something funny?
BILLY:	*Laughing.* Yes, Sir. He had it made.

BILLY goes to the curtain and draws it across, disclosing a wax image of HOLMES seated in a chair, back to the audience.

WATSON:	Good heavens, Billy!
BILLY:	Yes, Sir. It's like him, Sir. *Picks the head off and exhibits it.*
WATSON:	It's wonderful! But what's it for, Billy?
BILLY:	You see, Sir, he's anxious that those who watch him should think he's at home sometimes when he isn't. There's the bell, Sir. *Replaces*

head, draws curtain. I must go.
BILLY *exits.*

WATSON sits down, lights a cigarette, and opens a paper. Enter a tall, bent OLD WOMAN in black with veil and side-curls.

WATSON: *Rising* Good day, Ma'm.

WOMAN: You're not Mr Holmes?

WATSON: No, Ma'm. I'm his friend, Dr Watson.

WOMAN: I knew you couldn't be Mr Holmes. I'd always heard he was a handsome man.

WATSON: *Aside.* Upon my word!

WOMAN: But I must see him at once.

WATSON: I assure you he is not in.

WOMAN: I don't believe you.

WATSON: What!

WOMAN: You have a sly, deceitful face – oh yes, a wicked, scheming face. Come, young man, where is he?

WATSON: Really, Madam . . .!

WOMAN: Very well, I'll find him for myself. He's in there, I believe. *Walks towards bedroom door and gets behind settee.*

WATSON: *Rising and Crossing.* That is his bedroom. Really, Madam, this is outrageous!

WOMAN: I wonder what he keeps in this safe.

She approaches it, and as she does so the lights go out, and the room is in

267

darkness save for 'DON'T TOUCH' in red fire over the safe. Four red lights spring up, and between them the inscription 'DON'T TOUCH!' After a few seconds the lights go on again, and HOLMES *is standing beside* WATSON.

WATSON: Good heavens, Holmes!

HOLMES: Neat little alarm, is it not, Watson? My own invention. You tread on a loose plank and so connect the circuit, or I can turn it on myself. It prevents inquisitive people becoming too inquisitive. When I come back I know if anyone has been fooling with my things. It switches off again automatically, as you saw.

WATSON: But, my dear fellow, why this disguise?

HOLMES: A little comic relief, Watson. When I saw you sitting there looking solemn, I really couldn't help it. But I assure you, there is nothing comic in the business I am engaged upon. Good heavens! *Rushes across room, and draws curtain, which has been left partly open.*

WATSON: Why, what is it?

HOLMES: Danger, Watson. Airguns, Watson. I'm expecting something this evening.

WATSON: Expecting what, Holmes?

HOLMES: *Lighting pipe.* Expecting to be

268

	murdered, Watson.
WATSON:	No, no, you are joking, Holmes!
HOLMES:	Even my limited sense of humour could evolve a better joke than that, Watson. No, it is a fact. And in case it should come off – it's about a 2 to 1 chance – it would perhaps be as well that you should burden your memory with the name and address of the murderer.
WATSON:	Holmes!
HOLMES:	You can give it to Scotland Yard with my love and a parting blessing. Moran is the name. Colonel Sebastian Moran. Write it down, Watson, write it down! 136, Moorside Gardens, N.W. Got it?
WATSON:	But surely something can be done, Holmes. Couldn't you have this fellow arrested?
HOLMES:	Yes, Watson, I could. That's what's worrying him so.
WATSON:	But why don't you?
HOLMES:	Because I don't know where the diamond is.
WATSON:	What diamond?
HOLMES:	Yes, yes, the great yellow Crown Diamond, 77 carats, lad, and without flaw. I have two fish in the net. But I haven't got the stone there. And what's the use of taking *them*? It's the stone I'm after.
WATSON:	Is this Colonel Moran one of

	the fish in the net?
HOLMES:	Yes, and he's a shark. He bites. The other is Sam Merton the boxer. Not a bad fellow, Sam, but the Colonel has used him. Sam's not a shark. He's a great big silly gudgeon. But he's flopping about in my net, all the same.
WATSON:	Where is this Colonel Moran?
HOLMES:	I've been at his elbow all morning. Once he picked up my parasol. 'By your leave, Ma'm,' said he. Life is full of whimsical happenings. I followed him to old Straubenzce's workshop in the Minories. Straubenzee made the airgun – fine bit of work, I understand.
WATSON:	An airgun?
HOLMES:	The idea was to shoot me through the window. I had to put up that curtain. By the way, have you seen the dummy? *Draws curtain.* *WATSON nods.* Ah! Billy has been showing you the sights. It may get a bullet through its beautiful wax head at any moment. *Enter BILLY.* Well, Billy?
BILLY:	Colonel Sebastian Moran, Sir.
HOLMES:	Ah! the man himself. I rather expected it. Grasp the nettle, Watson. A man of nerve! He felt my toe on his heels. *Looks out of the window.* And there is Sam Merton

270

	in the street – the faithful but fatuous Sam. Where is the Colonel, Billy?
BILLY:	Waiting-room, Sir.
HOLMES:	Show him up when I ring.
BILLY:	Yes, Sir.
HOLMES:	Oh, by the way, Billy, if I am not in the room show him in just the same.
BILLY:	Very good, Sir. *Exit BILLY.*
WATSON:	I'll stay with you, Holmes.
HOLMES:	No, my dear fellow, you would be horribly in the way. *Goes to table and scribbles note.*
WATSON:	He may murder you.
HOLMES:	I shouldn't be surprised.
WATSON:	I can't possibly leave you.
HOLMES:	Yes, you can, my dear Watson, for you've always played the game, and I am very sure that you will play it to the end. Take this note to Scotland Yard. Come back with the police. The fellow's arrest will follow.
WATSON:	I'll do that with joy.
HOLMES:	And before you return I have just time to find out where the diamond is. *Rings bell.* This way, Watson. We'll go together. I rather want to see my shark without his seeing me. *Exit WATSON and HOLMES into bedroom.*
	Enter BILLY and COLONEL MORAN,

	who is a fierce, big man, flashily dressed, heavy cudgel.
BILLY:	Colonel Sebastian Moran. *Exit* BILLY.
	COLONEL MORAN *looks round, advances slowly into the room, and starts as he sees the dummy figure sitting in the window. He stares at it, then crouches, grips his stick, and advances on tip-toe. When close to the figure he raises his stick.* HOLMES *comes quickly out of the bedroom door.*
HOLMES:	Don't break it, Colonel, don't break it.
COLONEL:	*Staggering back.* Good Lord!
HOLMES:	It's such a pretty little thing. Tavernier, the French modeller, made it. He is as good at waxwork as Straubenzee is at airguns. *Shuts curtains.*
COLONEL:	Airguns, Sir, Airguns! What do you mean?
HOLMES:	Put your hat and stick on the side table. Thank you. Pray take a seat. Would you care to put your revolver out also? Oh, very good, if you prefer to sit upon it. COLONEL *sits down.* I wanted to have five minutes' chat with you.
COLONEL:	I wanted to have five minutes' chat with *you.* HOLMES *sits down near him and crosses his leg.* I won't deny

272

	that I intended to assault you just now.
HOLMES:	It struck me that some idea of that sort had crossed your mind.
COLONEL:	And with reason, Sir, with reason.
HOLMES:	But why this attention?
COLONEL:	Because you have gone out of your way to annoy me. Because you have put your creatures on my track.
HOLMES:	My creatures?
COLONEL:	I have had them followed. I know that they come to report to you here.
HOLMES:	No, I assure you.
COLONEL:	Tut, Sir! Other people can observe as well as you. Yesterday there was an old sporting man; today it was an elderly lady. They held me in view all day.
HOLMES:	Really, Sir, you compliment me! Old Baron Dowson, before he was hanged at Newgate, was good enough to say that in my case what the Law had gained the stage had lost. And now you come along with your kindly words. In the name of the elderly lady and of the sporting gentleman I thank you. There was also an out-of-work plumber who was an artistic dream – you seem to have overlooked him.
COLONEL:	It was you . . . you!

HOLMES:	Your humble servant! If you doubt it, you can see the parasol upon the settee which you so politely handed to me this morning down in the Minories.
COLONEL:	If I had known you might never—
HOLMES:	Never have seen this humble home again. I was well aware of it. But it happens you didn't know, and here we are, quite chatty and comfortable.
COLONEL:	What you say only makes matters worse. It was not your agents, but you yourself, who have dogged me. Why have you done this?
HOLMES:	You used to shoot tigers?
COLONEL:	Yes, Sir.
HOLMES:	But why?
COLONEL:	Pshaw! Why does any man shoot a tiger? The excitement. The danger.
HOLMES:	And no doubt the satisfaction of freeing the country from a pest, which devastates it and lives on the population.
COLONEL:	Exactly.
HOLMES:	My reasons in a nutshell.
COLONEL:	*Springing to his feet.* Insolent!
HOLMES:	Sit down, Sir, sit down! There was another more practical reason.
COLONEL:	Well?
HOLMES:	I want that yellow Crown Diamond.
COLONEL:	Upon my word! Well, go on.

274

HOLMES:	You knew that I was after you for that. The real reason why you are here tonight is to find out how much I know about the matter. Well, you can take it that I know *all* about it save one thing, which you are about to tell me.
COLONEL:	*Sneering.* And pray what is that?
HOLMES:	Where the diamond is.
COLONEL:	Oh, you want to know that, do you? How the devil should I know where it is?
HOLMES:	You not only know, but you are about to tell me.
COLONEL:	Oh, indeed!
HOLMES:	You can't bluff me, Colonel. You're absolute plate glass. I see to the very back of your mind.
COLONEL:	Then of course you see where the diamond is.
HOLMES:	Ah! then you do know. You have admitted it.
COLONEL:	I admit nothing.
HOLMES:	Now, Colonel, if you will be reasonable we can do business together. If not you may get hurt.
COLONEL:	And *you* talk about bluff!
HOLMES:	*Raising a book from the table.* Do you know what I keep inside this book?
COLONEL:	No, Sir, I do not.
HOLMES:	You.
COLONEL:	Me!

HOLMES:	Yes, Sir, *you*. You're all here, every action of your vile and dangerous life.
COLONEL:	Damn you, Holmes! Don't go too far.
HOLMES:	Some interesting details, Colonel. The real facts as to the death of Miss Minnie Warrender of Laburnum Grove. All here, Colonel.
COLONEL:	You – you devil!!
HOLMES:	And the story of young Arbuthnot, who was found drowned in the Regents Canal just before his intended exposure of you for cheating at cards.
COLONEL:	I – I never hurt the boy.
HOLMES:	But he died at a very seasonable time. Do you want some more, Colonel? Plenty of it here. How about the robbery in the train deluxe to the Riviera, February 13th, 1892? How about the forged cheque on the Credit Lyonnais the same year?
COLONEL:	No, you're wrong there.
HOLMES:	Then I'm right on the others. Now, Colonel, you are a card-player. When the other fellow holds all the trumps it saves time to throw down your hand.
COLONEL:	If there was a word of truth in all this, would I have been a free

man all these years?

HOLMES: I was not consulted. There were missing links in the police case. But I have a way of finding missing links. You may take it from me that I could do so.

COLONEL: Bluff! Mr Holmes, bluff!

HOLMES: Oh, you wish me to prove my words! Well, if I touch this bell it means the police, and from that instant the matter is out of my hands. Shall I?

COLONEL: What has all this to do with the jewel you speak of?

HOLMES: Gently, Colonel! Restrain that eager mind. Let me get to the point in my own humdrum way. I have all this against you, and I also have a clear case against both you and your fighting bully in this case of the Crown Diamond.

COLONEL: Indeed!

HOLMES: I have the cabman who took you to Whitehall, and the cabman who brought you away. I have the commissionaire who saw you beside the case. I have Ikey Cohen who refused to cut it up for you. Ikey has peached, and the game is up.

COLONEL: Hell!

HOLMES: That's the hand I play from. But there's one card missing. I don't

	know where this king of diamonds is.
COLONEL:	You shall never know.
HOLMES:	Tut! tut! don't turn nasty. Now, consider. You're going to be locked up for twenty years. So is Sam Merton. What good are you going to get out of your diamond? None in the world. But if you let me know where it is . . . well, I'll compound a felony. We don't want you or Sam. We want the stone. Give that up, and so far as I am concerned you can go free for so long as you behave yourself in the future. If you make another slip, then God help you. But this time my commission is to get the stone, not you. *Rings bell.*
COLONEL:	But if I refuse?
HOLMES:	Then, alas, it must be you, not the stone. *Enter BILLY.*
BILLY:	Yes, Sir.
HOLMES:	*To COLONEL.* I think we had better have your friend Sam at this conference. Billy, you will see a large and very ugly gentleman outside the front door. Ask him to come up, will you?
BILLY:	Yes, Sir. Suppose he won't come Sir?
HOLMES:	No force, Billy! Don't be rough

278

	with him. If you tell him Colonel Moran wants him, he will come.
BILLY:	Yes, Sir. *Exit BILLY.*
COLONEL:	What's the meaning of this, then?
HOLMES:	My friend Watson was with me just now. I told him that I had a shark and a gudgeon in my net. Now, I'm drawing the net and up they come together.
COLONEL:	*Leaning forward.* You won't die in your bed, Holmes!
HOLMES:	D'you know, I have often had the same idea. For that matter your own finish is more likely to be perpendicular than horizontal. But these anticipations are morbid. Let us give ourselves up to the unrestrained enjoyment of the present. No good fingering your revolver, my friend, for you know perfectly well that you dare not use it. Nasty, noisy things, revolvers. Better stick to airguns, Colonel Moran. Ah! . . . I think I hear the fairy footsteps of your estimable partner. *Enter BILLY.*
BILLY:	Mr Sam Merton. *Enter SAM MERTON, in check suit and loud necktie, yellow overcoat.*
HOLMES:	Good day, Mr Merton. Rather damp in the street is it not? *Exit BILLY.*

MERTON:	*To* COLONEL. What's the Game? What's up?
HOLMES:	If I may put it in a nutshell, Mr Merton, I should say it is *all* up.
MERTON:	*To* COLONEL. Is this cove tryin' to be funny – or what? I'm not in a funny mood myself.
HOLMES:	You'll feel even less humorous as the evening advances, I think I can promise you that. Now, look here, Colonel. I'm a busy man and I can't waste time. I'm going into the bedroom. Pray make yourselves entirely at home in my absence. You can explain to your friend how the matter lies. I shall try over the Barcarolle upon my violin. *Looks at watch.* In five minutes I shall return for your final answer. You quite grasp the alternative, don't you? Shall we take you, or shall we have the stone? *Exit Holmes, taking his violin with him.*
MERTON:	What's that? He knows about the stone?
COLONEL:	Yes, he knows a dashed sight too much about it. I'm not sure that he doesn't know *all* about it.
MERTON:	Good Lord!
COLONEL:	Ikey Cohen has split.
MERTON:	He has, has he? I'll do him down a thick 'un for that.

280

COLONEL:	But that won't help us. We've got to make up our minds what to do.
MERTON:	Half a mo'. He's not listening, is he? *Approaches bedroom door.* No, it's shut. Looks to me as if it was locked. *Music begins.* Ah! there he is, safe enough. *Goes to curtain.* Here, I say! *Draws it back, disclosing the figure.* Here's that cove again, blast him!
COLONEL:	Tut! it's a dummy. Never mind it.
MERTON:	A fake, is it? *Examines it, and turns the head.* By Gosh, I wish I could twist his own as easy. Well, strike me! Madame Tussaud ain't in it! *As MERTON returns towards the COLONEL, the lights suddenly go out, and the red 'DON'T TOUCH' signal goes up. After a few seconds the lights readjust themselves. Figures must transpose at that moment.*
MERTON:	Well, dash my buttons! Look 'ere, Guv'nor, this is gettin' on my nerves. Is it unsweetened gin, or what?
COLONEL:	Tut! it is some childish hanky-panky of this fellow Holmes, a spring or an alarm or something. Look here, there's no time to lose. He can lag us for the diamond.
MERTON:	The hell he can!
COLONEL:	But he'll let us slip if we only tell him where the stone is.

281

MERTON:	What, give up the swag! Give up a hundred thousand!
COLONEL:	It's one or the other.
MERTON:	No way out? You've got the brains, Guv'nor. Surely you can think a way out of it.
COLONEL:	Wait a bit! I've fooled better men than he. Here's the stone in my secret pocket. It can be out of England tonight, and cut into four pieces in Amsterdam before Saturday. He knows nothing of Van Seddor.
MERTON:	I thought Van Seddor was to wait till next week.
COLONEL:	Yes, he *was*. But now he must get the next boat. One or other of us must slip round with the stone to the 'Excelsior', and tell him.
MERTON:	But the false bottom ain't in the hat-box yet!
COLONEL:	Well, he must take it as is and chance it. There's not a moment to lose. As to Holmes, we can fool him easily enough. You see he won't arrest us if he thinks he can get the stone. We'll put him on the wrong track about it, and before he finds it *is* the wrong track, the stone will be in Amsterdam, and we out of the country.
MERTON:	That's prime.
COLONEL:	You go off now, and tell Van

Seddor to get a move on him. I'll see this sucker and fill him up with a bogus confession. The stone's in Liverpool that's what I'll tell him. By the time he finds it isn't, there won't be much of it left, and we'll be on blue water. *He looks carefully round him, then draws a small leather box from his pocket, and holds it out.* Here is the Crown Diamond.

HOLMES: *Taking it, as he rises from chair.* I thank you.

COLONEL: *Staggering back.* Curse you, Holmes! *Puts hand in pocket.*

MERTON: To hell with him!

HOLMES: No violence, gentlemen; no violence, I beg of you. It must be very clear to you that your position is an impossible one. The police are waiting below.

COLONEL: You – you devil! How did you get there?

HOLMES: The device is obvious but effective; lights off for a moment and the rest is common sense. It gave me a chance of listening to your racy conversation which would have been painfully constrained by a knowledge of my presence. No, Colonel, no. I am covering you with a .450 Derringer through the pocket of my dressing gown. *Rings bell. Enter BILLY.* Send them up, Billy. *Exit* BILLY.

COLONEL: Well, you've got us, damn you!

MERTON: A fair cop. . . . But I say, what about that bloomin' fiddle?

HOLMES: Ah, yes, these modern gramophones! Wonderful invention. Wonderful!

CURTAIN

How Watson Learned
the Trick

Watson had been watching his companion intently ever since he had sat down to the breakfast table. Holmes happened to look up and catch his eye.

'Well, Watson, what are you thinking about?' he asked.

'About you.'

'Me?'

'Yes, Holmes, I was thinking how superficial are these tricks of yours, and how wonderful it is that the public should continue to show interest in them.'

'I quite agree,' said Holmes. 'In fact, I have a recollection that I have myself made a similar remark.'

'Your methods,' said Watson severely, 'are really easily acquired.'

'No doubt,' Holmes answered with a smile. 'Perhaps you will yourself give an example of this method of reasoning.'

'With pleasure,' said Watson. 'I am able to say that you were greatly preoccupied when you got up this morning.'

'Excellent!' said Holmes. 'How could you possibly know that?'

'Because you are usually a very tidy man and yet you have forgotten to shave.'

'Dear me! How very clever!' said Holmes, 'I had no idea, Watson, that you were so apt a pupil. Has your eagle eye detected anything more?'

'Yes, Holmes. You have a client named Barlow, and you have not been successful in his case.'

'Dear me, how could you know that?'

'I saw the name outside his envelope. When you opened it you gave a groan and thrust it into your pocket with a frown on your face.'

'Admirable! You are indeed observant. Any other points?'

'I fear, Holmes, that you have taken to financial speculation.'

'How *could* you tell that, Watson?'

'You opened the paper, turned to the financial page, and gave a loud exclamation of interest.'

'Well, that is very clever of you Watson. Any more?'

'Yes, Holmes, you have put on your black coat, instead of your dressing gown, which proves that you are expecting some important visitor at once.'

'Anything more?'

'I have no doubt that I could find other points, Holmes, but I only give you these few, in order to show you that there are other people in the world who can be as clever as you.'

'And some not so clever,' said Holmes. 'I admit that they are few, but I am afraid, my dear Watson, that I must count you among them.'

'What do you mean, Holmes?'

'Well, my dear fellow, I fear your deductions have not been so happy as I should have wished.'

'You mean that I was mistaken.'

'Just a little that way, I fear. Let us take the points in their order: I did not shave because I have sent my razor to be sharpened. I put on my coat because I have, worse luck, an early meeting with my dentist. His name is Barlow, and the letter was to confirm the appointment. The cricket page is beside the financial one, and I turned to it to find if Surrey was holding its own against Kent. But go on, Watson, go on! It's a very superficial trick, and no doubt you will soon acquire it.'

A Gaudy Death

Conan Doyle Tells the True Story of Sherlock Holmes's End

To interview Dr Conan Doyle, the creator of Sherlock Holmes, is not an easy matter. Dr Doyle has a strong objection to the interview, even though he has no personal antipathy to the interviewer. Considerations, however, of his long and friendly relationship with the firm of George Newnes Ltd, in the pages of whose popular and universally read STRAND MAGAZINE Sherlock Holmes lived, and moved, and had his being, overcame Dr Doyle's reluctance to be interviewed, and he consented to give the following particulars, which will be read with interest by his admirers all over the world.

Tit-Bits,
15 December 1900

Before I tell you of Sherlock Holmes's death and how it came about, it will probably be interesting to recall the circumstances of his birth. He originally made his appearance, you will remember, in a book which I wrote called *A Study in Scarlet*. The idea of the detective was suggested by a professor under whom I had worked at Edinburgh, and in part by Edgar Allen Poe's detective, which, after all, ran on the lines of all other detectives who have appeared in literature.

In work which consists in the drawing of detectives there are only one or two qualities which one can use, and an author is forced to hark back upon them constantly, so that every detective must really resemble every other detective to a greater or less extent. There is no great originality required in devising or constructing such a man, and the only possible originality which one can get into a story about a detective is in giving him original plots and problems to solve, as in his equipment there must be of necessity an alert acuteness of mind to grasp facts and the relation which each of them bears to the other.

At the time I first thought of a detective – it was about 1886 – I had been reading some detective stories, and it struck me what nonsense they were, to put it mildly, because for getting the solution of the mystery the authors always depended on some coincidence. This struck me as not a fair way of playing the game, because the detective ought really to depend for his success on something in his own mind and not on merely adventitious circumstances, which do not, by any means, always occur in real life. I was seedy at the time, and, not working much, had leisure to read, so I read half a dozen or so detective stories, both in French and English, and they one and all filled me with dissatisfaction and a sort of feeling how much more interesting they might be made if one could show that the man deserved his victory over the criminal or the mystery he was called upon to solve.

Then I began to think, suppose my old professor at Edinburgh were in the place of one of these lucky detectives, he would have worked out the process of effect from cause just as logically as he would have diagnosed a disease, instead of having something given to him by mere luck, which, as I said just now, does not happen in real life.

For fun, therefore, I started constructing a story and giving my detective a scientific system, so as to make him reason everything out. Intellectually that had been done before by Edgar Allen Poe with M. Dupin, but where Holmes differed from Dupin was that he had an immense fund of exact knowledge to draw upon in consequence of his previous scientific education. I mean by this, that by looking at a man's hand he knew what the man's trade was, as by looking at his trousers leg he could deduce the character of the man. He was practical and he was systematic, and his success in the detection of crime was to be the fruit, not of luck, but of his qualities.

With this idea I wrote a small book on the lines I have indicated, and produced *A Study in Scarlet*, which was made *Beeton's Christmas Annual* in 1887. That was the first appearance of Sherlock; but he did not arrest much attention, and nobody recognized him as being anything in particular. About three years later, however, I was asked to do a small shilling book for *Lippincott's Magazine*, which publishes, as you know, a special story in each number. I didn't know what to write about, and the thought occurred to me, 'Why not try to rig up the same chap again?' I did it, and the result was *The Sign of Four*. Although the criticisms were favourable, I don't think even then Sherlock attracted much attention to his individuality.

About this time I began thinking about short stories for magazines. It occurred to me that a serial story in a magazine was a mistake, for those who had not begun the story at the beginning would naturally be debarred from buying a periodical in which a large number of pages were, of necessity, taken up with a story in which they had no particular interest.

It occurred to me, then, that if one could write a serial without appearing to do so – a serial, I mean, in which each instalment was capable of being read as a single story, while each retained a connecting link with the one before and the one that was to come by means of its leading characters – one would get a cumulative interest which the serial pure and simple could not obtain. In this respect I was a revolutionist, and I think I may fairly lay claim to the credit of being the inaugurator of a system which has since been worked by others with no little success.

It was about this time that *The Strand*

Magazine was started, and I asked myself, 'Why not put my idea in execution and write a series of stories with Sherlock Holmes?' whose mental processes were familiar to me. I was then in practice in Wimpole Street as a specialist, and, while waiting for my patients to come, I began writing to fill up my waiting hours. In this way I wrote three stories, which were afterwards published as part of *The Adventures of Sherlock Holmes*. I sent them to *The Strand Magazine*. The editor liked them, seemed keen on them, and asked for more. The more he asked for the more I turned out, until I had done a dozen. That dozen constituted the volume which was afterwards published as *The Adventures of Sherlock Holmes*.

That dozen stories being finished, I determined they should be the end of all Sherlock's doings. I was, however, approached to do some more. My instincts were against this, as I believe it is always better to give the public less than it wants rather than more, and I do not believe in boring it with this sort of stuff. Besides, I had other subjects in my mind. The popularity of Sherlock Holmes, however, and the success of the new stories with the common thread running through them brought a good deal of pressure on me, and at last, under that pressure, I consented to continue with Sherlock, and did twelve more stories, which I called *The Memoirs of Sherlock Holmes*.

By the time I had finished those I was absolutely determined it would be bad policy to do any more Holmes stories. I was still a young man and a young novelist, and I have always noticed that the ruin of every novelist who has come up has been effected by driving him into a groove. The public gets what it likes, and, insisting on getting it, makes him go on until he loses his freshness. Then the public turns round and says: 'He has only one idea, and can only write one sort of story.' The result is that the man is ruined; for, by that time, he has probably himself lost the power of adapting himself to fresh conditions of work. Now, why should a man be driven into a groove and not write about what interests him? When I was interested in Holmes I wrote about Holmes, and it amused me making him get involved in new conundrums; but when I had written twenty-six stories, each involving the making of a fresh plot, I felt that it was becoming irksome this searching for plots – and if it were getting irksome to me, most certainly, I argued, it must be losing its freshness for others.

I knew I had done better work in other fields of literature, and in my opinion *The White Company*, was worth a hundred Sherlock Holmes stories. Yet, just because the Sherlock Holmes stories were, for the moment, more popular, I was becoming more and more known as the author of Sherlock Holmes instead of as the author of *The White Company*. My lower work was obscuring my higher.

I therefore determined to stop my Holmes stories, and as my mind was fully made up I couldn't see any better way than by bringing Holmes to an end as well as the stories.

I was in Switzerland for the purpose of giving a lecture at the time when I was thinking out the details of the final story. I was taking a walking tour through the country, and I came to a waterfall. I thought if a man wanted to meet a gaudy kind of death that was a fine romantic place for the purpose. That started the train of ideas by which Holmes just reached that spot and met his death there.

That is really how I came to kill Holmes. But when I did it I was surprised at the amount of interest people took in his fate. I never thought they would take it so to heart. I got letters from all over the world reproaching me on the subject. One, I remember, from a lady whom I did not know, began 'you beast.'

From that day to this I have never for an instant regretted the course I took in killing Sherlock. That does not say, however, that because he is dead I should not write about him again if I wanted to, for there is no limit to the number of papers he left behind or the reminiscences in the brain of his biographer.

My objection to detective stories is that they only call for the use of a certain portion of one's imaginative faculty, the invention of a plot, without giving any scope for character drawing.

The best literary work is that which leaves the reader better for having read it. Now, nobody can possibly be the better – in the high sense in which I mean it – for reading Sherlock Holmes, although he may have passed a pleasant hour in doing so. It was not to my mind high work, and no detective work ever can be, apart from the fact that all work dealing with criminal matters is a cheap way of rousing the interest of the reader.

For this reason, at the outset of my career it would have been bad to devote too much attention to Sherlock Holmes. If I had continued with him I should by this time have worn him out, and also the patience of the public, and I should not have written 'Rodney Stone', 'Brigadier Gerard', 'The Stark Monro Letters', 'The Refugees', and all the other books which treat of life from many different standpoints, some of which represent my own views, which Sherlock Holmes never did.

There is one fact in connection with Holmes which will probably interest those who have followed his career from the beginning, and to which, so far as I am aware, attention has never been drawn. In dealing with criminal subjects one's natural endeavour is to keep the crime in the background. In nearly half the number of the Sherlock Holmes stories, however, in a strictly legal sense no crime was actually committed at all. One heard a good deal about crime and the criminal, but the reader was completely bluffed. Of course, I could not bluff him always, so sometimes I had to give him a crime, and occasionally I had to make it a downright bad one.

My own view of Sherlock Holmes – I mean the man as I saw him in my imagination – was quite different from that which Mr Paget pictured in *The Strand Magazine*. I, however, am eminently pleased with his work, and quite understand the aspect which he gave to the character, and am even prepared to accept him now as Mr Paget drew him. In my own mind, however, he was a more beaky-nosed, hawk-faced man, approaching more to the Red Indian type, than the artist represented him, but, as I have said, Mr Paget's pictures please me very much.

The Mystery of
Sasassa Valley

Do I know why Tom Donahue is called 'Lucky
Tom'? 'Yes: I do; and that is more than one in
ten of those who call him so can say. I have
knocked about a deal in my time, and seen
some strange sights, but none stranger than the
way in which Tom gained that sobriquet and
his fortune with it. For I was with him at the
time. – Tell it? Oh, certainly; but it is a longish
story and a very strange one; so fill up your
glass again, and light another cigar while I try
to reel it off. Yes; a very strange one; beats
some fairy stories I have heard; but it's true sir,
every word of it. There are men alive at Cape
Colony now who'll remember it and confirm
what I say. Many a time has the tale been told
round the fire in Boers' cabins from Orange
State to Griqualand; yes, and out in the Bush
and at the Diamond Fields too.

I'm roughish now sir; but I was entered at
the Middle Temple once, and studied for the
bar. Tom – worse luck! – was one of my
fellow-students; and a wildish time we had of
it, until at last our finances ran short, and
we were compelled to give up our so-called
studies, and look about for some part of the

297

world where two young fellows with strong arms and sound constitutions might make their mark. In those days the tide of emigration had scarcely begun to set in towards Africa, and so we thought our best chance would be down at Cape Colony. Well – to make a long story short – we set sail, and were deposited in Cape Town with less than five pounds in our pockets; and there we parted. We each tried our hands at many things, and had ups and downs; but when, at the end of three years, chance led each of us up-country and we met again, we were, I regret to say, in almost as bad a plight as when we started.

Well, this was not much of a commencement; and very disheartened we were, so disheartened that Tom spoke of going back to England and getting a clerkship. For you see we didn't know that we had played out all our small cards, and that the trumps were going to turn up. No; we thought our 'hands' were bad all through. It was a very lonely part of the country that we were in, inhabited by a few scattered farmers, whose houses were stockaded and fenced in to defend them against the Kaffirs. Tom Donahue and I had a little hut right out in the Bush; but we were known to possess nothing, and to be handy with our revolvers, so we had little to fear. There we waited, doing odd jobs, and hoping that something would turn up upon a certain night, something which was the making of both of us; and it's about that night sir, that I'm going to tell you. I remember it well. The wind was howling past our cabin, and the rain threatened to burst in our rude window. We had a great wood-fire crackling and sputtering on the hearth, by which I was sitting mending a whip, while Tom was lying in his bunk groaning disconsolately at the chance which had led him to such a place.

'Cheer up, Tom – cheer up,' said I. 'No man ever knows what may be awaiting him.'

'Ill-luck, ill-luck, Jack,' he answered. 'I always was an unlucky dog. Here have I been three years in this abominable country; and I see lads fresh from England jingling the money in their pockets, while I am as poor as when I landed. Ah, Jack, if you want to keep your head above water, old friend, you must try your fortune away from me.'

'Nonsense, Tom; you're down in your luck tonight. But hark! Here's someone coming outside. Dick Wharton, by the tread; he'll rouse you, if any man can.'

Even as I spoke the door was flung open, and honest Dick Wharton, with the water pouring from him, stepped in, his hearty red face looming through the haze like a harvest-moon. He shook himself, and after greeting us sat down by the fire to warm himself.

'Whereaway, Dick, on such a night as this?' said I. 'You'll find the rheumatism a worse foe than the Kaffirs, unless you keep more regular hours.'

Dick was looking unusually serious, almost

frightened, one would say, if one did not know the man. 'Had to go,' he replied – 'had to go. One of Madison's cattle was seen straying down Sasassa Valley, and of course none of our blacks would go down *that* Valley at night; and if we had waited until morning, the brute would have been in Kaffirland.'

'Why wouldn't they go down Sasassa Valley at night?' asked Tom.

'Kaffirs, I suppose,' said I.

'Ghosts,' said Dick.

We both laughed.

'I suppose they didn't give such a matter-of-fact fellow as you a sight of their charms?' said Tom from the bunk.

'Yes,' said Dick seriously – 'yes; I saw what the niggers talk about; and I promise you, lads, I don't want ever to see it again.'

Tom sat up in his bed. 'Nonsense, Dick; you're joking, man! Come, tell us all about it. The legend first, and your own experience afterwards. – Pass him over the bottle, Jack.'

'Well, as to the legend,' began Dick '– it seems that the niggers have had it handed down to them that Sasassa Valley is haunted by a frightful fiend. Hunters and wanderers passing down the defile have seen its glowing eyes under the shadows of the cliff; and the story goes that whoever has chanced to encounter that baleful glare, has had his after-life blighted by the malignant power of this creature. Whether that be true or not,' continued Dick ruefully, 'I may have an opportunity of judging for myself.'

'Go on, Dick – go on,' cried Tom. 'Let's hear about what you saw.'

'Well, I was groping down the Valley, looking for that cow of Madison's, and I had, I suppose, got half-way down, where a black craggy cliff juts into the ravine on the right, when I halted to have a pull at my flask. I had me eye fixed at the time upon the projecting cliff I have mentioned, and noticed nothing unusual about it. I then put up my flask and took a step or two forward, when in a moment there burst apparently from the base of the rock, about eight feet from the ground and a hundred yards from me, a strange lurid glare, flickering and oscillating, gradually dying away and then reappearing again. – No, no; I've seen many a glow-worm and firefly – nothing of that sort. There it was burning away, and I suppose I gazed at it, trembling in every limb, for fully ten minutes. Then I took a step forwards, when instantly it vanished, vanished like a candle blown out. I stepped back again; but it was some time before I could find the exact spot and position from which it was visible. At last, there it was, the weird reddish light, flickering away as before. Then I screwed up my courage, and made for the rock; but the ground was so uneven that it was impossible to steer straight; and though I walked along the whole base of the cliff, I could see nothing. Then I made tracks for home; and I can tell you, boys, that until you remarked it, I never knew it was raining, the whole way along. – But hello! what's the matter with Tom?'

What indeed? Tom was now sitting with his legs over the side of the bunk, and his whole face betraying excitement so intense as to be almost painful. 'The fiend would have two eyes. How many lights did you see, Dick? Speak out!'

'Only one.'

'Hurrah!' cried Tom – 'that's better!' Whereupon he kicked the blankets into the middle of the room, and began pacing up and down with long feverish strides. Suddenly he stopped opposite Dick, and laid his hand upon his shoulder: 'I say, Dick, could we get to Sasassa Valley before sunrise?'

'Scarcely,' said Dick.

'Well, look here; we are old friends, Dick Wharton, you and I. Now, don't you tell any other man what you have told us, for a week. You'll promise that; won't you?'

I could see by the look on Dick's face as he acquiesced that he considered poor Tom to be mad; and indeed I was myself completely mystified by his conduct. I had, however, seen so many proofs of my friend's good sense and quickness of apprehension, that I though it quite possible that Wharton's story had had a meaning in his eyes which I was too obtuse to take in.

All night Tom Donahue was greatly excited, and when Wharton left he begged him to remember his promise, and also elicited from him a description of the exact spot at which he had seen the apparition, as well as the hour at which it appeared. After his departure, which must have been about four in the morning, I turned into my bunk and watched Tom sitting by the fire splicing two sticks together, until I fell asleep. I suppose I must have slept about two hours; but when I awoke, Tom was still sitting working away in almost the same position. He had fixed the one stick across the top of the other so as to form a rough T, and was now busy in fitting a smaller stick into the angle between them, by manipulating which, the cross one could be either cocked up or depressed to any extent. He had cut notches too in the perpendicular stick, so that by the aid of the small prop, the cross one could be kept in any position for an indefinite time.

'Look here, Jack!' he cried, whenever he saw that I was awake. 'Come and give me your opinion. Suppose I put this cross-stick pointing straight at a thing, and arranged this small one so as to keep it so, and left it, I could find that thing again if I wanted it – don't you think I could, Jack – don't you think so?' he continued nervously, clutching me by the arm.

'Well,' I answered, 'it would depend on how far off the thing was, and how accurately it was pointed. If it were any distance, I'd cut sights on your cross-stick; then a string tied to the end of it, and held in a plumb-line forwards, would lead you pretty near what you wanted. But surely, Tom, you don't intend to localize the ghost in that way?'

'You'll see tonight, old friend – you'll see tonight. I'll carry this to the Sasassa Valley. You get the loan of Madison's crowbar, and come with me; but mind you tell no man where you are going, or what you want it for.'

All day Tom was walking up and down the room, or working hard at the apparatus. His eyes were glistening, his cheek hectic, and he had all the symptoms of high fever. 'Heaven grant that Dick's diagnosis be not correct!' I thought, as I returned with the crowbar; and yet, as evening drew near, I found myself imperceptibly sharing the excitement.

About six o'clock Tom sprang to his feet and seized his sticks. 'I can stand it no longer, Jack,' he cried; 'up with your crowbar, and hey for Sasassa Valley! Tonight's work, my lad, will either make us or mar us! Take your six-shooter, in case we meet the Kaffirs. I daren't take mine, Jack,' he continued, putting his hands upon my shoulders – 'I daren't take mine; for if my ill-luck sticks to me tonight, I don't know what I might not do with it.'

Well, having filled our pockets with provisions, we set out, and as we took our wearisome way towards the Sasassa Valley, I frequently attempted to elicit from my companion some clue as to his intentions. But his only answer was: 'Let us hurry on, Jack. Who knows how many have heard of Wharton's adventure by this time! Let us hurry on, or we may not be first in the field!'

Well sir, we struggled on through the hills for a matter of ten miles; till at last, after descending a crag, we saw opening out in front of us a ravine so sombre and dark that it might have been the gate of Hades itself; cliffs many hundred feet high shut in on every side the gloomy boulder-studded passages which led through the haunted defile into Kaffirland. The moon rising above the crags, threw into strong relief the rough irregular pinnacles of rock by which they were topped, while all below was dark as Erebus.

'The Sasassa Valley?' said I.

'Yes,' said Tom.

I looked at him. He was calm now; the flush and feverishness had passed away; his actions were deliberate and slow. Yet there was a certain rigidity in his face and glitter in his eye which showed that a crisis had come.

We entered the pass, stumbling along amid the great boulders. Suddenly I heard a short quick exclamation from Tom. 'That's the crag!' he cried, pointing to a great mass looming before us in the darkness. 'Now Jack, for any favour use your eyes! We're about a hundred yards from that cliff, I take it; so you move slowly towards one side, and I'll do the same towards the other. When you see anything, stop, and call out. Don't take more than twelve inches in a step, and keep your eyes fixed on the cliff about eight feet from the ground. Are you ready?'

'Yes.' I was even more excited than Tom by this time. What his intention or object was, I could not conjecture, beyond that he wanted to examine by daylight the part of the cliff from which the light came. Yet the influence of the romantic situation and of my companion's suppressed excitement was so great, that I could feel the blood coursing through my veins and count the pulses throbbing at my temples.

'Start!' cried Tom; and we moved off, he to the right, I to the left, each with our eyes fixed intently on the base of the crag. I had moved perhaps twenty feet, when in a moment it burst upon me. Through the growing darkness there shone a small ruddy glowing point, the light from which waned and increased, flickered and oscillated, each change producing a more weird effect than the last. The old Kaffir superstition came into my mind, and I felt a cold shudder pass over me. In my excitement, I stepped a pace backwards, when instantly the light went out, leaving utter darkness in its place; but when I advanced again, there was the ruddy glare glowing from the base of the cliff. 'Tom, Tom!' I cried.

'Ay, ay!' I heard him exclaim, as he hurried over towards me.

'There it is – there, up against the cliff!'

Tom was at my elbow. 'I see nothing,' said he.

'Why, there, there, man, in front of you!' I stepped to the right as I spoke, when the light instantly vanished from my eyes.

But from Tom's ejaculations of delight it was clear that from my former position it was visible to him also. 'Jack,' he cried, as he turned and wrung my hand – 'Jack, you and I can never complain of our luck again. Now heap up a few stones where we are standing. – That's right. Now we must fix my sign-post firmly in at the top. There! It would take a strong wind to blow that down; and we only need it to hold out till morning. O Jack, my boy, to think that only yesterday we were talking of becoming clerks, and you saying that no man knew what was awaiting him too! By jove, Jack, it would make a good story!'

By this time we had firmly fixed the perpendicular stick in between two large stones; and Tom bent down and peered along the horizontal one. For fully a quarter of an hour he was alternately raising and depressing it, until at last, with a sigh of satisfaction, he fixed the prop into the angle, and stood up. 'Look along, Jack,' he said. 'You have as straight an eye to take a sight as any man I know of.'

I looked along. There, beyond the further sight was the ruddy scintillating speck, apparently at the end of the stick itself, so accurately had it been adjusted.

'And now, my boy,' said Tom, 'let's have some supper, and a sleep. There's nothing more to be done tonight; but we'll need all our wits and strength tomorrow. Get some sticks and kindle a fire here, and then we'll be able to keep an eye on our signal-post, and see that nothing happens to it during the night.'

Well sir, we kindled a fire, and had supper with the Sasassa demon's eye rolling and glowing in front of us the whole night through. Not always in the same place though; for after supper, when I glanced along the sights to have another look at it, it was nowhere to be seen. The information did not, however, seem to disturb Tom in any way. He merely remarked: 'It's the moon, not the thing, that has shifted;' and coiling himself up, went to sleep.

By early dawn we were both up, and gazing along our pointer at the cliff; but we could make out nothing save the one dead monotonous slaty surface, rougher perhaps at the part we were examining than elsewhere, but otherwise presenting nothing remarkable.

'Now for your idea, Jack!' said Tom Donahue, unwinding a long thin cord from around his waist. 'You fasten it, and guide me while I take the other end.' So saying he walked off to the base of the cliff, holding one end of the cord, while I drew the other taut, and wound it round the middle of the horizontal stick, passing it through the sight at the end. By this means I could direct Tom to the right or left, until we had our string stretching from the point of attachment, through the sight, and on to the rock, which it struck about eight feet from the ground. Tom drew a chalk circle of about three feet diameter round the spot, and then called to me to come and join him. 'We've managed this business together, Jack,' he said, 'and we'll find what we are to find, together.' The circle he had drawn embraced a part of the rock smoother than the rest, save that about the centre there were a few rough protuberances or knobs. One of these Tom pointed to with a cry of delight. It was a roughish brownish mass about the size of a man's closed fist, and looking like a bit of dirty glass let into the wall of the cliff. 'That's it!' he cried – 'that's it!'

'That's what?'

'Why, man, a *diamond*, and such a one as there isn't a monarch in Europe but would envy Tom Donahue the possession of it. Up with your crowbar, and we'll soon exorcize the demon of Sasassa Valley!'

I was so astounded that for a moment I stood speechless with surprise, gazing at the treasure which had so unexpectedly fallen into our hands.

'Here, hand me the crowbar,' said Tom. 'Now, by using this little round knob which projects from the cliff here, as a fulcrum, we may be able to lever it off. – Yes; there it goes. I never thought it could have come so easily. Now, Jack, the sooner we get back to our hut and then down to Cape Town, the better.'

We wrapped up our treasure, and made our way across the hills, towards home. On the way, Tom told me how, while a law-student in the Middle Temple, he had come upon a dusty pamphlet in the library, by one Jans van Hounym, which told of an experience very similar to ours, which had befallen that worthy Dutchman in the latter part of the seventeenth century, and which resulted in the discovery of a luminous diamond. This tale it was which had come into Tom's head as he listened to honest Dick Wharton's ghost story; while the means which he had adopted to verify his supposition sprang from his own fertile Irish brain.

'We'll take it down to Cape Town,' continued Tom, 'and if we can't dispose of it with advantage there, it will be worth our while to ship for London with it. Let us go along to Madison's first, though; he knows something of these things, and can perhaps give us some idea of what we may consider a fair price for the treasure.'

We turned off from the track accordingly, before reaching our hut, and kept along the narrow path leading to Madison's farm. He was at lunch when we entered; and in a minute we were seated at each side of him, enjoying South African hospitality.

'Well' he said, after the servants were gone, 'what's in the wind now? I see you have something to say to me. What is it?'

Tom produced his packet, and solemnly untied the handkerchiefs which enveloped it. 'There!' he said, putting his crystal on the table; 'what would you say was a fair price for that?'

Madison took it up and examined it critically. 'Well,' he said, laying it down again, 'in its crude state about twelve shillings per ton.'

'Twelve shillings!' cried Tom, starting to his feet. 'Don't you see what it is?'

'Rock-salt!'

'Rock fiddle; a diamond.'

'Taste it!' said Madison.

Tom put it to his lips, dashed it down with a dreadful exclamation, and rushed out of the room.

I felt sad and disappointed enough myself; but presently remembering what Tom had said about the pistol, I, too, left the house, and made for the hut, leaving Madison open-mouthed with astonishment. When I got in, I found Tom lying in his bunk with his face to the wall, too dispirited apparently to answer my consolations. Anathematizing Dick and Madison, the Sasassa demon, and everything else, I strolled out of the hut, and refreshed myself with a pipe after our wearisome adventure. I was about fifty yards away from the hut, when I heard issuing from it the sound which of all others I least expected to hear. Had it been a groan or an oath, I should have taken it as a matter of course; but the sound which caused me to stop and take the pipe out of my mouth was a hearty roar of laughter! Next moment, Tom himself emerged from the door, his whole face radiant with delight. 'Game for another ten-mile walk, old fellow?'

'What! for another lump of rock-salt, at twelve shillings a ton?'

' "No more of that, Hal, an you love me," ' grinned Tom. 'Now look here, Jack. What blessed fools we are to be so floored by a trifle! Just sit on this stump for five minutes, and I'll make it as clear as daylight. You've seen many a lump of rock-salt stuck in a crag, and so have I, though we did make such a mull of this one. Now, Jack, did any of the pieces you have ever seen shine in the darkness brighter than any fire-fly?'

'Well, I can't say they ever did.'

'I'd venture to prophesy that if we waited until night, which we won't do, we would see that light still glimmering among the rocks. Therefore, Jack, when we took away this worthless salt, we took the wrong crystal. It is no very strange thing in these hills that a piece of rock-salt should be lying within a foot of a diamond. It caught our eyes, and we were excited, and so we made fools of ourselves, and *left the real stone behind*. Depend upon it, Jack, The Sasassa gem is lying within that magic circle of chalk upon the face of yonder cliff. Come, old fellow, light your pipe and stow your revolver, and we'll be off before that fellow Madison has time to put two and two together.'

I don't know that I was very sanguine this time. I had begun in fact to look upon the diamond as a most unmitigated nuisance. However, rather than throw a damper on Tom's expectations, I announced myself eager to start. What a walk it was! Tom was always a good mountaineer, but his excitement seemed to lend him wings that day, while I scrambled along after him as best I could. When we got within half a mile he broke into the 'double', and never pulled up until he reached the round white circle upon the cliff. Poor old Tom! when I came up, his mood had changed, and he was standing with his hands in his pockets, gazing vacantly before him with a rueful countenance.

'Look!' he said – 'look!' and he pointed at the cliff. Not a sign of anything in the least resembling a diamond there. The circle included nothing but flat slate-coloured stone, with one large hole, where we had extracted the rock-salt, and one or two smaller depressions. No sign of the gem.

'I've been over every inch of it,' said poor Tom. 'It's not there. Some one has been here and noticed the chalk, and taken it. Come home, Jack; I feel sick and tired. Oh! Had any man ever luck like mine!'

I turned to go, but took one last look at the cliff first. Tom was already ten paces off.

'Hello!' I cried, 'don't you see any change in that circle since yesterday?'

'What d'ye mean?' said Tom.

'Don't you miss a thing that was there before?'

'The rock-salt?' said Tom.

'No; but the little round knob that we used for a fulcrum. I suppose we must have wrenched it off in using the lever. Let's have a look at what it's made of.'

Accordingly, at the foot of the cliff we searched about among the loose stones.

'Here you are, Jack! We've done it at last! We're made men!'

I turned round, and there was Tom radiant with delight, and with a little corner of black

313

rock in his hand. At first sight it seemed to be merely a chip from the cliff; but near the base there was projecting from it an object which Tom was now exultingly pointing out. It looked at first something like a glass eye; but there was a depth and brilliancy about it such as glass never exhibited. There was no mistake this time; we had certainly got possession of a jewel of great value; and with light hearts we turned from the valley, bearing with us the 'fiend' which had so long reigned there.

There sir; I've spun my story out too long, and tired you perhaps. You see when I get talking of those rough old days, I kind of see the little cabin again, and the brook beside it, and the bush around, and seem to hear Tom's honest voice once more. There's little for me to say now. We prospered on the gem. Tom Donahue, as you know, has set up here, and is well known about the town. I have done well, farming and ostrich-raising in Africa. We set old Dick Wharton up in business, and he is one of our nearest neighbours. If you should ever be coming up our way sir, you'll not forget to ask for Jack Turnbull – Jack Turnbull of Sasassa Farm.

My Favourite Sherlock Holmes Adventures

How Conan Doyle made his list

When this competition was first mooted I went into it in a most light-hearted way, thinking that it would be the easiest thing in the world to pick out the twelve best of the Holmes stories. In practice I found that I had engaged myself in a serious task. In the first place I had to read the stories myself with some care. 'Steep, steep, weary work,' as the Scottish landlady remarked.

I began by eliminating altogether the last twelve stories, which are scattered through *The Strand* for the last five or six years. They are about to come out in volume form under the title *The Case-Book of Sherlock Holmes*, but the public could not easily get at them. Had they been available I should have put two of them in my team – namely, 'The Lion's Mane' and 'The Illustrious Client'. The first of these is hampered by being told by Holmes himself, a method which I employed only twice, as it certainly cramps the narrative. On the other hand, the actual plot is among the very best of the whole series, and for that it deserves its place. 'The Illustrious Client', on the other hand, is not remarkable for plot, but it has a certain dramatic quality and moves adequately in lofty circles, so I should also have found a place for it.

However, these being ruled out, I am now faced with some forty odd candidates to be weighed against each other. There are certainly some few an echo of which has come to me from all parts of the world, and I think this is the final proof of merit of some sort. There is the grim snake story, 'The Speckled Band'. That, I am sure, will be on every list. Next to that in popular favour and in my own esteem I would place 'The Red-Headed League' and 'The Dancing Men', on account in each case of the originality of the plot. Then we could hardly leave out the story which deals with the only foe who ever really extended Holmes, and which deceived the public (and Watson) into the erroneous inference of his death. Also, I think the first story of all should go in, as it opened the path for the others, and as it has more female interest than is usual. Finally, I think the story which essays the difficult task of explaining away the alleged death of Holmes, and which also introduces such a villain as Colonel Sebastian Moran, should have a place. This puts 'The Final Problem', 'A Scandal in Bohemia' and 'The Empty House' upon our list, and we have got our first half-dozen.

But now comes the crux. There are a number of stories which really are a little hard to separate. On the whole I think I should find a place for 'The Five Orange Pips', for though it is short it has a certain dramatic quality of its own. So now only five places are left. There are two stories which deal with high diplomacy and intrigue. They are both among the very best of the series. The one is 'The Naval Treaty' and the other 'The Second Stain'. There is no room for both of them in the team, and on the whole I regard the latter as the better story. Therefore we will put it down for the eighth place.

And now which? 'The Devil's Foot' has points. It is grim and new. We will give it the ninth place. I think also that 'The Priory School' is worth a place if only for the dramatic moment when Holmes points his finger at the Duke. I have only two places left. I hesitate between 'Silver Blaze', 'The Bruce-Partington Plans', 'The Crooked Man', 'The Man With the Twisted Lip', 'The "Gloria Scott"', 'The Greek Interpreter', 'The Reigate Squires', 'The Musgrave Ritual' and 'The Resident Patient'. On what principle am I to choose two out of those? The racing detail in 'Silver Blaze' is very faulty, so we must disqualify him. There is little to choose between the others. A small thing would turn the scale. 'The Musgrave Ritual' has a historical touch which gives it a little added distinction. It is also a memory from Holmes's early life. So now we come to the very last. I might as well draw the name out of a bag, for I see no reason to put one before the other. Whatever their merit – and I make no claim for that – they are all as good as I could make them. On the whole Holmes himself shows perhaps most ingenuity in 'The

Reigate Squires', and therefore this shall be twelfth man in my team.

It is proverbially a mistake for a judge to give his reasons, but I have analysed mine if only to show any competitors that I really have taken some trouble in the matter.

The list is therefore as follows:

1. The Speckled Band
2. The Red-Headed League
3. The Dancing Men
4. The Final Problem
5. A Scandal in Bohemia
6. The Empty House
7. The Five Orange Pips
8. The Second Stain
9. The Devil's Foot
10. The Priory School
11. The Musgrave Ritual
12. The Reigate Squires